# COLLIDE

## BY

## RILEY HART

Edited by Marion at Making Manuscripts

**Cover photo by jackson photografix**

Cover Design by B Design

# CHAPTER ONE

"Motherfucker!" Noah Jameson slammed his hands down on the steering wheel of his piece-of-shit car. This wasn't the first time she'd given him trouble. Hell, he'd put a good amount of money into her before he left, and now she was giving him crap again.

Which should be a sign he should give her up. But she also happened to be a '69 Mustang, and there wasn't a chance he was throwing in the towel. Noah should have known he'd have car trouble. It went right along with everything else going on in his life. Seemed he couldn't trust much of anything to be dependable— even his damn car.

Noah picked up his cell phone, which of course wasn't charged. Not that he had anyone to call in Blackcreek, anyway. He hadn't been here since he was thirteen years old. Hell, he wasn't even sure what he was doing here now. All he knew was he'd needed to get away, and Blackcreek, Colorado, was the first place he'd thought about. Probably the only place he'd ever considered home—but then, that could have been more because of a person and not a place.

Hell, maybe this car business was a sign that what he was doing didn't make any sense. Noah didn't run. He'd been forced to do enough of that as a kid, but then...this was different. He wasn't trying to escape his own wrongdoings. He was looking for something he left behind—that feeling of home. A feeling he hadn't experienced since leaving seventeen years before.

Cursing again, Noah got out of the car, shoved his dead cell phone into the pocket of his worn jeans, and locked her up. He let his feet start to carry him into the town he'd spur-of-the-moment decided to come back to.

Without a job.

Or a place to stay.

And now with a fucked-up car.

Not that he thought he would have much trouble. He was good with money and had some saved. Plus what his father had left him when he passed. Finding a building to open a shop he could fill with his furniture, hopefully, wouldn't be hard, either. Maybe this time he could actually buy something. Have the kind of roots he hadn't known growing up or during the years he'd spent in the army.

Thinking about the army made him think of David—somewhere he definitely didn't want his thoughts going. He'd become his dad. The one who didn't know how to fall for the right person. That's all he'd thought about when David screwed around on him.

*How the hell did I become my dad?*

At least with Noah, when he ran, he did it alone. Didn't drag his cheating lover along, the way his dad had with his mom.

Christ. Being cheated on had done a number on him. He didn't usually let the past run him so much. But then, he'd given a lot to David, too. More than any other man he'd been with. For David, he'd gone back into the closet at twenty-nine years old. He'd spent enough time there while in the service, and had sworn he'd never go back.

As he walked toward town, Noah took in the scenery. It always felt like a middle-of-nowhere town, and in a lot of ways it was, but in others it wasn't. It was only an hour and a half from Denver, but felt secluded, tucked away in the mountains and trees. Enough of a distance to keep the slow pace Noah loved, but close enough to give him options.

It didn't take long for him to walk the last couple miles into Blackcreek.

Noah stood by the sign welcoming him to the city. Hell, the place looked exactly like it did seventeen years ago. He looked at Main Street, lined with old-school businesses. It was a blast from the past—all the wood stores and old, hand-painted signs.

What the fuck was he doing back here?

He wanted to turn back but keep going forward at the same time.

Walking past a pharmacy and an ice cream shop, Noah kept on. If he remembered correctly, there was a gas station and a shoe-box hotel not too far up the street. A little after that, there was a mechanic. He had his first kiss with the daughter of the guy who used to own it. He hadn't known what the hell he was doing. Luckily, Mary hadn't, either.

Yeah, he changed a bit since he'd been here. There'd only been a few kisses with girls after that, and he'd slept with a couple, too, but none of them did much more for him than the first. It had never been women he had wanted.

Noah stood at the corner of Main and Berry Road, trying to decide where he wanted to go first—the mechanic or the hotel (assuming both were still there). Knowing the answer to that would probably help him decide if he needed to secure a room or get someone back for his car first.

Distracted, Noah took a step down off the curb. When he did, he saw a truck coming from the corner of his eye. Before he could move, the truck hit him. Pain blasted through him, knocking him on his ass.

Christ.

Noah grabbed his chest, like that would somehow take the ache away. Just what he didn't fucking need. Pain pierced him again as Noah tried, but failed, to get up. He'd kill whoever was behind the wheel of the truck. Forget that he hadn't been paying attention when he'd crossed the street, and that the driver obviously only rolled into him. He'd been through enough in the past few weeks that there was no way he was taking the blame for this one.

*****

"Motherfucker!" Cooper Bradshaw jumped out of his truck, panic flooding his veins. He'd fucking hit someone. Yeah, he'd been going slow—hopefully too slow to cause any real damage—but that didn't make him feel any better. Any time a one-and-a-half ton truck ran into something else, or in this case, someone else, you could pretty much bet on who the winner would be.

As he raced to the guy on the ground, Cooper hoped that whoever he was, he wasn't hurt too badly.

"Oh shit," he cursed, looking down. The guy had short, dark hair, his eyes squinted closed. He was tall and...familiar... A smile spread across Cooper's face. "Noah? Noah Jameson? Wow. Long time no see. How ya been?"

Noah cocked a brow at him, and Coop realized that probably wasn't the best thing to say when you mowed down your best friend from childhood.

"Run over," Noah replied.

Cooper jerked himself out of the past to take care of what needed to be done. "Sorry, man. Where does it hurt?" He knelt down, still in shock that he not only hit someone, but that it was his old friend.

"Still don't know how to watch where you're going, I see." Noah smiled, and some of the tension eased out of Cooper's shoulders. Holy shit. Noah Jameson was sitting in front of him.

"Still blaming other people for your crap, I see. You're the one who walked out onto the street without looking, just like you tried to go for that ball I'd already called." They'd been ten when Noah moved next door. Coop was outside playing football with some friends, and Noah pushed his way right into the game by going for the same catch Coop had. They'd collided in mid-air, fell on their asses, and then were best friends for the next three years.

He'd stolen his first dirty magazine with the man on the road right now. Snuck downstairs at night to watch his first porno with him. Talked about girls with him. Spied on girls with him. Yeah, they'd been young, but they'd been a team.

"You still didn't have to run me down, ya bastard." Noah flinched as he tried to get up. Coop cursed.

"Maybe we should call an ambulance. What hurts?"

Noah shook his head. "Hell no. My ribs are sore. I don't need an ambulance. I need a bed and about ten Ibuprofen."

When Noah tried to get up again, Cooper held onto his arm to help him. Once he was on his feet, Noah leaned against the truck. "Jesus." Coop shook his head. "I can't believe you're back, let alone that I ran your ass over. I'd say let's catch up, but I'd feel better if we got you to the hospital first."

Noah winced again and grabbed his side. "I'm sure my ribs are just bruised, so they won't be able to do much."

He was probably right, but Coop wasn't willing to take chances. "You got a car?" he asked, trying to show his friend he wasn't taking no for an answer.

"Broken down on the side of the road."

Coop knew it made him an asshole, but he laughed. It wasn't every day your car broke down and then you got hit by one. "Bad day?"

Noah shook his head but grinned, reminding Cooper exactly of the boy he used to know. "You don't even know the half of it."

Cooper reached for him. "Let me help you in the truck. I'll drive you over to get checked out, and then we'll head out for your car."

He watched as Noah took a deep breath and winced. He had a feeling if it hadn't been for that wince, his old friend would try to say no about the hospital.

When he tried to help Noah, his old friend shook him off. Cooper wasn't surprised. He'd been like that when they were young, too. Hell, he was like that himself. No reason he couldn't get to the truck by himself.

Once Noah was in, Coop *did* close the door for him before jogging around to the driver side. A car went around them before Cooper pulled away. Noah's eyes were closed as he leaned against the seat. Worry lit a fire inside Coop. "You doing okay over there?"

"Do you always stress so much? You didn't used to fret like a woman." Noah didn't look at him as he spoke. Cooper tried not to laugh. He remembered Noah used to get pissy when he was hurt.

"You didn't used to complain so much, either." Cooper laughed and shook his head. "So how are ya? Where you been all these years?"

Noah grunted in reply, and Coop felt like an ass for asking. He knew what it had been like for Noah. How many schools he'd been to and cities he'd lived in before coming to Blackcreek. Noah used to tell him that he'd do anything to stay here. Anytime they got in trouble for causing hell in town, Noah always worried it would make things bad between his parents again, and make him have to leave. Not that they'd done anything too bad.

He also knew that on Friday his friend had been there, and by Sunday, when Cooper got home from a trip with his aunt, Noah had been gone. There's no way he could have known he was leaving if Coop hadn't. They'd sworn to leave together if it ever came to that. Not that he didn't know that those were silly promises kids made— but Cooper knew Noah would have rather done anything than move from Blackcreek.

They were quiet for the thirty-minute drive to the hospital. Cooper sat in the waiting room with his feet up on another chair, while Noah went back to see the ER doctor. He tried to ignore the unease in his stomach. He didn't see how any real damage could be done, but you never knew with stuff like that.

"Cooper Bradshaw. What did I do to deserve a visit from you today?" A woman sat beside him. Coop looked over and smiled at Adrianna. She was an ER nurse who he'd gone out with a few times. He took in her pouty lips, red hair, and full breasts.

She was a woman he suddenly wanted to go out with again, very soon. They had a good deal between them.  She was busy with the hospital, had a five-year-old kid and not a lot of free time. He wasn't looking for anything serious. It wasn't that Cooper was anti-relationship or anything, he just wasn't sure they were for him. More power to anyone who wanted to settle down, but he enjoyed his lifestyle too much to change it. Adrianna was okay with no strings. They got together when her daughter was with her dad, or when one of them was looking for a good time. No strings, no attachment, no emotions. Just sex.

"I was thinking the same thing about you." Coop gave her a smile. The slow, easy one that women seemed to like.

"You're such a flirt."

Cooper winked at her. "You like it."

The doors to the emergency room slid open. "Mr. Bradshaw?" one of the nurses asked. "You're here with Mr. Jameson?"

Cooper pushed to his feet. A shuffle of footsteps sounded from behind him. "Yeah? Is everything okay?" he asked.

Cooper's palms were all sweaty and his heart slammed. Hell, he'd been out here flirting with a woman after maiming his friend. That pretty much tossed him into asshole territory.

"He's fine. His ribs are bruised. We have him wrapped and gave him some pain medicine. He's a little loopy in here. He warned us he gets like that with pain medicine. Are you going to take him home? He can't drive."

He nodded his head. Cooper had no clue if Noah had somewhere to stay, but he'd make sure he got him where he needed to be. "Sure. What do I need to know?"

The nurse finished giving him information, and then said she'd be right back with Noah. "Looks like you have plans. I was just getting off work, too." This time it was Adrianna who winked at *him*. Cooper cursed. He definitely could use a few hours with her.

Or a night.

"Sorry. I'm the one who hit him so I feel a little obligated to make sure he's okay. Are you busy tomorrow?" But then, that wasn't all it was, either. He'd want to catch up with Noah no matter if he'd hit him or not.

"Work."

"Day after?"

"Date."

Cooper didn't flinch. They weren't committed, and they both knew she wouldn't stay single forever and he wouldn't want to settle down. "Call me if it doesn't work out."

"I'm fine. I can walk! See?" Noah's voice came from behind him.

He looked back to see Noah walking with his arms out like he was trying to prove he could walk a straight line. Coop laughed. "Jesus. You still can't handle yourself?" he teased. At twelve, they'd stolen a few beers from Cooper's uncle. Halfway through one of them, Noah was toasted. Looked like pain pills affected him the same way. Smiling, he shook his head.

"Not you, too." Noah had a big, goofy smile on his face.

"I'll see you later," Adrianna told Cooper.

Coop told her goodbye, then grabbed Noah's arm. He was surprised Noah let him help him to the truck.

"Where you staying?" he asked once they were in the truck.

"No clue. Just ended up here." Noah pushed the button so the window went up and down, up and down, like he was eight years old. "Needed to get away. Packed. Ended up in Blackcreek."

Cooper looked over, trying to read the expression on his old friend's face. The fact was, he didn't know him anymore. Didn't know what the tone of his voice meant—if it meant anything. That honestly made him a little sad. He'd known everything about this man when they were kids.

"I have an extra room. You're welcome to use it."

"Don't know how long I'll be here."

"I was planning on renting it out."

Noah's head rolled to the side, flopping around as though he couldn't hold it up. This look Cooper recognized: Noah didn't believe him.

"I'm not shitting you. Just bought the house. It could use some work, but it's huge. I can put your ass to work."

"You don't know me anymore. You sure you want a stranger in your house?" Noah almost sounded sad when he said that.

"Eh. I'm sure I can still kick your ass. That's all that matters."

Noah started playing with the window again. He looked fascinated by the damn thing. Those pills must have really fucked him up. When the window got boring, Noah closed his eyes. He was almost out by the time Cooper pulled up at his house. Noah put his arm around him as Cooper helped him inside. He went straight for the guest room. His old friend was like dead weight, so trying to help him up the stairs wasn't an easy feat. Noah leaned right out of his arms and dove into bed, and then groaned and cursed before clutching his side.

"Dumbass." Cooper shook his head. "Where's your car? I'll get it towed in and grab your prescription. Don't think you won't owe me, though." Cooper felt this crazy thrill of happiness. It was fun teasing Noah. It always had been.

Noah's face was in the pillow as he mumbled his answer. Somehow, Cooper managed to understand him.

Cooper walked to the door, but paused there. "Get your ass feeling better. We'll go out and meet some women," he joked.

"Nope," Noah mumbled. "I'm gay." That easily, he was passed out again. Cooper couldn't help but laugh. Jesus, the man really couldn't handle pain pills.

# CHAPTER TWO

Noah rolled over in bed, all of his muscles stiff. He felt like he'd been hit by a truck. As soon as the thought struck him, he realized how ridiculous it was considering that's exactly what happened. Cooper Bradshaw had collided right into him.

All these years later and he still didn't watch where the hell he was going.

Noah tried to get up and groaned at the foggy feeling in his head. It wasn't his ribs that bothered him at all. No, he felt like he was swimming through muddy water, and the only thing that made him feel like that was Demerol. Why didn't he tell them he couldn't take it?

Fighting his way through the murk, Noah stood. He was a little shaky on his feet but kept on going. The only way to get out of this was to push himself. He needed a hot shower...something to drink. Then maybe he would start feeling like himself again.

As much as a shower called him, he not only didn't know where it was, but his mouth felt like it was stuffed with cotton balls. So, kitchen first, shower second.

Coop's house. He couldn't believe he'd landed himself in his old friend's place. Cooper had been the best friend Noah ever had. After they left Blackcreek, he stopped trying. Didn't want to make new friends because it would hurt when he had to leave them.

Noah padded his bare feet down the stairs, wondering where his shoes were, how they'd gotten off, and how the hell long he'd been out. When he got to the bottom, it opened into a large living room with oversized dark-green furniture and a big-ass flat-screen on the wall.

"H'llo?" His voice came out raw and scratchy. Damn Demerol.

"In the kitchen," Cooper's voice sounded from the other side of the living room. Noah followed it until he found Coop standing at the stove in a pair of jeans and nothing else. The years had been good to his friend. His muscles were firm and defined. His skin golden and sun-kissed, and fuck if he didn't have a six-pack. Noah fucking loved that.

He walked over and fell into the kitchen chair. "I feel like hell. My brain is all foggy."

Cooper laughed. He was always laughing at something. That's one of the things Noah remembered about him. He loved to laugh. "No shit. I thought you died in there. I went in a few times to make sure you were still breathing."

Noah watched as the other man scooped eggs onto two plates, walked over, and set one in front of Noah. It was strange how comfortable it felt sitting with Cooper. Almost as if no time had passed at all.

"You should eat. You're supposed to take your pain pills with food."

Noah's stomach growled as he stared at the food in front of him. Until Cooper sat the plate down, he hadn't realized how hungry he was. "Thanks, man. Mind if I get something to drink?" Noah stood.

"What do you want? I'll grab it."

"I'm not helpless. Point me in the right direction, and I can do it." Noah didn't like having people take care of him. Didn't like to cross those lines of getting too close. Not anymore. He'd broken his own rule when he got semi-serious with David, and look where that left him? Not that Cooper would be someone he'd end up in a relationship with, because he was pretty sure Cooper wasn't gay, but he wasn't up for letting anyone in again, either.

"Third cabinet over for the cups; drinks in the fridge." Cooper sat down and started to eat.

Noah poured himself some orange juice, trying not to wince with each of his movements. Maybe he was hurt more seriously than he thought. Definitely time to get another of those pain pills. Well, depending on what they were.

With slow steps, Noah walked over and sat back at the table, drinking down half of the orange juice with one gulp. "Thanks, man. I really appreciate you bringing me here, and for breakfast. We don't really know each other anymore—"

"I hit ya. It's the least I could do. Your car's outside, too. She's a beauty. Not running, but she sure is pretty."

Noah laughed, and when he did, a sharp stab of pain went through him. He grabbed his side. "Shit, that hurts. Don't make me laugh."

"How long are you planning on hanging around?" Cooper asked before taking a bite of his eggs.

Wasn't that a good question? All he'd known was that he needed a fresh start, and Blackcreek had called to him. "I don't know. I'm thinking for good. Like I said, just packed up and left."

Cooper nodded. "And like I said yesterday, I have a room. Might as well rent it out to you rather than someone else. If you're interested." Cooper set his fork on his empty plate and leaned back in the chair. He had stubble along his jaw, his dark blond hair cut short. His blue eyes were full of mischief, like they had been when they were kids. Hell, they'd caused some trouble together years ago.

Looking at him, Noah realized how much he'd truly missed his friend. Sure, he'd known it as a kid. It had pretty much wrecked him. Noah had isolated himself for a long time after that, but seventeen years had passed. He wouldn't have thought seeing Cooper would still mean so much, but given that Cooper had been his one real friend from when he was a kid, it made sense.

And renting a room was probably a smart idea. It would be a whole lot less money than getting an apartment. Again, he had the cash, but he also wanted to get his furniture business off the ground.

There was only one problem. He had no idea how Coop would react to him being gay. It wasn't a problem for him. They would only be roommates, but that didn't mean Coop would be comfortable with it.

"You don't mind sharing a house with a gay man?"

Cooper was taking a drink right as the question left Noah's mouth. He immediately started choking on his OJ and coughing like crazy.

Well, there was his answer. "You okay?" he asked.

Coop was still hacking away, but nodded his head before he took another drink to calm himself. "Jesus, way to spring that on someone."

A ghost of a memory from the day before snuck into his head. "I'm pretty sure I told you yesterday."

"You could hardly speak straight." Coop's blue eyes widened. "Not *straight*, straight. I mean, you were all messed up because of the pain meds. I didn't...I wasn't..."

Another laugh jumped out of Noah's mouth. He tried to hold his ribs, but it didn't stop the pain from shooting through him. He'd never seen Coop so flustered in his life.

"Asshole," Coop grunted. "It's not that funny."

Maybe it wasn't, but Noah needed to laugh. It felt good, too. Well, besides the killer pain in his ribs. "Shit. You're right. I'm sorry, but pain meds or not, people don't say they're gay if they aren't."

Cooper crossed his arms, and with that movement, the laughter left the room. This was game time. Where Noah would find out if his friend would want him to leave all because of who he was attracted to. He couldn't read the look in Coop's eyes. Didn't know him well enough anymore to know what his intense stare meant.

"We used to talk about girls together, man."

"I was a kid. I was confused. I can promise you, I'm not confused any longer." He held Cooper's gaze so he would understand Noah was serious. This was who he was, and he was okay with that. "Do you have a problem with it?"

"Are you going to hit on me?" Coop tossed back at him.

"You're not my type." Actually, the man couldn't have been *more* his type. Dark-blond hair, sexy eyes, strong, muscled frame. Wasn't like he could tell him that, though. "Plus, you don't hit on every woman you meet, do you? Because I'm attracted to men doesn't mean I can't control myself around them."

"That's what I thought, so don't ask stupid questions. You're my friend. I'm not going to slam the door in your face because you have bad taste."

This time Noah held in the laugh, but fuck it was hard. Still, he wrapped an arm around his ribs while he shook his head. The response was so typical of the Cooper he'd known all those years ago.

"More women for me." Coop winked, but then he shifted in his seat. His eyes didn't quite catch Noah's. He wanted to be comfortable with it, but Noah could tell it wasn't going to be as easy as Cooper wanted it to be.

\*\*\*

Noah Jameson was gay.

Yes, he'd said so the night before, and logically, Coop realized the meds wouldn't make him say that if he wasn't, but hearing it today made it more real. It wasn't that Cooper was homophobic or anything. He was all for the right to live and love who the hell you wanted. For everyone to have that benefit. But it wasn't every day you found out your childhood best friend was gay.

The same friend he told about a boner he got over kissing a girl at twelve. Maybe it shouldn't, but it made things a little weird.

"So, what do you do?" he asked Noah. Cooper crossed his arms over his chest and remembered he didn't have a shirt on. Was it strange that he wasn't wearing one? He knew if a woman sat at the table with him, shirtless, he wouldn't be able to pay attention to anyone but her.

He shifted in his seat again.

"I make wood furniture. Some indoor, some outdoor. It started out as a hobby when I was home from the service," he replied. "Hoping to open a store and have a workshop attached. You?"

Noah took a drink of his orange juice. Cooper felt naked. Noah stood and grabbed his plate, then reached over for Cooper's, and his eyes shot to his friend's hand.

"Christ. What do you think? I'm going to jump you? This isn't going to work out." Noah picked up the other plate, put them in the sink, and started walking out of the room.

Guilt curdled Cooper's stomach. What the hell was wrong with him? "I'm sorry. I'm being a prick. But you have to admit it's a lot to take in. I didn't expect it, but I'm okay with it."

Noah turned to him. "Glad to know I have your approval."

"Fuck." He ran a hand through his hair. "That's not what I meant. You're not making this easier, you know."

Noah closed his eyes and took a deep breath, which probably hurt. Cooper couldn't help but wonder if there had been people with whom his friend's sexual orientation *hadn't* been okay with; if Noah had had problems. But then, he'd said he'd been in the service, so that made sense. The thought of people giving Noah shit for being who he was sent anger coursing through him. This was Noah—the guy who always had Cooper's back when they were kids.

"You are who you are. Don't be a hot head because it surprised me. You always were getting pissed about something."

This made Noah open his eyes. He shook his head, but he didn't look upset anymore. "That's because you never took anything seriously. You were always getting us into trouble."

"I was always helping us find fun. Now come on, before I have to kick your ass like I did all those years ago. Remember that?"

"I remember you ramming into me and us rolling around in the yard, because neither of us knew how the hell to fight. If I remember correctly, I ended up on top, though."

Cooper let the memory dance around in his head. Maybe Noah was right. Hell, they'd only been ten years old. He couldn't even remember what they'd been fighting about. But then another thought crowded his brain… Had Noah known then? Or at least been questioning it? Had moments like wrestling around meant something different to Noah? Cooper shoved those thoughts away.

"Sit your ass down and I'll grab your pills. They only gave you Vicodin. Probably because you can't handle yourself."

"I need to work on my car."

"Doubt that's happening today. You got hit by a truck yesterday, remember?" Cooper walked over, grabbed the pill bottle and tossed it to Noah, who caught it.

They sat back at the table and his friend took one of the pills.

"I'm a fire fighter," he told Noah. Cooper didn't want to look him in the eye because he knew Noah understood how important that was to him.

"It's a good way to honor them. Your parents."

Cooper gave a simple nod at that. It was ridiculous that after all these years, he still couldn't talk about losing his parents in the fire. He'd been almost ten when he came to Blackcreek to live with his Uncle Vernon, and they'd never made him talk. Even the times he probably should have, Vernon wouldn't go there. *It wasn't how a man dealt*, he'd said. But the fact that Noah just understood him? That spoke volumes.

"I just bought the house, so I'm working on it in my spare time. I do three twelve-hour shifts a week, so it gives me lots of spare time."

Cooper watched as Noah eyed the kitchen. It wasn't that his house was falling apart or anything, but it was old. A big old place, with wood floors and a lot of windows. Sure it needed some tender love and care, but Cooper had loved it on sight.

"I'll be glad to help," Noah told him.

"I'll take you up on that."

For about forty-five minutes, they talked about Noah's car, jobs, and renting the room. They joked a little about their childhood, but didn't delve too far into it. Finally, Noah stood. "I really need a shower. Do you mind?"

Coop stood, too. "Of course not. I'll help you get your stuff out of the car." He knew Noah wouldn't let him get it by himself, no matter his injury. Cooper didn't blame him, because he would be the same way.

Considering he was moving, Noah didn't come with a lot of stuff: a couple of boxes and a few bags. It took less than five minutes for them to get everything into what would be Noah's room.

"There's no bathroom in your room. The shower in my bathroom's broken. Until I get around to fixing it, we're going to have to share the one in the hall."

"Not a problem, man. I appreciate you letting me stay here."

Cooper thought he saw something in Noah's stare that made him wonder if Noah was really trying to say something else. As quickly as it had come it was gone, though, so he figured he must have imagined it.

"What are friends for? I'll take ya out sometime and we'll..." Shit. He'd done it again. Almost said they'd go find some women. He'd never really had an openly gay friend before. Like he said, it didn't bother him, but it was...different.

"Have a beer?" Noah finished for him, making Cooper feel like an ass.

"Yeah. We'll have a beer."

When Noah turned around to head for the bathroom, Cooper didn't move. He didn't know why, but he couldn't stop himself from watching his old friend go.

The last thing Cooper thought as Noah closed the door was that he didn't look like he was gay to him. Then he realized what a stupid thing that was to think. "Jesus. What the hell is wrong with me?" He took one more look at the closed bathroom door, then walked away.

# CHAPTER THREE

Noah didn't do much for the next few days. His ribs were killing him, and he wanted to give Cooper a little space. Noah believed that Cooper would really be okay with his sexual orientation, otherwise he wouldn't be staying here. After a while you got a feel for people, and he trusted Coop. He also knew it was a shock to his friend, so he thought it would be better to lay low.

But after three days, he was getting a little stir crazy keeping himself in his room. He needed to get out and scour for shops—not that he could do much until his ribs were healed a bit more, but if he couldn't work, he planned to at least get something done on his car.

Noah threw on a pair of jeans, an old T-shirt and his shoes before heading outside. Cooper wasn't home so Noah had the place to himself, which was good. He loved working on cars, but it was something he wanted to do on his own. It was the same with building furniture. He liked to concentrate, to get lost in what he was doing. Noah enjoyed nothing more than working with his hands.

Noah opened the hood, pulled out his tools, and bent over the engine. If he couldn't get this figured out, he'd have to bring her to the mechanic, which he didn't want to do. When he heard the rumble of a truck in the driveway, it felt like it was only five minutes later, though experience told him it was much longer.

Busy with what he was doing, he ignored it, until Cooper spoke from beside him.

"Finally got your lazy ass up, huh?" Coop teased.

"Run anyone down with your truck today?" Noah stood up.

"Shit. You got me there. I still can't believe I hit you."

Noah shook his head. "What's done is done. Just don't ask me to get in a vehicle with you behind the wheel again. I'm not sure I can trust ya."

Cooper leaned against the car, his almond-shaped eyes trained on Noah.

"What?" Noah asked.

This seemed to pull Coop out of his trance. "Nothin'. Need some help?"

It was on the tip of Noah's tongue to say no, but he didn't want to come off as an asshole, so he nodded. He was pretty sure it was the fuel pump, which he could take care of no problem. Unfortunately, he wasn't sure that was the only thing going on here.

They worked on the car for about an hour without talking much. It surprised Noah, because Cooper wasn't usually the type to keep quiet for long. He was always in the middle of something, drawing attention to himself. When they were young, everyone knew who Cooper was—or they thought they did. They saw the guy who tried to make people laugh. The class clown. Noah remembered a different side of him. Noah remembered the sleepovers, when Coop woke up screaming about the fire.

Every time he glanced at Cooper, his eyes would dart away, as though he could read Noah's train of thought. He knew better than that.

Noah stood and crossed his arms. "Ask."

"Don't fuck around, do you?" Cooper asked.

"No. And if I remember correctly, you don't, either, so if you have a question, ask it so we can get over this."

Cooper sighed. "I feel like a prick for even wondering, but...how? I mean, when we were younger, you weren't..."

"I was," Noah replied before walking away. Cooper followed him and they sat in chairs on Cooper's porch. "I was thirteen years old. I didn't know exactly what I wanted or who I was. It's not like people just made that a choice back then, but I can tell you, it wasn't the same for me as it was for you when we were stealing dirty magazines. I did it more because I thought I should, instead of wanting to."

Cooper nodded. "Makes sense…. So, when?"

"Why do you ask?" Noah tossed back.

"Because I'm curious. You're my friend. Nothing more, nothing less." But unlike the few other times, Coop's eyes didn't leave him. They seemed to be taking Noah in, studying him in a way Noah didn't understand.

"I guess I was about fifteen. I always knew I felt different, but that's when I started to realize exactly how. The internet helped. Lots of good porn out there." Both men laughed, and Noah was glad to see his old friend could still laugh with him.

"Where'd you go, man?"

The change of subject surprised him. Noah hated the tension that tightened his muscles with the question. "Michigan. Same as it always was. One day things were okay, the next they weren't and we were leaving." Noah remembered running next door, trying to find Cooper to tell him, but he'd forgotten his friend had left with his aunt.

His uncle Vernon had opened the door and as soon as he did, Noah's mom was yelling at him to get home. That easily, he'd lost his best friend. That easily, he'd had to move again.

"Tried to write a few times," Noah added. "My parents sent them for me, but I never heard back. I'm sure you were busy."

Cooper cocked his head as though that surprised him. "Didn't get 'em."

Noah believed him. Partly because it was something so small that there would be no reason to lie, but also because even with the time that had passed, he felt like he still knew Cooper. Coop had never lied to him when they were young.

He'd talked to Noah about things he didn't share with other people, just like Noah had done with him, even when the words felt like they'd rip a hole through his insides.

*"Coop?" Noah held the flashlight in his hand, trying to decide if he wanted to turn it on or not. He probably shouldn't if Coop was sleepin'.*

*"What's up?" Cooper's voice sounded all groggy.*

*"Nothin'. Go back to sleep." Noah rolled over, his sleeping back rustling as he tried to concentrate on the crickets chirping in the distance.*

*"I can't go back to sleep now. You already ruined it," Cooper griped.*

"Not my fault you fall asleep so early. We're supposed to be campin' out."

"So, I have to stay up late cuz we're sleeping in my backyard?"

If he was going to be stupid like that, Noah wouldn't tell him anything. "Shut up."

The tent lit up when Cooper turned on a flashlight. Noah felt eyes on him, but didn't roll over to face Cooper.

"They fightin' again?" Cooper whispered, and Noah wondered how his friend knew. It wasn't like Cooper had witnessed it or anything. When things were calm, his parents got along awesome. The only thing Coop knew was Noah's stories. Still, he was right...kind of.

"No...not really fightin', but I think she's doing it again."

Cooper didn't have to ask what. "How come?"

"There was a cigarette on the side of the back porch when Dad made me clean the yard. It was half-smoked, but you could tell it wasn't old." Neither of Noah's parents smoked.

"Maybe she had a friend over? Or maybe your dad did. Oh! I bet one of them smokes and they don't want you to know."

Noah didn't reply because he knew it hadn't been his mom's or dad's. He didn't know how, but he knew his mom was messing with some guy again. Which meant it wouldn't be long until the fighting started. Until they'd decide to go, to get that fresh start that never came. Until Noah would be forced to leave his best friend.

He flinched when he felt Coop's hand on his shoulder. "We'll tell 'em you're not going. I bet Uncle Vernon and Aunt Autumn will let you stay with us. Then we can hang out all the time. We'll be like brothers."

"Yeah?" Noah asked, knowing he shouldn't believe it, but not having it in him not to trust Coop.

"Yep."

Noah closed his eyes, suddenly feeling okay to go to sleep. Cooper was right. Autumn and Vernon let him stay at their house all the time. Plus, they took Cooper in when his parents died. They'd probably do the same for Noah so he could stay here.

"You're my best friend. We'll run away if we have to," Cooper told him.

Noah wanted to tell him thank you, but he thought that would sound way too girlie. "Then we wouldn't have to go to school anymore, either."

"Awesome. We could do whatever we wanted." There was a pause, and then, "I got your back, Noah. You and me? We'll always be a team."

Noah hoped so. "I got yours, too."

When he woke up in the morning, Cooper's hand was still touching him.

***

"Hey, you in there, man?" Cooper kicked at Noah's chair. "You're spacing off."

"If I wasn't, I am now. Thanks for kicking me." Noah said the words with a smile on his face, but he looked upset to Cooper. In a lot of ways, Cooper felt like a fucking idiot for even thinking that. It wasn't like he really knew Noah all that well anymore, but he also remembered seeing the same look on his face when they were kids. Remembered Noah kind of disappearing into his own head when he had too much shit on his mind.

That didn't mean he knew what to say about it, so Coop said the only thing he could think of. "Want a beer?"

Noah laughed. "Nope."

"No? I'm not sure I understand."

Noah laughed again, and it felt more real than the first one. Coop knew he was always good for a laugh. People came to him expecting a good time. Even when he was younger. It was a hell of a lot easier to try to make people laugh than to deal with other shit.

Noah stood. Coop still couldn't get over his old friend being back. He didn't think anyone knew him as well as Noah used to.

"Let me rephrase. I want a beer, I just don't want it here. I'm going stir crazy, man. I need out of the house tonight."

Now that was a language Cooper could understand. "That's what I'm talkin' about. I could use a few games of pool and a couple beers."

It was obviously too early to do much of anything, so they hung around the house for a few hours. They watched SportsCenter for a while. Cooper threw some burgers on the grill and they ate dinner comfortably, as though years hadn't separated them. Afterward, Cooper took a shower, and then Noah jumped in next.

Noah came out wearing a pair of jeans and a white T-shirt. Cooper hated admitting to himself that he noticed how the shirt stretched across Noah's chest. Not because he dug men or anything. Hell, not because he ever really noticed them, but... "You cold, or just happy to see me?" he teased Noah.

"Fuck you. They're piercings."

Holy shit. "You have your nipples pierced? Didn't that hurt?" On reflex, Cooper touched his own chest. He wasn't letting any needle get close to him like that.

"Like a motherfucker. The guys like it, though." Noah winked at him.

Cooper tensed a little. He wasn't going to lie. It was weird as hell to hear stuff like that. Clearing his throat, he said, "Yeah...well, I'd like it, too, if a woman had her nipples pierced. Maybe I should bring up the idea to one of them..." But then his eyes were drawn to Noah's chest again.

Noah chuckled, which helped the misplaced tension Cooper felt. He didn't understand why he kept feeling out of sorts. It wasn't anything Noah did. He kept getting thrown for a loop where Noah was concerned. It wasn't a feeling he was used to.

"You haven't changed a bit." Noah walked over and opened the door. Cooper followed him out. When they climbed into Coop's truck, Noah spoke again. "You were always trying to get me into some kind of trouble where girls were concerned. *It's just a magazine, Noah. Look at this video I found, Noah. Holy shit, do you think girls can really do that, Noah?*"

As he drove down the road, Cooper laughed. "If I remember correctly, I didn't have to try very hard. You were always up for that kind of shit."

At that, Noah shrugged, sobering slightly. "You were, so I was. Wanted to fit in with ya. Didn't want to be different than my best friend."

Cooper couldn't help but turn his head Noah's way. Hell, they'd been thick as thieves, but Noah never said something like that to him before. Damned if it didn't make Coop's chest swell with pride. Noah was a good guy, and to think he'd always wanted to fit in with Cooper...well, that meant something. He'd been devastated when Noah left. It hit him the same as when he'd lost his parents—like he'd been abandoned. Especially when he'd never heard a word from him.

"Stop getting sappy. You know you never have to try and be anything other than what you are with me. I mean, I was always cool enough for both of us, anyway."

Like Cooper hoped he would, Noah laughed. "Fuck off."

It was the perfect distraction for Cooper to ignore the flood of...contentment... Hearing that their friendship had meant to Noah even a portion of what it had meant to Coop. Which, as a kid, had been everything.

# CHAPTER FOUR

"Corner pocket." Cooper pointed his cue. Noah laughed.

"Yeah right. You're dreaming."

"Watch and learn, Stretch. Watch and learn." Cooper paused, wrinkling his forehead. Noah wasn't sure why until he said, "Holy shit. That just came out. I forgot about that name."

Noah had, too. "I haven't been called that since I was a kid."

"That's because no one besides me knew your secret. I swear to Christ, I used to think you had some kind of magic that made you be able to catch a ball like that. I mean, you were always taller than me, but it was like your whole body stretched out. Gumby or some shit." Cooper took a drink of his beer and then eyed the pocket.

"It's called jumping. Maybe you've heard of it?"

"I always thought you would have made a good basketball player." The cue stroked smoothly through Cooper's fingers as the solid, purple ball made it into the pocket he called.

"I played when I left here." Noah eyed the table, looking for his shot.

"No shit?"

"Yeah. I was always better at it. Gotta go with what you're good at."

Cooper pointed to a pocket. Noah nodded but Coop missed the shot.

"You know I'm about to clean the table, don't you?" He saw Cooper scowl. He always hated losing.

"Bastard."

Noah laughed before calling and then sinking his shot. He moved to the next and did the same. The whole time, he felt Cooper's eyes on him. He wanted to say it was because of the game, and it probably was, but it felt like he'd been doing it all evening. When Noah looked at him, Coop always turned away. He wasn't sure how that made him feel, considering Cooper seemed on and off with his comfort about him being gay. Though, discomfort wasn't what he would call the look in Cooper's eyes. Curiosity? Interest—even if not sexual? Or could it be? "Eight ball, side pocket," Noah called before hitting the ball in. As he did, a group of a few men and women approached them.

*Perfect.* They definitely needed to be joined by some other people. He didn't know if it was the couple beers he'd had, or the fact that the past always crept in when he was speaking to Cooper, but the air was thick between them in a way it hadn't been the first few days.

"Cooper, how's it going?" one of the guys asked. Noah watched as Cooper said hello and shook hands with the guys in the group.

Cooper nudged Noah, but then didn't step away. Their arms still touched as he went down the line of the group. "Russ, Travis, Danny, Lizzy, Jules, and Heather." Then he wrapped an arm around Noah's shoulders and shook him gently. "Guys, this is my old friend Noah."

Noah winced and tried not to curse when pain shot through his ribs.

"Shit, man. I'm sorry," Cooper told him, still clutching onto Noah.

He shook his head. "Hey. Nice to meet you guys."

"You, too," Russ said.

Noah pressed a hand to one of his sides. The pain was minimal now, but it still hurt like a bitch when Cooper shook him.

"What happened?" Travis asked.

When Noah went to nudge Cooper, he noticed Coop's arm was still on his shoulders. It only took him a second to realize he liked the weight of it there. Noah fought to shake off the feeling. "Some asshole hit me with his truck," he teased.

Everyone turned to Cooper. "And it automatically had to be me, or what?"

They all laughed, and then Heather nodded toward a table in the back. "You guys want to sit with us? I need a drink."

Noah felt Coop's eyes on him again, so he met them. Coop raised his brows as if to ask if Noah cared. The energy pulsing off Coop said he very much wanted to stay at the bar. He'd always been like that. When he got excited about something, he couldn't keep it in. He jumped in headfirst to whatever he felt at the time. Noah had always admired that about him.

"Sounds good to me." When he moved, Cooper took his arm away. Not that it was a big deal to have had it there. It was a friendly gesture, but he liked it in ways he probably shouldn't.

Noah ran a hand through his hair as he headed for the table with Cooper's friends. He didn't remember any of them from when they were younger, so he figured they must have come to town after he left.

They'd only sat down for about thirty seconds when the waitress came up and asked what they wanted. Cooper ordered a couple pitchers of beer before leaning back in the chair next to Noah. The scent of cologne hit Noah, making him wonder how he could smell it over the smoke and alcohol in the bar.

"You don't recognize me, do you?" the woman he thought Cooper called Jules asked him. She had curly black hair that went about halfway down her back, and dark eyes. Noah studied her, trying to place her, but couldn't.

"I dyed my hair. You guys used to call me Juju," she said.

A memory of a girl with red hair popped into his head. She used to play with them all the time. She was as tough as the boys out there. "Wow. I'm sorry. I didn't even recognize you. You've…"

"Lost a little bit of weight, too." She smiled at him. He wouldn't have said anything, but yeah, she had.

The woman looked completely different than the tomboy she used to be. She wore a tight skirt and form-fitting shirt, with cleavage he imagined Cooper probably really enjoyed.

"You look great," Noah told her, meaning it.

"Thanks. You're not so bad yourself." She gave him a playful smile.

About then, the beer came and everyone poured a glass. The table was small, all of them fitting tightly around it. Cooper's leg pressed against Noah's on one side, and Jules's leg on the other. He could feel the contrast even in that—the firmness of Cooper's body, compared to the softness in hers. It was that feeling—the masculinity of a man—that drove him fucking wild. Shit, he should not be feeling this way about Coop.

"You just move to town?" Danny asked.

"Yep." Noah nodded.

"He's renting a room at my place. Once he stops lazin' around, and those damn ribs heal, he's going to help me fix up the house." Cooper laughed.

"You mean the ribs you rammed your truck into?" Noah tossed back at him.

"*Rolled.* I *rolled* into you, man. There's a difference."

Noah took a drink of his beer. "No, there's not."

"I think I'm going with Noah on this one," Jules added, and everyone at the table laughed.

After that, they all broke off into their own conversations. Jules asked Noah question after question about his life, which he answered, enjoying seeing another old friend again.

"What about a wife? You married or have kids?" she asked. Cooper quieted beside him, cleared his throat, and then shifted uncomfortably. It made Noah's muscles pulse. Was he embarrassed of Noah being gay? Afraid of Noah telling his friends?

Noah crossed his arms. "Not married and no kids. How about you?" The fact was, Noah hadn't planned to tell her. Being gay wasn't something he was embarrassed about *or* something he hid. Those days were over for him. But he also didn't feel the need to declare his sexuality in the middle of the bar. If she'd asked one of the other guys, it's not like they would specify if they were married to a woman or not. And he'd answered her question honestly. Still, Cooper's reaction bothered him more than he wanted to admit.

***

Cooper listened while Jules told Noah about her recent break-up. She'd been dating the same asshole for about five years. He'd cheated on her a few times before she finally walked away from him. On the other side of Cooper, Heather was speaking to him. Coop tried like hell to pay attention, but he kept getting drawn back into Noah and Jules's conversation.

He hadn't told her he was gay. Cooper didn't know why that bothered him so much. Maybe "bothered" wasn't the right word. But why in the hell he couldn't stop wondering about it, he didn't know.

Cooper shifted in his seat, his movement automatically making his leg press against Noah's more firmly. It was a reflex to move it, which he almost did, but then for some reason he just...didn't.

Noah glanced over his shoulder at Coop, his eyebrows pushed together, before Jules pulled his attention away. *He's wondering what I'm doing.* I'm *wondering what I'm doing...* But then, it wasn't like there was a ton of space at the table. There was nothing wrong with sitting back comfortably.

So he brought his attention back to Heather, who really was incredibly gorgeous—nice plump lips, and curves he loved—and listened to her talk.

It was forty-five minutes later when Cooper told her he'd be right back. He went to the bathroom and took a piss, tired and ready to go home all of a sudden. Hell, he hadn't even gotten to spend a whole lot of time with his old friend. They'd missed the days when they could go out and drink legally, and he'd looked forward to hanging out with him. Not that he hadn't been excited about seeing his other friends as well, but he didn't know they'd take over the night like they did.

He hardly made it two steps out of the bathroom door when Heather said, "Hey."

That easily, his body started to heat. He understood what the husky tone in her voice meant. *This* is what he should be focusing on. Not how much he got to talk to his friend.

"Are you following me, sweetheart?" He took a step toward her.

"Do you want me to follow you?" she tossed back.

"Now what kind of question is that?" Another step closer. But then he remembered he had Noah out there waiting on him. They'd ridden in together. It wasn't like he wanted to pile Heather in the truck with them and take her home.

Plus, that made him an ass if he came to spend some time with his friend and took a woman home instead. It would be different if Cooper had come out by himself or something. "Maybe—"

"Maybe nothing." Heather's lips lifted up to his. That was all it took for Cooper to forget the reasons he almost told her, *maybe another time*. He took the kiss over, delving his tongue into her mouth and backing her against the wall. She moved against him, her hand rubbing the growing erection under his jeans.

"Ah, fuck. Sorry."

Cooper jerked back at the sound of Noah's voice just as he turned to walk away.

"What's up? Something wrong?" he asked, and then realized his friend probably needed the john.

"Nothing. I just…" Noah's words drifted off, as though he couldn't say what he wanted to.

Cooper turned to Heather. "Can we pick this up another time?"

"No, hell no. Don't mind me." Noah turned to leave again.

Cooper's pulse spiked slightly, and he realized he was kind of grateful for the cock block, which was a fucked-up thought. He couldn't think of one *good* reason he should be grateful for that.

"Nah, we're good. Wait up." He winked at Heather. "We're gonna get going, okay?"

She smiled and shook her head. "You're such a charmer, Cooper Bradshaw. It's probably a good idea we don't go there tonight, anyway."

"Thanks, sweetheart." Leaning forward, he kissed her forehead before he went to Noah.

They were halfway to the table when Noah said, "You didn't have to bail on her. I just had a bit of a situation."

Coop made one of his eyebrows kick up. "Jules?"

"Yeah." He rubbed a hand over his chest. Cooper wondered how it felt when Noah rubbed his piercing, and then promptly stumbled a little. *Why the fuck am I wondering that?*

"I wasn't thinking at first," Noah continued. "But I can see where her thoughts are going and I'm trying to avoid something awkward."

"That easily? Jules hasn't paid attention to any man since she left the prick."

"I have that effect on people." Noah winked at him, and Cooper found himself smiling.

They made it back to the table by then, and Coop automatically gave Noah a cover. "Hate to be the downer of the night, but I need to head back early tonight. I have some shit to take care of early tomorrow, and Noah's driving me home." He hit his friend's arm.

"Drink a little too much?" Russ asked.

Cooper nodded, figuring that was as good an excuse as any, even though he wasn't acting drunk.

They said their goodbyes, and Coop watched as Noah told Jules it was nice to see her again. Her eyes skimmed up and down Noah like he'd seen women do to him a million times. Cooper looked at him, too. He was about two inches taller than himself. Noah's muscles were long, lean and defined. His hair had dried sticking up in different directions, like he'd run his hands through it. Stubble covered his square jaw, making Cooper wonder why he hadn't shaved.

He shrugged. The guy probably had women falling over him all the time. *And why the hell am I thinking about this stuff?*

"Why did you shrug?" Noah asked.

Coop took a step back. He didn't know. Hell, he didn't even know why he'd been looking at Noah. "I'm drunk, remember? I do random shit for no reason when I'm drunk. Let's get going."

It was still hot as hell when they stepped outside. The parking lot was darker than it should've been, one of the lights having gone out.

"You really need me to drive? I'm sober," Noah asked him.

"So am I, and I don't trust anyone enough to let them drive my truck. She's my baby. We'd be sitting here to sober up before that happened." Cooper pulled the door open and climbed in. Noah did the same on the other side.

"I forgot you used to want one. Even when we were kids you talked about how you wanted a big-ass truck one day, so you could run everything off the road. Little did I know that seventeen years later, that would be me."

"Holy shit." Cooper started the truck. "I forgot about that. And I'm never going to live this down, am I, Stretch?" he teased.

"Not until you do something else I can talk shit about."

Even when they were kids, Coop remembered Noah always had a comeback for whatever he said. They used to give each other hell all the time, trying to see who could outdo each other. It was a toss-up on which one of them would win. Tonight he decided to let it go.

As they drove through the dark toward the house, he asked, "What happened with Jules?" Cooper rubbed the back of his neck, wondering if it was okay to ask that.

"Nothing, really. It felt good to visit with an old friend, but...hell, you know how it goes? She started getting closer to me and touching me. I could see it in her eyes, but then I was kind of stuck. I would have come off as an asshole if I said, 'oh, and by the way, I like cock as much as you probably do."

Cooper's stomach dropped out at that.

"Shit. I'm sorry. I shouldn't have said that. I didn't mean to make you uncomfortable."

Coop didn't reply because he wasn't sure what to say. Noah talked about men the way he did women. He was used to it from the guys, but again, it was usually about the opposite sex.

Noah sighed. Coop noticed him lower himself in his seat. "I forget sometimes. When we were kids, you were the only person I really told shit to. I've only been back a little while, and my mind jumped right back to seventeen years ago. I don't think before I speak."

That made Cooper's stomach drop even farther. Noah could talk to him however he wanted. That's what friends were for. "You and me? We're cool, man. You don't have to watch what you say. I just...I guess I forget sometimes, too. I'll get used to it."

A question popped into his head then. Coop almost didn't ask it, but hell, he didn't really work that way. He just went for it, no matter what it was. "About Jules...have you ever?"

"Fucked a woman?" Noah asked.

"Yeah." Coop had no idea why he wanted to know.

"Sure I have. Didn't change anything, though."

Cooper made a turn, and then glanced at Noah. "That's not what I mean. You know me. I'm nosey."

"When I was fifteen and started to really realize I was gay, it freaked me the hell out at first. Met a girl. She was eighteen. We had sex, and yeah, I got off, but...it wasn't right. Then once when I was in the army. I didn't want to get caught with a man, and I was horny. I was only with a woman once that first year but it wasn't the same. It's just...not what I want. Been all men since then. Was a little hard sneaking around in the service, but I managed."

Cooper nodded, not sure if Noah was even looking at him. He appreciated the hell out of his friend's honesty. "Different strokes, I guess," Coop told him.

Noah was quiet for a few minutes. Even though Coop's eyes were on the road, he knew Noah was looking at him. He didn't know why he was asking if Noah had been with women. The only way he could describe it was that they were friends, and he wanted to try and understand him.

But then...that wasn't right, either. He'd been irritated when Noah spoke with Jules tonight. Probably because he was worried about her getting hurt. What else could it be?

Finally Noah replied, "Yeah...different strokes."

# CHAPTER FIVE

It had been three weeks since their night at the bar. Noah's ribs hardly ever hurt now, so he'd spent a bunch of time working on his car. He finally got the thing going. Now, he had to hope the damn thing kept running.

"I'm gonna go grab some more wood." Noah picked up his T-shirt from where he'd tossed it on one of the postsand wiped the sweat from his forehead. They had their priorities straight deciding to build the deck out back before working on anything inside the house. It would be perfect for barbequing. Who needed an updated inside when you could be outdoors?

"Need any help?" Coop looked over at him and rubbed a hand over his short hair. God damn, he'd grown up nice. No matter how hard Noah tried, he couldn't *not* notice Coop. Strong, sexy and cocky always drew his eye. His jeans rode low on his hips, and Noah wished like hell Cooper was gay so he'd have even the slightest chance to be able to lick the "v" that disappeared below his jeans. To unzip his pants and let his tongue trace Cooper's dick.

*Stop it. Stop those fucking thoughts right there, man.* This was the first real friend he ever had, and probably the best one. Thoughts like that would screw everything up. Only, they'd been happening more and more... And he could have sworn Cooper knew Noah couldn't help but look at him, and he didn't seem to mind it.

*In your dreams, man.*

"Nah, I'm good. I got it." He threw the shirt back down before heading over to the shed that held all their supplies for the deck. Noah grabbed a heavy load, maneuvering the long boards around the door before heading around back again.

Noah dropped them to the ground beside Cooper.

"We're getting it knocked out pretty fast."

"Sure are." Noah handed him one of the pieces of wood and they laid it on the frame. It was another hot day today, the sun beating down on them.

"We should plant some more trees back here. And I can put us up a patio cover in a few hours." As soon as the words left Noah's mouth, he started to backtrack. "A cover for you, I mean." Even though he'd been here for a month now, this wasn't his place. Sure he was renting a room from Coop, but that wouldn't last forever. He wasn't sure why he'd said that. He'd always just kind of felt comfortable with Cooper. From the first time they collided jumping for that football, he'd felt a connection with his friend.

"You live here, don't ya?" Cooper replied, as he laid out another board.

"I do, but that doesn't make it my house."

"It's not like I don't have the room, man. And you're putting in the work, too. You'll be here enjoying it."

Noah could tell by the tone of his voice what he was doing. "Still doesn't make it my house. Now stop trying to argue with me just to hear yourself speak."

Laughing, Cooper picked up the electric screwdriver and put a few screws into place.

It took them another hour and a half to get the rest of the boards laid out. They were quiet some of the time, and talked about random shit the rest of it.

"I think that's good for today." Cooper leaned against the deck.

"Too old to keep going?" Noah teased. It was early evening already, but he liked any excuse he could find to give his friend shit.

"Fuck off." Coop shoved Noah's arm and smiled. "I'm going easy on you."

"Easy isn't the way I like it." Noah winked at him. Ah, hell. Why did he keep getting himself into trouble where Cooper was concerned? Coop's eyes held a flash of surprise, and Noah almost apologized again, but this time he let it go. "I'm gonna head inside."

He began to walk past Cooper when Coop reached out and grabbed his arm. Damned if he didn't like that rough, calloused hand on him a little too much.

He didn't let go when Noah stopped moving.

"It's cooling off. Why don't we relax out here for a while with a beer or something? I think we deserve it after how we both worked our asses off today."

Even though Noah had been the one to say he was going inside, he didn't want to. All he'd wanted to do was avoid any chance of awkwardness there could be between them. And to get his head on straight after the way he'd been eyeing Coop all day.

But a beer sounded nice. There was nothing wrong with having a drink with a friend on a warm summer night.

"I could use a beer or two." He looked down at Cooper's hand still holding his arm. When he did, Cooper jerked it away.

"We have leftover pizza in there, too."

They always ordered an extra one so they could eat off it for a couple days. Neither of them were very good cooks.

They went into the house. Coop threw some ice into a small cooler and pushed a few beers inside for each of them, while Noah filled two plates with pizza and tossed them in the microwave. It only took a couple minutes before they were both sitting in lawn chairs out back with their feet up, the cooler between them and a plate of pizza on each of their laps.

"So, is it good to be back?" Coop asked him.

Noah finished chewing before he replied. "It is. This place has always felt like home to me."

"Yeah, I remember you saying that when we were kids. I thought you were crazy as hell."

Cooper's parents had died, and he'd moved here about six months before Noah had showed up. "You were still adjusting. Doesn't mean you didn't love it, though. I remember." Cooper was Blackcreek and Blackcreek was Cooper. At least where Noah was concerned.

Coop nodded, and Noah couldn't help but wonder if he was remembering some of their childhood adventures.

"Without running the risk of sounding like a sap, I'll admit it got better after you got here. Hell, we had fun, didn't we?"

Noah looked over as Cooper took a drink of his beer. He watched Coop's neck as he swallowed it down, wishing he could taste his skin. Christ, he was horny. He needed to get out of the house more, and do it without Cooper. But it seemed that whenever Cooper wasn't working, they were always together. "We did."

And then, because he thought it was a good idea, he changed the subject. "I'm thinking it's about time I start looking into getting my business going." He'd been reluctant when he first moved back, because coming to Blackcreek had been a spur-of-the-moment decision, anyway. There'd been the chance he wouldn't want to stay—that being here wouldn't feel quite the same way it had when he was a kid. In the short month he'd been back, Noah knew he wanted to stay.

"No shit? That's good. Making things more permanent."

"Eh," Noah shrugged. "Figure this is as good a place as any." He felt Cooper's eyes on him, probably glad his friend was moving back for sure, but Noah couldn't meet his gaze. He needed to nip this attraction he felt, now. "It'll be some work getting it off the ground. Will probably be slow in going, so it's best I get started now."

"I'm glad you're stayin', man. Seriously, you're welcome here as long as you want." Coop set his plate on the ground.

"You just like the free labor." Both men laughed.

The sun began to lower, the air slightly cooling but not enough to really matter. Behind Coop's yard was nothing but trees and open sky. Noah loved it. He always had. Blackcreek was beautiful.

"Tell me about the army," Cooper asked, his voice thoughtful and deep.

"Not much to tell. It was the military. Tough as hell. Spent a little time in Iraq. It's not something I really like to talk about."

"Sorry. Didn't mean to pry."

This time Noah couldn't help but look over at him. Coop smiled, and it was still that same confident, mischievous smile as when they were kids. But then he cocked his head a little...seemed to dissect Noah in a different way. Becaushe didn't want to speak about his time in the army, maybe?

Noah cleared his throat. "You didn't pry. All you did was ask a question."

"And you said you had a..."

"Boyfriend?" Noah chuckled.

"Bastard. Yeah, you were seeing someone before you came back? Hell, I've never been serious about anyone. It's just not something I see for myself. Were you guys?"

Noah groaned. The last thing he wanted to do was talk about David—especially to Cooper. He knew what Noah went through as a child. It made him feel like a chump that he had fallen for someone who would do the same shit his mom had.

"I thought we were serious." Before Coop had the chance to ask him what happened, Noah continued. "And why am I not surprised you've never been serious about someone?"

His friend laughed. "Variety is way too much fun to only have one flavor for the rest of your life."

They both laughed again, helping Noah dodge the David bullet, and to stop wondering why Cooper would be curious about his relationships, anyway.

***

Coop watched as Noah's chest and stomach heaved in and out with laughter. Eyed the bar piercing through his nipples. And Jesus...wondered how they would feel against his tongue. What it would be like to run his hand over Noah's firm muscles.

He whipped his head around and looked out at the trees. What the hell was wrong with him? He'd never in his life admired another man the way he just had his friend. *But it isn't the first time with Noah... And Noah wasn't just another man...* When it came to Noah, things were always *more*.

It wasn't as though it happened all the time, but there had definitely been moments in the past couple weeks. It freaked him the hell out. The only way he could describe it was... Damn, he couldn't really, but maybe it was because things with Noah had always been on another level. Even their friendship when they were kids.

Coop drained the rest of his beer before grabbing another.

"What's wrong with you?" Noah asked.

His first instinct was to ask him how he knew, but that suddenly confused him as well. Noah had always known him so much better than anyone else. He noticed things about Cooper that no one else did. "Nothing," he gritted out, before realizing he was being an ass. The last thing he wanted to do was draw attention to his fucked-up behavior. "It's a gorgeous night and I'm holding a beer, after building a deck today. What could be wrong? The only thing that would make it better is a woman to celebrate with."

Out of the corner of his eye, he saw Noah nod. Before either of them had the chance to speak again, Coop's cell beeped in his pocket. Leaning back, he pulled the thing out and then groaned at the name that flashed on the screen.

"Your uncle?"

"Yeah. Which really isn't a big deal. I don't know why I acted like that. He did raise me, after all."

Cooper hit talk on the phone and then said, "Hello."

"If it isn't my nephew, who likes to pretend he's too busy for his family. You're breaking your aunt's heart, Cooper."

Cooper winced. When things started out like this, it was never a good sign. It wasn't that Vernon was a bad man. He supported his family, didn't drink or do drugs. The man loved his wife something fierce and would do anything for her—a quality Cooper respected. But he was also tough as nails. He'd been older than Coop's dad by fifteen years, and even though he took Cooper in and treated him as a son, he never let Cooper forget that fact, either. That he hadn't wanted kids, they'd been set in their ways, but took Cooper in anyway, because that's what family did. He was hard and he expected the same out of Coop—even to the extent that he said it was weak to dwell on the death of his parents.

*"They're gone, kid, and I know it hurts, but you gotta push that aside. There's nothing you can do about it. The sooner you realize that, the better. Toughen up, be a man, and leave it in the past."*

That had been the first night Cooper had a nightmare about his parents dying in the fire. He didn't want to leave them behind—hadn't wanted to leave her trapped, but his Mom had told him to. Now his uncle was telling him to leave them behind as well.

"I know. I need to get out there and visit you guys. Things have been crazy around here." Which was partially true, and partially a lie. Yes, he'd been busy at the station and around the house, but he definitely had time to do other things.

63

"We're only half an hour away. You know it's easier for you to get out here than for her to get to you. She loves you like a son, Cooper, and always has. Not comin' round for months is no way a son treats the woman who raised him."

Guilt burned through his gut. Vernon was right. "I'll be out there soon. Promise." And he would. It was an asshole move for him to stay away so long, after all they'd done for him. He didn't even know why he did.

"There ya go. That's what I want to hear."

"So how's everything going?" Coop asked. He looked over at Noah to apologize with his eyes that he had to take a call, and Noah nodded his understanding.

"Good, good. They got a couple new officers at the station. A bunch of Nancy's, according to Jim. Have you met 'em?"

Coop froze at that, hoping like hell Noah didn't hear him through the phone. How many times had Vernon talked like that when Coop was a kid, and he never thought twice about it? He had no doubt the new cops weren't really gay, and he also knew Vernon meant that in the most derogatory way possible.

"Aren't you supposed to be retired? Why are you still worried about what's going on at the station?"

"Once a cop, always a cop. You should feel like that about your job, too, if you take it seriously."

That comment hit Coop like a punch to the gut. Being a good fireman was, and always had been, the most important thing to Cooper. There were certain things he owed his aunt and uncle, and he figured being a good fire fighter was something he owed his parents.

"You know there's nothing more important to me than doing my job well." He didn't add anything more than that because it would only lead to an argument.

It was only a minute or two later that Vernon ended the call.

"Sounds like he hasn't changed much," Noah said. Coop didn't reply because he didn't need to. They both knew what his friend said was true. It was this odd relationship with all of them. Even as kids, Noah had liked Cooper's uncle, too. He'd loved when Vernon took them all camping or fishing, and Noah had stayed at his house any night he could. But then, Noah always got pissed when Vernon and Cooper got into it.

"Don't let him make you feel like shit, man. He's always done that. You're good at what you do, and there's never been anything wrong with the way you grieved your parents," Noah added.

*Smoke. That's all he could see was smoke all around him. And it was so hot. So, so hot it felt like his skin was melting off him.*

*"Go! You need to go, Cooper."*

*"No!" He shook his head. "Not without you."*

*Mom was on the floor, a beam holding her down. Fire was all around him, smoke so thick it was difficult to see her clearly. There was a pop and a hiss from behind her, so loud that Cooper heard it over everything else around them.*

*"Baby...go. I need you to go. Run as fast as you can. Do what I say, Cooper, now!"*

*Another pop. A wall on the other side of the room crashed down.*

*"Go! Now, Cooper. Get out of here, right now!"*

*And he did. Cooper ran, screaming and crying the whole way.*

*Something grabbed ahold of his arm.*

*"Coop! Wake up. You're dreaming."*

*Cooper jerked out of sleep at the sound of Noah's voice. Nausea crawled up his throat. He couldn't believe he had the dream in front of Noah. It was their very first sleepover, and now he'd think Coop was a baby.*

*"You were screaming," Noah said as the bedroom door opened and the light turned on.*

*"What in the hell is going on in here?" Uncle Vernon opened the door.*

*Coop froze. He didn't want to tell his uncle he had the dream again. Didn't want his uncle to say he was being ridiculous and make Noah think him a baby even more.*

*"Cooper? Noah?" Vernon asked. "What are you guys doing? We told you it was time to settle down and go to bed."*

*Still, Coop couldn't make his voice work.*

*"It was me," Noah said.*

*Coop's eyes flashed toward his friend.*

*"I couldn't sleep and was playing a trick on Coop. I didn't mean to be so loud." Noah's lie sounded so true, even Coop would have believed him if he didn't know better.*

*"If you can't listen to my rules, kid, you won't be allowed to stay here."*

*"Yes, sir." Noah looked toward the ground.*

*"Now get to bed. You nearly gave us a heart attack." Uncle Vernon turned off the light and closed the door.*

*It took Coop forever to talk. "Bet you think I'm a wuss now."*

*"No."*

*The nausea started to melt away. He should have known Noah wouldn't make him feel stupid. "Thanks...for covering... He doesn't get it."*

*"Was it about your parents?" Noah asked.*

*"Yeah."*

*A pause. "I get it."*

*And, Coop somehow knew his friend did. Even though he still had his mom and dad, he got it.*

*"Do you think he won't let me come over no more?" Noah asked.*

*"No...it's all talk." He believed that. Yeah, Uncle Vernon was tough, but he wouldn't take away Coop's best friend. "If he tried, I wouldn't let 'em."*

*Noah was quiet for a minute. "I bet I'd have dreams, too...if that happened to me."*

*And for the first time, Coop didn't feel like such a baby because of the nightmares. If Noah said he would have them, too, it must be normal to not be able to forget.*

*"Thanks, Noah." Into the darkness, Coop smiled. He had the coolest best friend in the world. His smile stretched even bigger when Noah's hand touched his shoulder.*

A warm hand came down on Cooper's shoulder and snapped him out of the memory. Turning, he took in the sight of his friend as Noah let his hand fall away. It was like the years had wiped away some of those memories. He'd been devastated when Noah left— when he didn't hear a word from him—but over the years, those feelings faded. He'd been young and lived a whole lot of life since then. But having him back now made those feelings flare to life again. Had he ever had a friend he felt as close with as he did Noah? Someone he trusted with everything inside him, and who would always be there for him?

He didn't think so. At thirty years old, there had never been anyone who touched him as deeply as Noah.

"Thanks, man." He knew it has probably been at least a minute since Noah had spoken to him, but he didn't call Cooper on it.

Noah stretched, the corded muscles in his arms straining and tightening. His stomach tensed, showing off his six-pack beneath all that golden skin.

Lust shot through Cooper. His balls started to ache.

*What. The. Fuck.*

Still, he didn't turn away. That had always been how he went about life—full speed ahead. He regretted running away from his parents, even though he'd only be a snot-nosed, nine-year-old kid. He didn't want any other regrets in his life, so he took a second to visually get his fill. To try and make sense of what the hell these thoughts and desires meant.

Noah didn't seem to notice. He ran a hand through his dark hair. Cooper admired the veins in his hands, and the dragon tattoo on his upper back that he'd seen the first time Noah had been shirtless in front of him. He shifted his eyes to Noah's face. To the curve of his lips, and how he'd made Cooper smile that night and so many others.

And then he remembered the call with his uncle. How much he would disappoint him if he ever knew Cooper was eying Noah like this. And why he hell was he? He was straight. He liked women. Always had.

Cooper pushed to his feet. He needed to get himself under control and find a way to wipe these feelings away. "I think I'm about ready to go in."

"Yeah, me, too." Noah stood as well. They left the chairs in the lawn, but Cooper picked up the cooler as Noah grabbed the plates.

After they put things away, they stood in Cooper's kitchen. Silent. It wasn't even dark yet, but still, Coop said, "I think I'm going to head to my room. I'm not feeling too hot." Really, he needed to get his fucking head on straight.

"Yeah…me, too. Maybe watch a movie or something."

Cooper nodded and then went to walk away. Noah stopped him, putting an arm around his shoulder. "Don't let it get to ya, man."

Coop's body flamed. The spot where their bodies met, a wildfire burned inside him, flaring out from there.

Nodding again, he pulled away, because…Jesus, because…he didn't want to. That meant he needed to back up and get out of here. Now.

***

A hand shoved beneath Coop's boxer-briefs...but that wasn't right, was it? He always slept naked, and he was in his bed.

Any questions or thoughts were cut off when the hand wrapped tightly around his cock. And he was hard. He was already so fucking hard.

"Oh, God." Cooper dropped his head back as the hand started to stroke. Quick, strong pulls up and down his dick. Another hand touched his balls, adding the perfect amount of pressure as it played with them. Those touches somehow traveled the length of his sensitive body. A low buzz of excitement gained strength inside him as the skilled, rough hand jerked him off.

It had only been about five seconds, but it was already the best fucking hand job he'd ever had.

A thumb brushed the tip, spread pre-come around, before stroking him again.

His body jerked as he was flipped to his stomach, a hard weight on his back. A masculine voice in his ear said, "I told you, I didn't like it easy."

Cooper thrashed, scrambling into a sitting position in his bed. The room was pitch black, silent except for his quick, panting breaths. Sweat dripped from him.

He'd dreamed about another man.

About Noah.

Holy shit.

Cooper ran a hand down his chest but it didn't feel the same as Noah's had. No, not Noah, just a dream. He didn't stop until he reached the erection between his legs, trying to find some of the pleasure he'd just imagined.

He was hard as hell, with a picture of his best friend in his head. What the fuck was up with him?

His body tensed when he ran his finger over his head, and the hole there. Then he stroked. Stroked the same way he had a million times, but different because this time he chased that feeling from the dream.

The dream of Noah.

It didn't matter right now. Cooper needed some fucking relief. He squeezed his hand tighter around his cock and jerked-off, thinking about another man.

Thinking about Noah.

# CHAPTER SIX

Noah loved his balls to be played with, even when it was himself doing the touching. He cupped them, rubbed, as his other lubed fist rapidly jerked up and down his cock. Each time he reached the head, he rubbed it with his thumb, reveling in the feel of it rasping over the little hole there.

He was such an ass to be masturbating at the thought of his straight best friend, but that knowledge didn't stop him from thrusting his hips as he jacked off. From squeezing tighter and stroking faster as his other hand teased his sac.

He was right there—his orgasm right at the surface, fighting to break free. Noah wanted to hold it off, to keep feeling his hand working himself. But damn, he needed to come, too. Needed the release, because he was wound so fucking tight.

So, Noah let himself do it, let himself pretend it was Cooper's hand on him. Let himself imagine Coop's thumb rubbing the pre-come from where it beaded at his head. His hips thrust faster, and then his balls drew up tight. A jet of come flew up, landing on his abdomen. He jerked again and shot more, pleasure rushing through him before he went limp on the bed.

Noah got up, grabbed a towel and cleaned off. He dropped back into bed, flinging an arm over his head and closing his eyes. Jesus, this lust for Coop hit him hard and fast. Though he guessed, if he was being honest with himself, it wasn't much of a surprise. He'd always been more deeply connected to Cooper than he had anyone else in his life. Only when he was a kid, it was just friendship. Now it was all mixed-up, and fucked-up, by the fact that he wanted him. Noah needed to find a way to get over this before he did something stupid and screwed everything up.

***

Noah slept like shit the whole night. Deciding it wasn't worth it to stay in bed, tossing and turning, he got up early. It couldn't be any later than six, if it was even that. He pulled on a pair of shorts and headed for the shower.

Noah let the hot water pour over him until it started to turn cold. Nothing relaxed him like a hot shower. Okay, maybe one thing did, but considering he didn't really know many people in this town—none of them being gay—he didn't think sex was going to happen any time soon.

After washing up in lukewarm water, Noah got out, dried off, and wrapped his towel tightly around his waist. If there wasn't a reason for Cooper to be up early, he never was. The man slept like the dead. He could pass out anywhere, which Noah usually could, too, but he rose fairly early every day.

Coop's habit of sleeping in was exactly the reason he didn't expect to walk out of the bathroom, round the corner, and slam right into him.

Cooper had his shirt off, his hair sticking up as though he'd run his hands through it a million times, just the way Noah had imagined him when he'd jerked off last night. "Shit. Sorry." He went to pull back but Cooper was already doing the same. His eyes down the hall, to the floor, on the ceiling, anywhere other than on Noah.

"No problem. Easy to do. I mean, not easy. Well it is, but...fuck. I gotta take a piss." Cooper moved around him, with clothes and a towel in his hand, as though he was taking a shower. He slammed the bathroom door behind him.

What the hell was that?

Did he already fuck-up somehow? Cooper's reaction made him think he did.

Shaking his head, Noah made his way back to his room. He dressed and then found random shit to do for a little while. He needed to get out of the house for a while today. Get some fresh air away from Cooper, and get some perspective or something.

And start getting his life together. He'd sat around for a month. Granted he'd been hurt, but it was still too long. His father used to fall apart when his mom played her games. That wouldn't be Noah.

When he made his way into the kitchen, Coop was sitting at the table with a cup of coffee. This time, with his shirt on. Thank God.

"I'm going to head out. I want to grab some parts for the shower, and maybe see if there's any buildings or shops I can look into." It was probably a good idea to get Cooper's shower fixed so they didn't have the same problem again.

Coop nodded. "Let me know if you need me to ask around. And give me the receipt for whatever you buy, and I'll pay ya back."

"Thanks. I will. Town's not too big, I'm sure I'll figure something out."

"Depending on when you get back, I might not be here. I talked to Adrianna, this woman I see from time to time. We're going out, and then I'm staying at her place tonight." Cooper grinned at him.

A knot formed in Noah's gut that he had no business feeling. Coop had a right to go out. It surprised him this was the first time Cooper had made plans with a woman. "Guess I don't need to tell ya to have fun," Noah tried to tease, but the words were awkward on his tongue.

"Definitely not." He stood and Noah looked at him. For the first time all morning, Cooper met his eyes.

Coop stood there for a second, staring at him as though he wanted to say something else. Noah waited, but it never came. "Have a good one. I'll see ya tomorrow or something."

Hell, maybe Noah would go out, too. Maybe a night with a man was what he needed to get his mind off Cooper.

***

Cooper stood at the counter in the busy bar. It wasn't the same one he'd taken Noah to the other night. He decided to take Adrianna to Rowdies. Things were a little upbeat here. A band played in the back. The dance floor so packed, it looked like people could hardly move.

They always tried to go places that weren't right in town. Rumors spread so fast in Blackcreek, and since neither Adrianna or Cooper wanted anything serious with each other, it made things easier.

"You're awfully quiet, Cooper." She looked up at him from the stool she sat on. Coop stood in front of her, close, Adrianna's back to the bar so she could see him.

And she was right. He was being quiet. But he wasn't sure why. "Nah. You're imaginin' things." He grinned at her and she smiled back. She really was a beautiful woman. He'd always loved red hair. Hers was this deep shade, with certain spots looking almost purple in some lights. Cooper touched it, let some of the strands slide through his fingertips. All that soft hair. This was what he needed to try and focus on. This and the fact that they both wanted the same thing from each other was just icing on the cake. She wasn't looking for a guy like Coop for the long haul. He guessed he wasn't the kind of guy she thought would be a good fit as her kid's stepdad.

She was right. Not that he didn't like kids. He just never saw himself as a father. The thought of getting hurt and leaving a child behind scared him too much.

Leaning forward, he put his mouth close to her ear. "It's been a while. How have things been with you?" His arms were on either side of her, palms on the edge of the counter.

"Too long. And things are good. Keeping busy at work." She had this husky, smoky voice that had always driven him wild. "How's your friend that you brought to the ER? He hurt his ribs, right?"

At that, Cooper pulled away and stood up straight. It would mean he'd have to talk louder so she could hear. Noah was the last person he wanted to talk to Adrianna about. Which made him an asshole. It wasn't his friend's fault Cooper had a fucked up dream about him, and started noticing him in ways he shouldn't. "All healed up."

Picking up his beer, he drank the whole thing and signaled for the bartender to bring another one. "You ready for more?" he asked, but the glass in Adrianna's hand was still half full. She held it up to show him.

"I'm good. So, he's new in town, right? How'd you guys end up friends so fast?"

Cooper fought his groan. She was only being friendly and making conversation, but the point in tonight was to get his mind off Noah, not to keep thinking about him.

*It was a fluke. A weird night. I'm not attracted to Noah.*

"He and I were friends as kids. He up and disappeared while I was away with my aunt one weekend, and I never heard from him again. Not till he came back last month. Been seventeen years."

He hadn't needed to say all that. It pissed him off that he did.

Cooper grabbed the new beer and took a couple long pulls. "I want my hands on you. Come dance with me."

79

She smiled and set her drink down. Cooper joined his hand with hers and led her to the dance floor. The song was fast but he still pulled her tightly against him, moving slowly, letting his hands skate up and down her back. *Soft, soft, soft. That's what I want.*

They danced a few songs, Adrianna exploring as much as Coop. Afterward, they took a break and he ordered another drink, bullshitting about life and whatever else they could think to talk about. Anytime they went out, Adrianna never drank more than one.

The conversation continued on for a while. Each time Cooper went to ask her if she was ready to leave, he asked her another question instead. *I'm putting off going home with her. Why isn't Adrianna turning me on like she always has?*

Finally it was Adrianna who prompted, "Not that I'm not having a good time here with you, Coop, but you have to remember, I need to be home early for my daughter. She has a soccer game in the morning, and it's highly frowned upon for me, as the coach, to be late."

His pulse spiked. "I thought your daughter was with her dad tonight, so we were going to your place?"

She shook her head. "The soccer schedule got changed and she has the early game. It's not fair to her dad to lose time with her having to get her home early. He's taking her next weekend instead. I got a sitter for tonight." Her nose wrinkled, and he could tell she wondered what the big deal was. It wasn't as if she'd never come to his house before.

Coop shook his head. What the hell was his problem? It *shouldn't* be a problem. He had the right to bring a woman home, just like Noah had the right with a man.

Coop pushed to his feet, the chair accidentally falling backward. "Shit." He bent and picked it up. He needed to relax. Coop had no idea why he was so on edge.

"Let me go pay and we can go." He took care of the tab and then met Adrianna by the door. They had taken her car. There wasn't a place for Coop to hide his truck at her house, so she often drove. She always pulled her car around by the shed at his place.

"Ready?" he asked, as he held the door open for her.

"Always."

# CHAPTER SEVEN

"I'm hungry, and the food here is shit. There's a little diner about a mile east called Reds. I'll be there for the next half hour or so, grabbing something to eat." The brown-haired guy—Wes, who'd sat next to Noah at the bar—stood and walked out. Noah didn't watch him go. Didn't have to to know he'd enjoy the view. He was sexy as hell, strong jaw, with the right amount of stubble that Noah liked. He loved the way stubble felt against his skin.

He also knew that even though he rarely picked someone up at a bar, that's exactly what he would do tonight. It's what he came out for, after all.

It hadn't been ten minutes that he'd been here when he'd noticed Wes looking at him. At first he'd turned away each time Noah met his eyes. When Noah let his gaze linger enough, Wes got the message—Noah was gay, too. He'd come right up to the bar and took the stool next to him and ordered a drink. They bullshitted a little, not too much, because the last thing he wanted was to risk shit going down, but now Wes had solved that problem for them.

Raising a hand, Noah signaled the bartender over. "How much?"

He closed out his tab, not that it was large, before climbing into his Mustang to find Reds. As soon as he pulled in, he saw Wes through a window, sitting in a booth alone.

"Hey," he said a few minutes later as he approached Wes.

"Hey." Wes nodded to the seat across from him and Noah sat down. "I'm only getting coffee and a piece of pie."

That sounded about perfect to Noah. Would fill the hole, and be quick, too. The waitress approached them at that, and they both ordered their coffee and apple pie.

"Lived around here long?" Noah asked. He'd headed closer toward Denver, though not too far from home, figuring it would be much easier to meet someone. He'd almost gone all the way to the city to find a club downtown, but that wasn't really his scene. He didn't mind going if he had someone with him, but wasn't much into going alone.

"Nah. Not from around here. I live in California. I'm spending time with my sister while she's sick, helping her take care of her kid and all. I needed a night away, though." He shrugged. "I wasn't sure where to go."

There was a sadness to him that Noah hadn't noticed before. It immediately made him feel for the man. "Sorry to hear about your sister. I hope everything's okay."

He looked toward the window, making Noah realize that it probably wouldn't be.

The waitress returned and set their mugs and food in front of them. "What about you?" Wes asked, when she left.

"I actually live in Blackcreek. I've only been back about a month now, but I lived there for a few years when I was younger."

Wes nodded but didn't ask where Blackcreek was, making Noah wonder if he knew.

They spent about thirty minutes eating and talking. It wasn't about anything at all really, and he wondered if maybe picking someone up in a bar was even more of a rarity for Wes than it was for him. He liked the guy, though. There was something about him that Noah connected to.

After getting their bill, Noah asked, "Are you lookin' to leave with me?"

"As long as you know it's just tonight. I have too much shit on my plate right now."

"That's all I want, too." The problem was they obviously couldn't go to Wes's. Not with a sick siste, and her kid there. Hotels were always an option but, fuck he hated going there. It made him feel like his mother. Like he was sneaking away somewhere to do something he shouldn't.

*Coop won't be home tonight,* he said so himself. It felt weird as hell to bring someone to Cooper's house. It wasn't something they'd talked about, but again, he wouldn't be there. He made sure Noah knew to make himself at home. He paid rent to live there. "You want to follow me to my place? It's a bit of a drive, but…"

"Let's go." Wes stood and Noah did the same. Each took some money out of their pockets and tossed it on the table.

This was exactly what he needed. He'd fuck thoughts of Cooper out of his head, and maybe it would give Wes a little bit of peace, too.

The drive home felt quicker than it should. Noah was in a daze for part of it, but the second he closed the door behind them, he saw clear and knew what he wanted.

Sex. Release.

Noah's lips came down hard on Wes's. Their tongues battled for dominance, Wes obviously wanting it as much as Noah. The temperature in his body went up about a million degrees, his cock instantly going hard. This is what he loved about being with a man—the fight, the fact that he didn't have to hold back, and hoped like hell the other guy wouldn't with him, either.

Noah pulled away. "Take off your shirt."

Wes didn't need to be asked twice. He pulled the shirt over his head and dropped it to the floor. Noah only gave himself a few seconds to enjoy the view before backing Wes up until he hit the wall. There was a clattering sound, something on the wall, maybe, but he didn't take the time to pay attention.

Noah crushed his body against Wes's. Wes leaned forward but Noah pulled back, out of his reach. "What do you like?"

Wes smiled. "I'm verse, but tonight I want to be fucked. It doesn't mean I won't try and take control, though."

Just what he wanted to hear. He loved being in control, loved driving another man wild. Didn't mean he didn't like the battle for it, though.

Noah ripped his shirt over his head. Wes groaned, his eyes on the piercing in his nipples. Noah smiled. Like he'd told Cooper, men liked it.

*Shit.* Why did he have to go and think about Coop right now? The whole point was to get his friend *out* of his head.

He pressed his mouth to Wes's again. The other man's fingers went to the button on Noah's pants, pushing it through the hole, then ran his hand through Noah's hair. Noah let his lips trail down Wes's throat. Pulled him away from the wall, stumbling toward his room.

That's when he saw him. Cooper. Standing at the base of the stairs, in nothing but a pair of jeans like Noah and Wes. His eyes were riveted on them, blazing with fire that Noah wished could possibly mean Cooper wanted him. He could pretend that wasn't what he wanted, but he knew it would be a lie.

"Aw, fuck. You're with someone?" Wes asked.

Noah couldn't look away from Cooper when he answered. "No." His heart thundered, his hands fisted, yet he didn't know why. Noah forced himself to break eye contact with Coop and look at Wes. He owed him an explanation for whatever the hell his weirdness was. "He's my roommate."

Then he looked at Cooper again. "I didn't think you'd be home tonight."

He stood there for what felt like hours, studying Noah, before turning and walking up the stairs. Noah let out a heavy breath, his erection long gone. Too many thoughts crowded his brain, questions about Cooper's reaction, and then guilt for whatever confusion this caused Wes.

When he looked at the other man, he was already grabbing his shirt. Noah closed his eyes and shook his head before saying, "I'm sorry. I don't know what that was about."

"Then you're a fool." Wes pulled the black T-shirt over his head.

*I wish.* "It's not that. He's straight. He just found out I'm gay, and this is the first time he's seen me with someone. I'm guessing it was harder for him to accept than he thought."

Wes chuckled. "It would have been fun."

"Yeah...yeah it would have. Maybe we still could—"

"No."

Noah figured Wes was right. "Let me walk you out." He followed Wes to his truck. When they got there, he leaned over in the seat, scribbled something on a piece of paper, and handed it to Noah.

"Depending on Chelle, I'll be around for a while. Gimme a call if you ever want to have a drink again."

The tone of Wes's voice told him that's all it would ever be. And he was okay with that. He liked the guy. He could hang out with him. "Thanks for understanding—not that I really have a clue what's going on."

Wes nodded.

"Take care of your sister. I hope she's okay."

Wes started the truck, and he was gone. Noah sighed, but didn't have much time to try and figure out why in the fuck Cooper had walked away from him because he heard the house door close. Coop walked around the side of the house with a woman, to where he assumed they'd parked.

Fuck. Maybe that was it. Coop had brought someone home, and Noah having someone there at the same time made him uncomfortable.

Or maybe... He wished like hell Wes could have been right.

***

"Are you okay?" Adrianna asked Cooper as she climbed into her car.

No, he wasn't. He really fucking wasn't. "Yeah, I'm sorry tonight had to end before it really had the chance to get started. Something came up. I didn't realize my roommate was bringing someone home."

"No, it's fine. I need to be home early tonight, anyway. I'm just worried about you. You were white as a ghost when you came upstairs."

*That's because I saw my friend with another man. Saw them together and wanted...* "Rain check?" he asked.

"If you're lucky," Adrianna winked, started the car, and drove away.

Part of him wanted to stay out here all night but he forced himself inside. He couldn't look at Noah when he closed the door so he started pacing the living room instead. His muscles hurt they were so tense. His heart pounded harder than he ever remembered it beating before.

And his brain? Fuck, he wanted nothing but to turn the thing off. To turn anything off inside himself that could think, feel...or become aroused.

"What's wrong, man? You're scaring the hell out of me." Noah leaned against the living room wall, his arms crossed. Cooper groaned, wishing like hell he didn't look at the man. Didn't see concern in his eyes. His hair tousled from the hands that had been running through it. Wished like hell he would put on a shirt.

"Fuck!" Cooper punched the wall. Pain shot through his hand and up his arm, but he didn't care. He wanted more of it to help him block the thoughts he tried to evict from inside him.

"*Christ,*" Noah hissed. "Talk to me. What happened? Did it freak you out that I brought someone home? Did it make you more uncomfortable than you thought it would?"

Yeah. Only not in the way he expected. Cooper actually felt like he could cry. Scream. He didn't understand anything going on, and he wanted nothing more than to set fire to the thoughts. Burn them into ash so they could never form in his brain again. A dream was one thing, but this? This was... "What the fuck's wrong with me? There's something wrong with me."

He slid down the wall and crumpled to the floor. He sat there, back against the wall, but feeling like he had nothing to hold him up.

"Coop." Noah's voice cracked, and Cooper couldn't stop himself from looking at his friend. The pain and understanding in his dark brown eyes simultaneously comforted, scared, and embarrassed him. In that moment, Noah saw something in him Cooper knew no one had ever seen before. Saw deeper than Coop even knew was there.

And he couldn't turn away.

As much as the words scared him, he couldn't *not* share this. Couldn't *not* trust his friend with what he was feeling, even though it killed him. "I saw you with him." It was hell when the one person you always felt like you could tell everything to was the one to have you tied in knots. The one you wanted to run from. Needed to, yet Cooper couldn't make himself flee.

"Jesus. I saw you kissing that guy and…what the hell is wrong with me? I had a beautiful woman in my bed and…shit." Cooper shook his head. Slid both hands through his hair and yanked as though that would somehow change things. "I wanted to kill him."

*I wanted to be him…*

Dizziness hit him. All he could do was thank God he was already sitting down. Noah watched him. His eyes intense, looking, searching, always finding things inside Cooper that no one else could see.

They burned Cooper's skin and were bright with…fuck. He didn't even want to think of that.

Noah took a step toward him, but when Cooper shook his head, he stopped. He only had on jeans, the button undone, and Cooper hated himself for even noticing that. For looking at the cut of his abs, the long muscles of his arms.

He jerked his head the opposite direction. Still he couldn't quiet his brain that kept telling him he shouldn't be thinking the things he was, and everything else that begged him to explore his thoughts.

"Cooper," Noah started, but Coop squeezed his eyes shut, and Noah stopped talking. Which made no sense considering Noah couldn't even see his face, but somehow he'd known.

"I've never felt jealousy like that in my life." He spoke so softly he wondered if Noah could even hear him. Somehow he knew he could, which was good since he didn't have it in him to speak any louder. He saw Noah's hands on the other man's waist as he'd kissed him against the wall. Saw Noah's nails digging in. Saw how roughly Noah had practically slammed the other man into the wall. He hadn't had to be gentle. It had been rough and primal, and it splintered every fucking thing Cooper thought of himself. Hit buttons he didn't know he had, and sprouted feelings he wanted to forget.

"It's wrong. Tell me it's fucking wrong, Noah. That I shouldn't feel this way. It's not right."

He heard Noah come toward him. Knew his friend stood across from him, probably leaning against the back of the couch, but Cooper still couldn't make himself look at him.

"You think I'm wrong, Coop? The way I live my life? Is that what you're saying? That I shouldn't feel or be attracted to men?"

Cooper heard it. The pain, disappointment, and anger in Noah's voice.

"No." He finally managed to look at him. He was such a pussy, sitting on the floor like this, but couldn't make himself move. "If that's who you are, then there's nothing wrong with it." But it was different for Coop. Wrong for Coop. He wasn't gay. He loved women. He'd had a lot of them. He'd been raised to believe it should be one man and one woman.

"So why does it make it wrong for you to—"

"Wonder what your hands would feel like on me like that?" He hated himself for admitting it, but needed to say it, too. Needed the words out because they were the only truth he understood right now. "Wonder what it would be like to touch you? To feel you?"

Noah cursed and for the first time, Cooper couldn't read him. Had no idea what his friend was thinking. Probably because he didn't know what he was thinking, either.

"What's wrong with me?" Cooper hated the weakness in his voice, the need to even ask such a question. He knew who he was and what he wanted. He'd never been the type to try and bend to fit someone else, but this? Wanting another man? This was different.

"There's nothing wrong with you." Noah's voice was hard—not angry, but firm, telling Coop he believed what he was saying.

And then he took a step forward. And another one.

Cooper's heart stopped. It was like a fist tightened around his chest, keeping him from breathing.

Noah hadn't shaved, and Cooper noticed the stubble on his jaw. Why the fuck was he noticing that shit?

Cooper couldn't move as Noah kept walking toward him. Didn't know if he wanted to. He should, because he wasn't gay and shouldn't crave Noah to keep getting closer, but he did.

Noah stopped in front of him. Looked down at Coop while Coop looked up at his friend. His eyes said so much, but nothing at the same time. All Cooper knew was they were intense beams pointed right at him.

Noah kneeled in front of Cooper.

"What the fuck are you doing?" he asked, panicked. Forget that Noah hadn't even done anything yet.

"I don't know," Noah replied, the same confusion in his voice that Cooper felt. Noah reached out and touched Coop's hand that rested on his knee. He looked down to see it was red, swollen from punching the wall.

But that's not what he paid attention to. He watched Noah's fingers trace his muscles. Watched as a hand that matched his in size fucking *caressed* him.

He wanted to punch Noah.

Wanted to run.

Wanted to ask for more.

The touch shot up his arm as Noah explored. It wasn't like they'd never touched each other before, but this was different. This was...intimate, which in a lot of ways Cooper felt was a stupid word for what they were doing, but it was all he could come up with.

Noah's fingers traced his, as though he was drawing them. Then slowly...slowing trailed up his arm.

*Push him the fuck away!*

Cooper knew he shouldn't but he watched—fascinated—and just *felt*.

Noah's fingers brushed his hairs as they ran up his forearm. His bicep. Cooper shivered. Couldn't take his eyes away.

Noah reversed his path, heading down again. Cooper risked a glance at him to see awe in Noah's eyes as he watched what he was doing to Cooper. Which made no sense. This was normal for him. It was what he did, but that's the only way Cooper could explain it.

When he got to Cooper's wrist, he circled it with his fingers. They touched. A woman would never be able to wrap one hand fully around his wrist like that.

And he liked it—the way they matched in so many ways. The masculinity of another man's hand on him. He fucking did, and he tried to blame all sorts of things: having his friend back in his life after all these years, drinking tonight. None of it was true, though, and he knew it.

Noah lifted Cooper's hand toward him. Coop's dick ached, and the fist around his chest tightened. His brain screamed at him to use his fist to punch Noah in the face, but he didn't. He watched, savoring the large hand touching him. The way his body overheated, trying to burn any conflicting thoughts.

Watched as Noah bent toward his hand. Watched as Noah pressed his lips to Cooper's swollen knuckles. Watched as Noah's eyes squeezed tight, his mouth still pressed to Cooper's hand, the action somehow traveling up his arm, until he felt it everywhere.

And then, Noah's eyes opened. He pulled away and Cooper finally let a heavy breath escape his lungs. A plea for Noah to touch him again echoed through his brain.

"There's nothing wrong with you," Noah said, before he stood up. "Nothing at all."

He took a few steps backward and Cooper wanted to ask him to stop. Ask him where he was going. But he didn't. Couldn't. Part of him hoped Noah would walk out the door and never come back, because if Noah left, he could forget about wanting him. Coop could block these thoughts from his head and keep going the way he had been his whole life.

But the other part... It wanted to trap him here. To find a way to keep Noah to himself, so he could explore the desires inflaming him.

"Take care of your hand. You should clean it and wrap it. I...I..."
For the first time all evening, Noah skipped over his words, but found his ground quickly. "I have to go, before I do something both of us will regret in the morning."

And like that—no shirt and all—he walked away, grabbing his keys off the table, and slammed the door.

Cooper didn't stop him. All he could do was sit there and look at his hand.

# CHAPTER EIGHT

Noah's whole body fucking trembled. He had to try three times to get the key in the ignition. The second he did, he cranked the engine and sped out of the driveway as fast as he could. He had no idea where he was going. All he knew was he had to get the hell out of there. He had to fight against every nerve ending, every little thing in his body, that clawed and yanked and pulled at him to go back. To go inside the house and taste Cooper's mouth.

To feel every inch of hard, muscled skin with his hands and his tongue. To fuck him, over and over and over, even if it killed him.

Had he ever wanted anyone with the passion that he desired Cooper? His best friend? The person who helped him get through his pain because of his parents when he was a kid, and who had been ripped away from him? No, Noah hadn't known it at the time. He hadn't realized what Cooper meant to him, but since coming back home, he got it.

He'd probably always wanted Coop. Maybe always would.

The shitty part was, no matter how much that need filled him up, no matter how hard his cock was beneath the fly of his jeans, or how hard his heart slammed into his ribcage, he couldn't touch, taste, or have Cooper. He wouldn't risk losing him when Coop freaked out about it later.

It didn't matter that Noah saw Coop's desire, his curiosity, and maybe even a portion of the same need Noah felt. Cooper wasn't gay, didn't realize he was, or he didn't want to be. And Noah swore he would never hide whom he was with ever again. Not the way he had with David, only to get betrayed. And what chance did they really have, anyway? Coop had told him before that he didn't see himself ever being serious with someone. But hooking up and then breaking up risked their friendship.

Christ, he would do anything to have Cooper, though.

Noah didn't calm down all night. He drove around for hours before pulling off into a parking lot for a couple more. The sun just started to break over the horizon, his eyes heavy and rough like sandpaper, when he decided to go back home. He couldn't stay away forever. They'd have to deal with this sooner or later, so he might as well get it over with. Maybe Cooper slept it off. It could have been alcohol that inspired last night. Fuck, he hoped not. That was probably the stupidest thing he could wish for, but there was now a knot in his gut. It kept twisting and turning, doubled knot after doubled knot, tying him up more and more because of how much he wanted Coop.

As soon as he stepped into the house, he knew Cooper was up. Noah followed the smell of coffee to the kitchen where Cooper sat in the same jeans, with no shirt, like he'd been last night.

Like Noah still was, too.

"Coffee's fresh." Cooper's voice was rough, probably from lack of sleep.

"I smell it. Thanks." Noah walked over and poured himself a cup.

"Of course you do. That was a stupid thing to say. I just didn't know what to say instead."

Sorrow pierced through him. Cooper always knew what to do. He always had the answers, or at least played it off like he did. The only time he was lost was when he'd have those dreams about his parents. Noah hated that his friend felt that way now.

"It's not a stupid thing to say, and it's okay to be freaked out. No one would blame you." Noah sat across from him and they both sipped their coffee. That ball in his stomach kept getting bigger and tighter. What if Cooper asked him to move out? Told him he couldn't see him anymore? The thought made him want to hit something. One of Noah's hands balled into a fist at the idea of losing Cooper again.

Coop chuckled humorlessly. "Freaked out. That's a pretty safe word to use." He set his cup down and held Noah's stare with his intense blue eyes. "I wanted you last night, Noah. Fucking. Wanted. You."

Noah choked on his coffee, coughing before he found a way to settle down. He didn't know why. It was just like Cooper to spit it out like that.

"Hell, I'm scared as fuck that I *still* might want you, man. That I have for a while now, and I don't know what it means. I had a dream about you, Noah. I've never wanted a man before." He shook his head. Noah reached out for him before jerking his hand back. Christ, he didn't even know if he could comfort his own friend any longer. And a dream? Was it wrong that the thought of Cooper dreaming of him made Noah feel invincible?

"How do you feel about it?" As soon as the question fell out of his mouth, he wished he could take it back.

"Confused. How do you think I feel?" He leaned back in his chair. Closed his eyes, as if in thought. Shook his head and then opened them again. "I've never trusted a friend the way I do you. I've never talked to anyone the way I talk to you. Now I'm all fucked up because you're the one who has me turned inside out, yet you're the only person I can open up to about it."

God, was there anyone as honest as Cooper? He went through life no-holds-barred. Noah always respected that about him. This, it seemed, would be no different.

"You can still talk to me. You always can. I have to admit, I don't know what I'm doing here either, Coop. I'm not in your head, and don't know what you're thinking or feeling. Usually if I want someone and they want me, even if the world doesn't know about it, we fuck and deal with the rest later. I've never wanted someone who wasn't gay before. I—" Noah shifted.

"You want me, too?" Cooper's voice was soft...so soft Noah hardly heard him. He sounded so unsure as he asked Noah that question. It ripped his insides to shreds and damned if his cock wasn't hard, too.

"I don't know what the best thing to say is, man. I don't want to fuck this up and lose your friendship, but I can't lie to you, either. Of course I want you. I've never wanted anyone as badly as I want you. It's like embers that are always inside me, this slow burn that I can't stop. Hell, I don't know if I want to stop it." His brain knew he should. It was why he kept trying to, but inside? Stopping wasn't at all where his instincts led when it came to Cooper.

Cooper leaned forward, one of his hands shaking as he set it on the table. He stared at Noah, as if shocked by his words. Struggled a minute before he finally spoke. "I don't know if I want to stop, either...but I feel like I should. This isn't something I should want, but never experiencing it—you—that scares the hell out of me, too."

Lust like Noah had never felt exploded inside him. But it was more than that, too. Pride and gratitude that being with Noah sounded so important to Cooper, that he would actually regret walking away. Every little thing inside Noah fought for the chance to have Cooper. "Coop..."

"I've never even touched a man, Noah. I wouldn't know what to do. I don't know how I would react, but I crave it from you at the same time. All last night, I remembered what it felt like to see your hand on me. Jesus. I'm getting all sappy here." Cooper laughed, but Noah couldn't bring himself to do the same. His dick ached. His skin felt too tight. His hands itched to reach for Coop. To show him exactly how another man liked to be touched.

"You're not alone in this. I couldn't get you out of my head last night, Coop."

At that, Cooper's eyes shot toward him. His skin glistened with nervous sweat. Noah wanted to wrap himself up in nothing but Cooper.

"Try it again... Not a lot, just like last night. Go slow... Just...just...touch."

Noah almost came right there. His cock pulsed in his jeans as fear spiked to all new levels inside him. "No. I can't do that, man. I don't want you to hate me for it."

Cooper took another drink of coffee before turning to the side so he wasn't facing the table anymore. His thumb tapped against the top, as though he didn't know what to do with it.

"I'm asking you to do it. I need you to fucking do it. I have to know, man. I have to feel it to make sense of it." He turned his head to look at Noah. "You know I'd never hate you for anything."

Even if he wanted to, nothing would hold him back now. Slowly, Noah pushed to his feet. His legs were weak, but nothing was going to hold him back from going to Cooper. Nothing.

He couldn't explain how his body felt as he moved. Adrenaline ripping through him, begging him to hurry the fuck up, but like lead settled into his bones at the same time.

It was only a touch. He knew that, and no matter how much he wanted it, he would never take more than that today, but Christ did he want his hands on Cooper.

When he stood in front of his friend, Coop looked up at him. His nerves showed in the crease lines on his face. Noah almost backed up, but then he saw it. Cooper's eyes skating over his bare chest. A chest he had seen hundreds of times before, but never looked with the blaze of desire that he had right now. "Christ, you are so fucking brave."

"You know why," Coop rasped his reply.

"Don't do that. If you tell me to walk away right now, you're not running. You wouldn't be running today, just like you weren't running that night with your parents. You did what you were supposed to do, Coop."

He ignored the part about his parents and the fire when he spoke. "I'm not telling you to walk away."

Noah's desire amped up yet another notch. He went down to his knees in front of Coop, kneeling between his spread legs. "Where?" His voice actually cracked as he spoke.

"I don't know. My arms. My chest. Like last night, just go slow." Cooper closed his eyes.

"No. Open them. I need you to look at me. I need to know you see who's touching you. Or if you want me to stop."

Slowly, Cooper's blue eyes opened. Noah didn't waste any time after that. He reached out and let his fingers trail over Coop's right shoulder. They both watched his hand as he did it. Noah savored the heat of Coop's hot flesh.

"Both hands," Cooper whispered, so he did. His hands ghosted down each shoulder, to his chest. Fuck, he wanted to run his thumbs over each nipple. To get them hard, and see if Cooper liked it, but he held back.

Noah explored his stomach, his sides, traced the muscles in each section of his six-pack.

Cooper hissed. "Your hands are rough."

That was one of Noah's favorite parts about being with a man, the roughness. "Do you like it?"

Cooper's eyes left Noah's hands and met his stare straight on. "I like knowing it's you."

His already hard cock swelled even more. "You're testing me. I don't know how much I can handle."

Urgently, Noah jerked to his feet.

"Where are—"

"I'm not leaving." He stepped around the back of Coop, knowing he would lose it if he didn't try. Noah started by massaging Coop's shoulders, digging his fingers into his hard muscles, as Cooper sat in the chair.

"Fuck, man. That feels good."

Noah wanted more. He ran his hands over Coop's pecs. Brushed his thumbs over each nipple. When Cooper froze, so did he, but when his friend moaned out, "No. Don't stop," he started moving again.

He alternated between massaging his shoulders and playing with his hardening nipples. Noah breathed deeply, and so did Coop.

He plucked each nipple between his thumb and finger, making Cooper groan a sexy fucking groan, before his head dropped back against Noah's bare stomach.

Noah had to fight everything inside him not to take Cooper's mouth. That's when he knew to pull the breaks. "No more. Not right now," Noah told him, even though he thought the words could kill him. "If you decide you want to try more, I don't want it to be a rash decision."

Coop still leaned back into him and rested his head against Noah's abs.

"I know it wasn't much, but I liked it. I feel like it shouldn't be a big deal, but damn did I fucking like it."

"Me, too," Noah replied, running his hand through Cooper's hair. *Like* wasn't a strong enough word. "I don't want to push you but I have to tell you, it feels good seeing you like this. Touching your hair and feeling your head lean against me."

Coop paused before replying. "My...my dick's hard."

All that fucking honesty again. Noah moaned and, for the second time that morning, almost came in his pants. Damn, did he want to make his friend come. To open Coop's pants, pull out his cock, and take it deep to the back of his throat. "You're making me crazy, man. I am so fucking hard for you," he growled out.

Cooper pulled slightly away from him. "I can't..."

"I know. We go at your pace, or if you don't want to, not at all."

"I know."

With that, Noah forced himself to step away. "You need some space. I'm not going to crowd you. I'm going to my room. Might be there all day, but if you want anything, you come to me, okay? I don't want to fuck this up, but I also know your head has to be a mess right now. Take however much time you need. You work tomorrow, right?"

Cooper stood and faced him. Noah didn't let his eyes travel down, knowing if he saw the bulge in his friend's pants he wouldn't be able to walk away, but wishing he would've taken the time to kiss his injured hand again.

"Yeah." Coop shook his head. The look on his face told Noah everything was coming back to him. "I need to go to my room. We'll talk later."

"Hey." Noah grabbed his arm as Coop started walking away. "Are you okay? Tell me I didn't screw up."

There wasn't a pause before Cooper replied. "It's scary how okay I am. I just need to think. You only did what I wanted."

Noah let go and Cooper walked away. As soon as he heard a door shut, he went to his own room, stepped out of his pants, and wrapped a fist around his cock. The whole time he saw Cooper, and hoped like hell his friend was in his room doing the same thing while thinking of him.

***

It had been a long ass couple of days. Cooper had done his twelve-hour shifts plus extra because of a fire. He loved his job and loved saving people, but it took a lot out of him—both physically and emotionally.

Half the time spent not fighting fire, he was thankful as hell to be at work. He dreaded seeing Noah because...well, he'd asked the man to touch him. He'd had another man's hands on his chest and leaned his head against his stomach, and it had made his dick hard.

He'd enjoyed it, and he'd wanted more.

It helped that it was Noah, though. That fact made it easier to deal with, which led to the other half of the time, when he wanted his shifts to be over so he could go home and...he didn't know what yet.

It was a strange thing to even have to consider. Cooper wasn't sure exactly *what* he should be thinking about, or why he'd asked for time. What did it mean? That he wanted to fuck around with his best friend? That he wanted to *fuck* his best friend?

Cooper's whole body tensed, and not in a good way. How could he even think those words? He'd never wanted another man in his life. He slept with women and he enjoyed the hell out of it. But damn, the feel of having Noah's hands on him. It had been electric and dangerous and...strong? That didn't sound right, but there was a hardness there that sent heat shooting through his body that he didn't understand.

Hell, he didn't get any of it.

But he couldn't deny that part of him that wanted Noah. Wanted to explore this attraction, and to do those same things with Noah that he'd witnessed with the other man.

*How can I want a man? How the fuck can I want a man?*

Those questions hadn't left him alone since he'd seen Noah with that guy, so when he pulled his truck in front of his house he almost wanted to drive back out again and never come home.

But the truth was, Cooper didn't let himself run. He hadn't since that night, when he'd woken up to his lungs filled with smoke and there had been red all through his house. When he'd run outside, as his mom had told him to.

When he'd left her and his father to die.

After that day, even when something scared the fuck out of him or it was dangerous, or even if he just knew he shouldn't be doing it, Coop charged forward. He'd never again let himself be so weak that he took the easy way out.

Could he do that here? Could he really just forge ahead into a sexual relationship with Noah?

As weak as it made him, he didn't know if he could.

He still couldn't believe how bad he *wanted* to, however.

Before he sat out here all night, Cooper killed the engine and climbed out of the truck. Regardless of what happened, he wasn't going to be a pussy and hide. He'd say whatever came out, and then he and Noah would deal with it.

Yeah...too bad his insides didn't get that. His heart collided with his chest and his hands actually fucking shook.

"Hey," Noah was sitting on the couch, a boxing match on the TV. The volume was down and Cooper knew it was a façade. Noah was waiting for him.

*Jesus Christ, I started this and now I'm going to pull the brakes.* Guess there was his answer.

"Noah…" He dropped his gear by the door, which he never did, and slowly ambled into the living room.

"It's okay." His friend stood, obviously knowing what Cooper had been going to say before he said it.

"I'm sorry, man… Is this even something I should apologize for?" Without giving Noah time to respond, he continued. "This is such a fucked up situation. I know it…" He didn't even know what to say.

"It's *okay,*" Noah said again. He rubbed the back of his head like he always did when he was nervous. *Holy shit. How did I know that?* It wasn't the type of detail Cooper usually paid attention to, but here, he just *knew.*

"I want to…God damn, do I want to, but…I just can't." It didn't make sense. Whatever he was feeling right now would pass. People didn't suddenly turn gay.

"Then we shouldn't. I think I knew that from the beginning. I know how you are, man. You don't back down. You don't want to seem scared, and you're always looking for the next adventure. I can't be your adventure, Coop."

He shook his head. "That's bullshit. I wouldn't. Not with you—"

Noah stepped closer. Close enough that Cooper could see the outline of those fucking nipple rings through his shirt. He wanted to grab them with his teeth.

Coop stepped backward and Noah said, "You wouldn't mean to. And...hell, I just got out of a relationship with someone who wasn't ready for the world to know who he was."

The words hit him straight in the chest, reminding Cooper that this wasn't new for Noah. He'd been with men before. Fucked them. If Cooper were to be with him, would Noah expect to fuck him, too?

The shaking came back, rocking more than just his hands. His chest, head, heart, *world,* and anything else. No. He'd made the right decision. There was no way he could do this.

He studied Noah's hands. Imagined them on himself.

*Then why do I still want to...?*

"So...we're cool? I don't want to lose your friendship, man." Not after how it'd felt all those years ago.

"Yeah. We're cool. I'm going to head out for a few hours, okay? I have some stuff to take care of." Noah headed for the door.

"Where—" Cooper cut himself off. It didn't matter where Noah was going. "Don't do anything I wouldn't do," he teased. Noah looked over his shoulder and grinned at him before walking out. Christ, that fucking grin. But it hadn't been completely right, had it? It hadn't taken away the sadness in his eyes.

Cooper stood still, closed his eyes and breathed, trying not to wonder where Noah was going. Trying not to imagine him with another man. Trying not to remember the feel of his calloused hands rasping across his skin.

Trying not to miss it.

# CHAPTER NINE

Noah wouldn't let them lose their friendship again, so after he went off and pouted like a horny teenager that first night, he made himself get his shit under control. He made sure he didn't hide away in his room when Cooper was home, and they worked together on the house. They fixed Cooper's shower, and whatever else Noah could think of to get back to the place where there was no sexual tension between them.

It wasn't easy. Just like it wasn't easy to keep from admiring the way Cooper moved or how he spoke, but he found a way.

Cooper said it wasn't something he could do. Noah didn't lose himself in people who didn't want him. He learned that while growing up; seeing the way his father would do anything for his mom, regardless of how many times she hurt him.

He could tell things were a little harder for Coop at first, but like his friend always did, he came around. All it took was a few jokes and they were solid.

They were getting back to normal.

God Damn, he still wished he could have him, though.

"Hey. You decent?" Cooper said from behind Noah's bedroom door. It was only open a sliver.

*Do you wish I was, or I wasn't?* He wondered. "Yep." Coop slid the door open and Noah asked, "What's up?"

"One of the guys from the firehouse needs some help painting an old barn. Told him I'd come. He's looking for a few extra hands. You in?"

Noah shrugged before getting off his bed. "Sure."

Cooper didn't fully meet his eyes. "Sounds good. I'll meet you downstairs in ten."

Fuck. Maybe things weren't as back to normal as he thought they were. Noah was already wearing a pair of basketball shorts. They were what he lounged around the house in more often than not, anyway. Walking over to his dresser, he tried to push all thoughts of Cooper out of his mind before grabbing an old T-shirt and putting it on.

He pulled shoes out of his closet, put them on, and then headed for the living room to wait for Cooper. When Noah got there, Coop was sitting on his brown leather couch.

"You ready?" Cooper stood.

"Yeah, let's go." It was a quick drive to the guy's house. There were three other men standing out front when they arrived. Before they got out, Cooper looked like he was going to say something but didn't. A rock settled in the pit of Noah's stomach. He knew exactly what it had to do with. It wasn't like he'd been in town long enough for people to know a lot about him. He wasn't sure anyone even knew he was gay. It wasn't something that he hid, but he didn't go around introducing himself as 'Noah the gay guy', either.

And Cooper was worried.

But he'd still asked Noah to come. That meant something to him. "Stop stressin'. We're painting a barn. I swear, you're worse than a damn woman." Noah winked at him.

"Fuck you," Cooper replied, without any real venom behind his voice, but then he sobered. "You know how people in Blackcreek can get."

Noah nodded. "Yep. Been dealing with how people can get for years." And then he got out of the truckand started walking over. A few seconds later, he heard Cooper's door open and close behind him.

"Hey. About time you guys showed up," one of the guys said. They all shook hands and Coop introduced Lenny, Ryan, and Fredrick, who the barn belonged to.

"Nice to meet you, and thanks for helping. My wife has been asking me to get it done for a while now. I'm afraid if it's not done tonight, I'll be on the couch."

They all laughed.

Fredrick led them over and gave them supplies before they got started.

"Braden was supposed to come, too, but he met some chick and I guess their night isn't over yet," Fredrick told them as they started painting.

"Lucky motherfucker. He's always going home with someone. I miss that shit," Lenny added.

Cooper leaned over and whispered to Noah, "Lenny just got married," as Ryan said, "You just got married."

"Don't you know the sex stops then?" Lenny tossed back.

"Not for me. My girl can't get enough." This from Ryan, and it went on from there. The guys were all cool to hang around, sharing beer and stories. They were all fire fighters except for Noah, so a lot of the talk circled around that.

They asked Noah where he was from and how he knew Cooper. They talked about the army for a while, Ryan having spent four years in the service.

Noah was aware that Cooper didn't veer far from him. At first he'd been pissed, thinking that he was *really* worried one of these guys was some kind of homophobic asshole who would cause shit if he found out about Noah. When the other three guys were out of earshot, Noah grabbed a hold of Cooper's arm before he could walk away and asked him.

"What? No," Coop replied. "I'm not going to pretend they don't throw words around, but if I thought someone was that big an asshole, do you really think it's someone I would spend time with outside of work?"

He had Noah there. "Then why are you watching me like I need a goddamned babysitter?"

It was then that Cooper's eyes skated down Noah's body. That his jaw flexed, the left side with a tick. Lust took place of any anger Noah had. That look on Cooper's face said it all. It was because he still wanted him. Because he didn't *want* to stay away? Noah sure as hell wished that was the case. Wished like hell Cooper could make himself go there.

His friend jerked his arm away. "Won't happen again." And then, Cooper walked away. Noah thought about going after him, but he wasn't sure whether he would tell the other man he could have his eyes on Noah all he wanted, or that he needed to make up his fucking mind before Noah went crazy.

So he did nothing. He dipped the roller back in the paint and wondered if he was wrong, if they'd already fucked things up beyond repair.

*** 

Noah was right. Cooper had stuck to him like glue all day because...well, because he wanted to be with him. As crazy as it sounded, he realized he never felt alone when Noah was around.

Not that he should be feeling alone when he was with guys he knew from work, and in some ways he didn't, but in others, Cooper always felt a little shut off from other people. He never felt that with Noah.

Plus—and this was the part that he really needed to try and put a fucking stop to—he still couldn't keep his eyes off Noah. Every time he thought it was getting better, Noah would do something or say something, or move a specific fucking way, that would knock Cooper for a loop.

He'd seen beautiful women. He'd been with beautiful women, but he'd always been able to take his eyes off them. He hadn't felt that frenzied need that made him feel like he'd lose his mind if he didn't have them.

But he had it with Noah. Wasn't that some shit?

"Did you hear that someone's buying Rowdies?" Ryan asked everyone.

"No shit? I didn't know they were selling." Coop tried to focus on the conversation, instead of where his thoughts had been.

"I think it was sort of a last minute thing. I'm not sure why, but some guy is buying the bar." Ryan replied.

"I heard about that." Fredrick shook his head. "I heard he's some faggot from Denver."

Lenny chuckled.

Ryan kept painting.

Cooper's hand tightened on the roller in his palm so he didn't knock Fredrick out.

"Like a *fag* fag, or just some guy with big pockets?" Lenny asked.

"Like an 'I fuck guys' queer. He'd told them he and his *boyfriend* were parting ways when he came in to look at the place." Fredrick wore a look of disgust on his face. Cooper turned to look at Noah. The guy was about to come out of his fucking skin. That made two of them.

"Watch your fucking mouth, man," Cooper told Fredrick. The three men all eyed him.

"What's your problem, Bradshaw?" Lenny asked. He was smiling as he said it, probably not realizing how serious Cooper was.

"Besides that being a dickhead thing to say?"

"Hell, man. I didn't mean shit by it. If he admits he's a fag then why does it matter?" Fredrick really looked like he didn't get it. He didn't look like he was trying to be an asshole. But he was.

"I don't like that word." He never had.

"Chill out, guys. I want to get this painting done so I can get the hell out of here. He's right, Fredrick. It's kind of a dickhead word to use." Then Ryan looked at Cooper. "But it's also just a fucking word. You're not gay, so who cares?"

Cooper did. He opened his mouth to say so but Noah cut him off. "I dropped my roller. Is there a hose I can use to clean it off?"

Fredrick walked over to show him where it was it was, and everyone else got back to work. It was less than a half hour later that Cooper said he was done and he and Noah needed to leave.

"Why did you stop me from saying anything else?" he asked Noah when they were in his truck.

"Because he's an ass-backward, narrow-minded prick, but you also work with him. You don't need to cause problems for yourself there because that guy can't keep his mouth shut. Especially not over me."

But he would, because it was the right thing to do. And, he realized, because it was for Noah.

"But I also won't give him a free pass twice. I see him somewhere other than his home and he says something like that again, I won't be as forgiving." There was a sharp edge to Cooper's voice that Noah didn't often hear from the man. It was confident, and...sexy. Coop's senses went on high alert, his body suddenly buzzing.

He still wanted Noah Jameson, and he wasn't sure he wanted to keep fighting it.

# CHAPTER TEN

Noah sat up in his bed, wishing like hell he could sleep. He rubbed a hand over his bare chest and closed his eyes, but he knew sleep wouldn't come. He hated it when he got like this. When he was younger, he had a lot of trouble sleeping. His parents often fought at night, or sometimes that's when they would leave.

*It's easier to drive at night,* his parents would say. *Less traffic.*

He didn't wake up with nightmares like Coop used to, but he still felt haunted by the dark sometimes. It's when they'd left Blackcreek the first time. He'd run over to Cooper's house in the middle of the night, banging on the door, before being dragged away.

"Fuck." He dropped his head against the headboard. He didn't need to think about that night right now.

"Don't make me go alone!" Cooper's voice broke through the night. Before thoughts had the chance to form in Noah's head, he was out of the bed and running toward his friend's room. His heart jackhammered as he heard, "Please! I don't wanna go alone!" in Cooper's broken voice.

Christ, those nightmares. They'd been brutal when Coop was a kid.

Noah didn't pause at the closed door. He pushed right into the room and headed straight for Coop's bed.

"No! No!" Cooper's rough voice broke through the night.

Noah grabbed his shoulder, slightly shaking him. "Wake up, man. It's a dream. Wake up."

Cooper's blinds were open, the moon shedding enough light into the room that Noah saw his friend's wide eyes jerk open.

"You were dreaming," he told him, as though it wasn't obvious.

"The fire... Shit man, the fire. I...I still see them." Cooper had been through a lot in his life. He overcame it all with strength and determination. He didn't let his past hold him back. Noah always wished he was more like that. Cooper plowed into any situation, running never an option, because of that night. Now, his voice sounded so alone and so broken.

"You're good. We're okay. It's over." Noah wanted to snatch back the words. How fucking ridiculous could he sound? We're okay? This had nothing to do with him. These were Cooper's demons.

"They made me go alone, Noah. They left me all alone. I didn't want to go by myself. I'm so tired of being alone."

Noah squeezed his shoulder, not sure what else to do. This wasn't usually how it went. Yeah, Coop had nightmares, and Noah had woken him up and talked him through them before, but he'd never sounded so lost. That was usually reserved for Noah himself.

"You're not alone, man. You know that. Everyone loves Cooper Bradshaw." He hoped the playfulness in his voice helped.

Noah noticed the feel of Cooper's muscled shoulder beneath his hand. The stretch of his warm, taut skin. *Fuck, I'm such a prick.* He had no business thinking about that at a time like this.

Noah started to move his hand away, but Cooper grabbed it. "No...don't. Wanna feel you."

The moan was impossible to hold back. How bad had he wanted to hear words like that from Cooper? But not like this. Not when his friend was so raw. "Don't do this, Coop. Not tonight. You're emotional and not thinking straight."

Cooper's hand tightened on Noah's wrist. "No shit I'm emotional, and I haven't been thinking *straight* for a while, and you know it."

If this were any other situation, Noah would have laughed at that. Leave it to Coop to play on the word *straight*. But it wasn't any other situation, and as much as he wanted to crawl into bed with his friend and touch him everywhere, he couldn't.

He looked down at Coop, the moonlight on his muscled chest. His body chiseled and defined. Rough, yet smooth, with a light dusting of hair. It made it even sexier that it was Cooper. "If I touch you anymore tonight, I'm not going to want to stop. I won't do something you'll hate me for."

"I told you I could never hate you. I don't want to be alone. I don't want to close my eyes and see them. You always chase my demons away. I need you tonight, Noah. Just sit with me. Touch me. Ground me."

A primal desire to do just that reared to life in Noah, stronger and fiercer than anything he'd ever felt before. He wanted to do all those things Cooper said. He wanted to own him, to take care of him in a way he'd never done with another person.

There wasn't a chance he could walk away right now. Not after what Coop just said to him. His friend never admitted to needing much of anything, yet everything in what he said screamed he needed Noah right now. People failed Noah enough that he wouldn't do the same to someone else.

"What do you want from me? What do you need?" He didn't want to fuck this up.

"Just be here. Fuck, I sound like a pussy, but just don't leave."

Noah sat on the edge of the bed in nothing but his boxer briefs. He had no clue what, if anything, Cooper had on because his blanket covered him from the waist down.

He put his hand back on Coop's arm, then his shoulder, feeling each masculine curve and muscle in him. "I didn't know you still had nightmares." He couldn't think of anything else to say.

"Not often." Coop's eyes closed.

"Do you talk to anyone?"

Coop shook his head. "Not since I used to talk to you."

Noah's hand stilled on Cooper, but he tried to play it off like he wasn't about to fucking explode. "That shrink?"

Coop shook his head. "Didn't last long. My uncle didn't think I needed it." And then...then he began pulling on Noah's hand. "Lay with me. Jesus, I really want you down here with me, man."

Noah fought the urge to do just that. To do more than that. "You're killin' me here. You said you couldn't."

Cooper's eyes were on him. "I know. I fucking know what I said, and I don't mean to screw with you, but...I can't explain it. Everything inside me is calling for you. No matter how hard I try to push it away, you keep calling. I want to touch you. It's eating me alive how much, and I don't think I have the strength to hold it back anymore."

Noah's cock jerked, hardened to the point of pain. "I need to make sure you know what you're asking, Coop. I can't lay down there with you and not do more than hold you. I'm going to want to do more than touch you. You need to make sure it's what you want. I know this is hard for you, but I can't just get up and walk away this time. Are you hearing me?"

"I am." Then Cooper pulled again. This time, Noah went down. He lay next to every hard inch of his friend, their bodies aligned, muscle against muscle. Heat against heat.

Noah let his hand slide from Cooper's grasp and brought it up to his face, rubbed his thumb over Coop's bottom lip. "You are fucking sexy. I want to taste you, Coop. Are you going to let me kiss you?"

"Why don't you try and find out?" There was a slight hesitation in Cooper's voice. A small nervous shake that made Noah go slow. No matter what he'd said, if Cooper changed his mind, he'd walk out with no hard feelings. Fuck, he hoped he didn't, though.

He leaned over, paused right before their lips touched, to give his friend the chance to say no. But then...Cooper leaned forward, and it was his lips that touched Noah's first. It was all the confirmation he needed.

Noah's mouth came down hard on Cooper's, pushing him into the mattress. When he felt Coop's hands grab his shoulders, he kissed deeper, sliding his tongue between Cooper's lips, tasting him for the first time.

It took everything in him not to attack, touch, suck and kiss him everywhere, but Cooper moved tentatively beneath him, and Noah fought not to push too hard.

Their tongues moved together, Noah exploring every inch of Cooper's mouth. His body screamed at him for more. To touch him somewhere or do *something*. When his friend made a soft sound beneath him, Noah leaned away. "You okay?"

"Don't do that. I'm not a fucking virgin. If I can't handle something, I'll tell you. Now kiss me again."

A growl vibrated through Noah as his mouth crushed against Cooper's again. He was in an awkward position, leaning over his friend, so he scooted, climbed up, before lowering himself on top of Coop. "Too much?" he asked, his mouth sliding down Cooper's neck. "I promise, I won't try to fuck you. Just need to feel you." The blanket was between them, but when Noah flexed his hips, grinding against Cooper, he felt Cooper's hardened cock against his.

"Ah fuck." They both groaned at the same time.

"Do that again. Jesus, I can't believe I need you to do that again." Cooper's legs opened, and Noah settled between them, rubbing his dick against Cooper's.

Coop's hands slid down Noah's back, finding a home at his waist. Noah kept moving, kept rubbing them together, dry-humping like a horny teenager.

"This feels so different. Fuck, I feel like I could come right now."

Noah kissed him again. Harder. Wanting as much as he could have of him, in case this was the only time he got. When his mouth went to Cooper's neck again, he said, "Let me make you feel good."

"You are," Coop gasped. "You. So. Fucking. Are."

"I can make it better, Coop. Let me make you come. I really want your cock in my mouth. Let me please you."

Cooper froze beneath him and Noah feared he'd gone too far. He stopped, held completely still over Cooper, waiting to get the boot. *Please don't fucking kick me out.*

"You'd...you'd do that?"

Cooper's shock made him laugh. "Yes. I'd so fucking do that."

"Shit. That was a stupid thing to say. I'm not...I...hell, I'm out of my fucking element here."

"Then let me show you," Noah said to him again, moving his cock to rub against Cooper's.

He was pushing. He was really fucking pushing it, and he'd be lucky if Cooper didn't tell him to get lost. It was a lot, and it was fast, but Christ, Noah wanted him. Noah wanted to taste him and pleasure him.

"I know what feels good, Coop. I will know how to drive you fucking wild."

Cooper groaned beneath him, his hand fisting in Noah's hair. "Yes…"

***

*"Yes…"* Cooper's answer echoed in his head. He didn't regret it. There wasn't anything inside Cooper that wanted him to change his mind. Definitely not his body. He couldn't remember ever being so hard, so eager and *urgent* to be touched. That didn't mean there weren't nerves, too. This changed things. It changed everything he'd ever known about himself, and there were pieces of him that wanted to hide. Wanted to run. But this was Noah. That's what made the difference.

"Tell me you're sure, Coop. I need to hear that you want my mouth on you. I need to make sure we're on the same page here."

Noah's voice was deep and husky and…hot? So fucking hot, and that sent another dose of fear shooting through Cooper, but there was desire, too. So much desire that he couldn't stop himself from opening his mouth and saying, "Do it. Jesus, I need you to suck me." Softly, he pushed Noah's head down.

133

His friend laughed against his stomach before jerking away. Cooper's heart stopped and he reached for him, but Noah just pulled back the blanket before peering down at him. Cooper couldn't see his facial expressions clearly in the half-dark room, but Noah stared. Cooper slept nude, so every hard inch of him was on display. He'd never been unsure about his body, but the weight of Noah's gaze shook something deep inside him. Had he changed his mind?

The urge to run hit him again, but then Noah reached out and wrapped a hand around his cock, and Cooper hissed. Concentrated on the feel of a large hand on him and how it differed from a woman's smaller one.

"You are so damn hot I could look at you all night," Noah whispered. He leaned forward and sucked the head of Cooper's cock into the heat of his mouth.

"Ah, fuck," Cooper rasped out, and then Noah took him deeper, lying down, cupping Cooper's balls. His cock hit the back of Noah's throat.

Eyes closed, Coop let himself feel. He knotted his hand in Noah's hair. A hand fisted around his dick, Noah jacking him while he sucked. His other hand still played with his testicles, squeezing them gently. Damn it, he wanted to flex his hips. Cooper loved nothing more than being taken deep.

"What do you want, Coop?"

Cooper opened his eyes. Noah's voice, a husky reminder of who he was in bed with. *Noah, I'm with Noah.*

"Tell me how you like it. Deep?" Noah's mouth lowered all the way to the base of his cock before pulling off again. "What about your balls? Do you like them licked? Sucked?"

"Fuck," Cooper moaned when his friend pulled his testicles into the heat of his mouth.

"Oh, I know. You want to take control don't you, Coop? You want to fuck my mouth. I'll let you. Christ, I'll fucking let you."

That was all the invitation Cooper needed. He thrust his hips forward, burying himself in Noah's mouth. Noah took him all, swallowed so Coop felt this throat constrict around the tip of his prick. Already his balls drew tight, but he wasn't ready to let go yet. All he wanted to do was feel. To feel Noah. So he squeezed the base and pulled out. Noah, obviously knowing exactly what he wanted, took to playing with his balls again.

He sucked one, then the other, into his mouth. Licked his tongue down the seam. Cooper's whole body was afire. He felt sensitive everywhere, as though Noah's mouth touched him in more than one place.

Cooper couldn't form any thoughts. All he could do was focus on what Noah was doing to him. Holy shit, he'd never had a blowjob this good before. And he needed to come. Badly.

"Take me deep. I want your mouth," he mumbled, and Noah did. After licking the head, he lowered his mouth down over him again.

Cooper pumped his hips, this time not stopping at one or two. He fucked Noah's mouth over and over. That's when he felt it. The finger trailing under his balls, lower…lower.

"Ah, fuck." The orgasm slammed into him. Cooper tried to pull back but Noah didn't let him. Coop let go, his come shooting down the back of Noah's throat, and he kept going. Kept sucking, kept taking him deep as Cooper emptied his load into his friend's mouth.

Coop's whole body went limp, like someone had taken all the muscles out of his body. That felt… "I don't think I've ever come so hard in my life," he somehow managed to rasp out.

Noah chuckled. "You taste good. I could do that all night. Hell, I almost came myself just from having you in my mouth."

Desire already started to pool again, deep in his gut. Hearing Noah talk like that… Cooper had always been a vocal lover, but usually it was him doing the talking. It put his body on high alert, made it hungry for more, hearing it from Noah.

Noah. Who'd sucked his dick.

"You're tense. Realize what you did?" Noah asked.

Yes, and no. But hell, he liked it. He'd fucking loved it, and he didn't want Noah to think any differently. "I'm...I'm glad I did it. I'd do it again. I can't pretend it's not a lot to take in, Noah, but I'm also not going to sit here and say I didn't love it." He paused, trying to find his words. "That I didn't like knowing it was you. And...I don't want it to stop."

It took Noah a few minutes to reply. "Not tonight. This is a big deal, and it's been a long day.

"Really? I would have thought you could go all night?" He tried to tease, but really, Coop agreed with him.

"Oh, I can. Just because I'm going easy on you now doesn't mean I'll keep it up. I don't like easy, remember?"

Oh yeah. He remembered. "I had a dream about you saying that and woke up hard as hell."

Noah groaned, but Coop could hear the laughter there. "Christ, that mouth of yours. You're always saying shit that turns me inside out. I'm going to want to put it to use soon."

Coop's heart stuttered at that, but he ignored it. The bed shifted and then Noah stood. "But again, not now. I'll see you in the morning."

Cooper didn't let himself think—just spoke. "I want you in my bed." He figured that would be the best way to go about all this. Full steam ahead.

Noah stood there for a second without speaking. Coop thought he was going to tell him no, and Cooper would have to kick his friend's ass, but then Noah climbed back into bed with him.

"I should... You deserve some relief, too." He'd been a prick not to think about it sooner. It was an asshole move to get off and not offer something in return.

"Not tonight," Noah said simply. And maybe it really did make him an asshole, but he accepted the demand.

"Night." Cooper flexed his arm, not sure if he should wrap it around Noah or not.

"Night."

They didn't touch, didn't talk, and Cooper's nightmare didn't come back when he fell asleep.

# CHAPTER ELEVEN

It took Noah most of the night to fall asleep. He already had shit on his mind before he stepped foot into Cooper's room, and now he worried his friend would realize at any second what he'd done and kick Noah out. Even if that didn't happen, he still had to deal with the feel of Cooper's naked body next to him while he had a killer case of blue balls. He struggled not to shove his hand under his boxer briefs and give himself a little relief, too.

As soon as his hard-on would go away, Coop would move, or hell, let out a breath, and Noah would get hard again. He had the taste of Cooper on his tongue and the knowledge that his dick was within touching distance. All he had to do was reach out his hand and stroke. Lower his mouth and enjoy.

And those thoughts were exactly the reason he'd been awake most of the night.

As light began to slowly fit its way through the blinds on Cooper's window, his thoughts went black.

Noah trembled when what felt like a finger ran up the length of his cock. Even with his underwear as a barrier, it was still the best thing he'd ever felt. He needed to come, now.

Noah's hips thrust as the finger turned into the palm of a hand, pushing and running up his length. Waking up from this dream was the last thing he wanted to do.

Something brushed over his tip, the roughness of the fabric making him moan.

"Tell me you're awake, Noah. Tell me I can touch you."

Noah's eyes popped open at the sound of Cooper's voice. Cooper laid on his side, his hand hovering over Noah's black boxer briefs.

"You don't have to ask, man. You can do whatever you want to me." Part of him knew they should talk first, figure shit out, or he should at least make sure Cooper wasn't freaked out over what happened last night, but when the man said something like that, logic didn't matter. "Can I take my underwear off?" Noah asked him. Damned if he didn't hold his breath, waiting for the answer.

Coop looked at him. Noah saw determination in his gaze...saw lust, too, as his friend nodded his head.

"I don't think...I mean...last night. I don't know..."

Noah hoped like hell this didn't come back to bite him in the ass, but he leaned forward and silenced Cooper with his mouth. When Cooper immediately opened up for him, Noah let his tongue slip inside. It took everything in him not to climb on top of him and try to fuck Cooper right now. But he made himself pull back. Made himself speak. "I didn't ask you to. You do what you want. My body is at your disposal."

At that, Cooper laughed. Noah reached down to get rid of his clothes but Cooper stopped him. "I think I want to do it."

"Am I going to have to fight for control with you?" It wasn't that he didn't mind giving it up to Cooper. Or at least enjoy the hell out of the battle, to see who could come out on top.

"Shut up. I'm about to touch a naked dick that isn't mine for the first time. Let me do it without you yappin' in my ear." Cooper winked at him before he pulled Noah's boxer briefs down.

Noah lifted his hips, concentrated on the feel of Cooper's fingers brushing against his skin.

"Jesus…" Cooper whispered.

"Impressive, isn't it?" Noah fought to keep this light, even though he was a hair-trigger away from exploding.

Cooper didn't reply. Like he did everything in his life, he went for it, wrapping his hand around Noah's cock and stroking.

"Holy shit." Noah's whole body went rigid. This was Cooper. Cooper was touching him, and he'd be damned before he blew like a teenager getting a hand job for the first time.

"You feel good." There was a sort of awe in Coop's voice that made Noah smile.

"You do, too. Squeeze a little tighter."

Cooper did as his hand ran up and down Noah's shaft. Every few strokes he'd stop, his hand moving to Noah's balls and testing the weight. Running his thumb over the head, smearing pre-come as he rubbed.

"I can't believe I'm touching you, man. It's like I have this little voice in my head, telling me I shouldn't be doing this, but I want it so much, it doesn't matter. Each sound you make, the voice gets quieter."

He was making noises? News to Noah. He thrust forward and Cooper started to jack him off again, picking up speed, squeezing him nice and tight. He focused on every touch, the feel of a callous, or the sounds Cooper made.

Cooper's grip was firm. Every inch of Noah's shaft felt like it was on fire, electrified by the touch and knowing it was Cooper. Fuck, he felt like this was the first time he'd had a man's hand on him, his orgasm already so close.

"Wait." Noah laid his hand over Cooper's.

"I'm not done." Coop's eyes were on Noah's cock, on their hands together there. It made Noah's erection jerk. If he kept looking at him so intensely, he'd lose it now.

"I'm about to come."

"That's the point. I want...I want to see you. I want to make you feel like your whole fucking world is coming apart, like you did to me last night."

Noah groaned. "Ah, hell. How do you expect me not to come as soon as you say shit like that? Trust me, you'll like this. Then we can come together." Noah pulled his hand away. "Lie on your back."

It took Cooper a second, but then he did as Noah said. "Do you have lube?" Noah asked.

"No."

"Christ, Coop. What do you jackoff with?" Noah rolled over to lie on top of Cooper. He held himself up on his forearms. "Spit on your hand and wrap it around both of us."

Cooper's eyes widened for a second, but then as though he didn't want to look out of his element, he said, "I ran out. Plus, I usually jerkoff in the shower, bossy motherfucker." Then he did as Noah said. Coop spit in his hand, and then wrapped it around both their dicks. They were both big, so his fingers couldn't close, but it was good enough. Cooper didn't need any instructions from there. He worked both their cocks together. *Fuck,* was it ever good enough.

"You better come fast because I'm not going to last long." Noah pumped into Cooper's hand. Their pricks rubbed together, hard and hot.

"You and me both.  Holy shit, why does this feel so good?"

Their breaths mingled. Sweat slicked their bodies as they moved together. As they both fucked Cooper's hand. Noah bit his lip, trying to hold his orgasm off. All it took was looking down at Cooper, seeing him doing the same while his eyes were down, watching their cocks together.

"Fuck…I'm right here, man. I'm about to fucking lose it." Noah pushed again as Cooper's grip tightened. That was all it took. He groaned, his body tense, his movement not stopping as a jet of semen shot from his dick and all over Cooper's abs. When Cooper exploded, Noah erupted more, both their come pooling in the creases between Cooper's muscles.

Noah collapsed on top of him, not caring about the sticky mess between them. *No*, liking their spunk mixed together between them. A part of himself, mixed with the most important person in his life.

Neither of them moved except to breathe heavily. Finally, it was Cooper who spoke first. "I'm good at that."

Noah couldn't help but laugh, even though there was a part of him who felt like Cooper was taking this much too lightly. It had to be a huge deal for him. He'd only been with women, yet he got a blowjob from a man last night, and now he'd jerked Noah off. "You're a cocky bastard, is what you are."

"With good reason. Now get the hell off me. You're heavy."

Noah laughed again and stood. Cooper didn't look at him. Noah wondered if Cooper had regrets or if he was just looking too deeply into things. "I'm going to clean up. Meet me in the kitchen. I'll start the coffee. We need to talk."

No matter how much he wanted to forget talking and clean Cooper off with his tongue, before getting him all messy again, Noah walked out without a word.

***

It wasn't until Cooper stood in his bathroom cleaning not only his own, but Noah's jizz, off his stomach, that it really hit him what he just did. He'd jacked another man off. Their cocks had been together, hard, rubbing against each other until they'd both gotten off.

He'd slept in the same bed, naked with another man.

A guy had Cooper's cock in his mouth last night.

And he'd liked it.

*I fucking loved it. It was...normal, comfortable, incredible.*

What would people say if they knew? The guys at the firehouse? Forget other people. What mattered was his uncle, and he knew damn well what he would think.

Cooper's stomach dropped out, and he suddenly wanted to vomit. But then, he considered it had been Noah. Noah, his oldest and best friend, who had done all those things to him—with him. That made it different. Made the consequences worth it.

It wasn't as though they were getting married. Or like they'd be announcing their...whatever the hell it was they were doing, to the world. What was wrong with just chilling out and seeing what happened? Cooper didn't like regrets. What if he'd tried to pull his mom free? What if he could have saved at least her? He spent his life wondering that, and as crazy and scary as this whole thing was, he wouldn't let Noah be a regret.

Cooper finished wiping himself off, brushed his teeth, and then pulled on a clean pair of boxer briefs before making his way downstairs and to the kitchen.

Noah wore a pair of shorts as he stood at the coffee pot, pouring the water in. Cooper watched the muscles in his back move. The sexy as hell dragon tattoo on his back that Noah said he had randomly gotten while drunk one night. Watched his waist as he turned. He'd looked at Noah a million times and never noticed that there was something almost...beautiful about him.

He chuckled to himself, realizing that he sounded like a sap. Turning one of the kitchen chairs backward, he sat at it, leaning over the back. "Thanks for last night. That nightmare kind of snuck up on me. I'm trying not to be embarrassed."

Noah turned to him. "Not the first one I've seen. No need to be embarrassed."

No, it wasn't the first. Noah had heard a lot of them when they were kids.

Noah pulled two coffee cups from the cabinet, filled them both, and then set them on the table. There was already a sugar bowl there. Cooper watched as Noah grabbed the creamer from the fridge and then sat across from him.

They made their cups in silence.

This was ridiculous. "Why are we acting like someone died?"

Noah shook his head but Cooper could see a smile curling his lips, hiding behind his coffee cup.

"We need to take this seriously, Coop. You came in my mouth last night, and while I want nothing more than to taste you again, you can't tell me you're not the least bit confused by it. We go back too far to jump without thinking. That can't end well."

Cooper tried not to roll his eyes. This was typical Noah. He'd always been the one who wanted to think things through. Who'd try to get Cooper to stop whatever it was he wanted them to do. "I'm pretty sure we already jumped."

Noah sighed. "You know what I mean."

"You want to know what I think? I think what we did felt good. Neither of us have had a whole lot of good, Noah. Not when it came to how things felt on the inside. I'm not gonna sit here and try to pretend I understand this, or to give us a name, or even to lie and say that yeah, there isn't a part of me who thinks it would be smarter to forget it happened. A part of me who doesn't wonder what the hell is going on, or what this means to me, even exactly where it's going. But the bigger part of me doesn't give a shit about that stuff, and wants to keep going. Wants to see what this means."

Noah set his coffee cup down. "I'm not your experiment."

"Fuck you. You know that's not what I meant. You said you wanted to suck me off again. I can tell you, there's just about nothing in this world I want more than that, either. When I compare how I got off last night, and hell, this morning, to every other orgasm I've had? It was different. I'm not good with words. I don't know what it means, but let's not fuck it up before it even starts. Let's just..." Cooper shrugged. "See what happens. Not push it, but not fight it, either."

Cooper could tell Noah wasn't convinced. He ignored the nerves in his stomach, stood and walked over to him. "You always meant more to me than anyone else when we were kids... Maybe this is why. All I have to do is look at you and I get hard, man. That feels too good to just run away from."

Coop took a deep breath before hooking his thumb under Noah's chin and tilting is head up. Ignoring the thoughts in his head or the worry in Noah's eyes, he leaned forward and kissed him. Traced the seam of Noah's lips with his tongue before finding his way inside.

Their tongues stroked one another, tasted one another, a mix of coffee and mint. Just like he'd told Noah, his cock tented his boxer briefs.

"I don't have it in me to keep fighting this. Hell, I don't *want* to. You've always trusted me before. Do it now, too."

Noah smiled against his mouth. "You've always been a persuasive motherfucker."

"We had fun, though. Jesus, we had a lot of fun. Then, and now."

And they had. There wasn't anyone else Cooper had liked raising hell with more than Noah. Noah, who now ran his finger against Cooper's skin, on the edge of his underwear. Cooper stood up straight to make it easier for Noah to touch him.

Leaning forward, Noah pressed his lips to Coop's stomach. "I'm trusting you to know what you're doing. To know what you want."

He knew exactly what his friend was saying. Noah didn't trust easily, but he was giving that to Cooper. Putting his faith into him to not do something that would screw up their friendship. He hoped he deserved it.

"I'm trusting you, too."

"You think I don't know that? You're putting yourself out there, man. That's brave, but you always have been."

Cooper wasn't so sure about that. What he did know was things were much too serious for him. "Does it make me an asshole that I let you blow me last night, and now I expect you to help me finish the deck today?"

Noah laughed and playfully pushed him away. "I'm not doing anything until I finish my coffee. And no...you're not an asshole, as long as you know that soon I'm going to want to see my dick slide between your lips, too." Noah touched Cooper's mouth.

A thrill of excitement ran through him. Cooper figured that meant they were doing the right thing.

# CHAPTER TWELVE

Noah and Cooper spent the morning sanding the deck. They went straight from that to staining. It was as if this morning or last night didn't happen. They were back to two friends working together in the yard. Still, it didn't stop the wheels from turning in Noah's mind. He trusted Cooper. He did. But that didn't stop him from stressing out that he was getting himself right into the kind of relationship he wouldn't want to be in. Where David hadn't wanted to come out, Cooper just wasn't gay. Or at least, he never had been. That made it hard for Noah to see this going anywhere. It made him feel like he was doing the exact thing he said he would never do after David: Hide.

"You never told me how things went when you went looking at buildings." Cooper ran a hand over his forehead, wiping the sweat away.

"Good. There are a couple possibilities. I'm supposed to go and talk to a woman this week, which is good. I'm itching to get busy. I miss working with my hands."

Cooper cocked a brow at him. "You're not working with your hands now?"

"It's different. I get these ideas and I want to make stuff, but I don't have the space to do it, or a place to store it."

Coop nodded his head. "Furniture, huh? I'd like to see something you made sometime."

"Then I'll have to do it. Some of my shit is in storage back home. Once I get my own place, I'm going to have to go back and get it."

Cooper's brows pulled together. "Plenty of room here, if you haven't noticed."

"I can't rent a room from you forever. Pretty soon I have to look for a house, Coop. Might as well not move the stuff twice."

Cooper turned away and began staining again. Noah wanted to lean over and bite him. He always did pout when he didn't get his way. You'd figure he would have gotten over that by now.

"If you're nice, maybe I'll give you something." When Coop turned, Noah winked at him. Cooper rolled his eyes, obviously understanding that it might not be something he made that he gave to Coop.

"If you tease me, I might have to just take it."

"Good luck with that."

Once they finished the job, they worked in the yard for a little while longer. "I'm about done here. I need to run to the station and pick up my paycheck. Figured I'd go grab something for dinner after and bring it home to watch the game. First preseason game of the football season. That calls for celebration."

Noah laughed. It was. They used to watch football with his uncle when they were kids.

"You gonna be around?" Cooper asked.

The way he said it made Noah smile. It was almost like he was nervous. He almost teased Cooper but decided to keep his mouth shut. "I'll be here. I might screw around out here and get some shit done."

"Okay. I'm going to run in and shower before I head out. See ya later."

Noah groaned at the mention of a shower, wishing Cooper would ask Noah to join him.

Cooper paused for a second, opened his mouth, closed it, and then turned to walk into the house.

Noah watched him go, still wondering what the hell they were doing.

*** 

"Hey, man. How's it going?" Braden asked as he leaned against a wall at the firehouse.

Cooper walked over to him. "Pretty good. I came to grab my check and then I'll probably head home. What about you?" He and Braden had gone out and grabbed a drink a few times. He hung out with him more than anyone else at the station.

"Just got off. I could go home, but where's the fun in that? I was thinking of hitting the bar. Maybe playing some pool or something. Wanna go?"

Hell. He didn't know why he hadn't seen that one coming. Any other time he would have, but tonight... well he had other things in mind for tonight. Exactly what he didn't know, but they damn sure included being home with Noah. "Nah. My buddy who's renting a room from me is expecting me. We're watching the game."

"Bring him with us. The more the merrier. And it's not like the game won't be on there."

Which was true, but for some reason Cooper still found himself saying, "Maybe next time. I don't really feel like going out tonight." *Because I'm going home to the man who sucked my dick last night.*

It wasn't as if that was all Noah was to him, though. Still, his thoughts almost made him take it back. Almost made him tell Braden he'd go out. That they'd drink some beer and maybe meet some women, and it would be like any other night. That would be the easy thing to do. Even though no one knew what he was doing with Noah, if they kept it up, people would find out. It would be hell at work. Hell with his uncle. Maybe going out wasn't just the easy thing, but the right thing.

But it wasn't what Cooper wanted. Crazy as it was, he wanted Noah.

"Maybe next week." Cooper backed up as he spoke. "We'll catch the game next time and I'll kick your ass at pool."

"Yeah right, Bradshaw." Braden laughed.

Coop ran into the office and grabbed his check. Luckily, he didn't run into anyone else on the way. Once he got back to the truck, he tried to figure out what to get for dinner. He could always barbeque, but it was getting close to game time. Plus, they'd worked in the yard most of the day. He knew he didn't feel like cooking, and figured Noah probably didn't, either. He probably should have asked Noah what he wanted.

*What the fuck am I doing?* It was dinner and a game with his friend. Why was he acting like this was a big deal? Coop ran by the pizza place and grabbed a large pepperoni and some wings before heading home.

It was about ten minutes before kick-off when he got home. Cooper set the food on the coffee table and then yelled up the stairs to Noah. "Stop primping and get your ass down here. It's almost game time."

By the time Cooper came out of the kitchen with a couple beers in his hands, Noah was jogging down the stairs, his hair wet, telling Coop that he spent most of the time he'd been gone working in the yard. That he'd caught him right after his shower. Noah wore a pair of gray sweats, low on his hips, and no shirt. Cooper's eyes trained in on the cut of his abs, the trail of hair disappearing beneath his clothes.

It struck him that he was checking out another man, enjoying the way his body moved and each hard plain of it. It was a shock to his system, blasting electricity into him, but not enough to make him turn away. *This is really happening. I'm into Noah...*

"You keep looking at me like that, and it's not the game you'll be watching, but my mouth swallowing your cock." Noah's voice was all sex. It sent desire racing through him, ricocheting off all his insides, and heading straight to his crotch. He was already getting hard.

"Holy fuck. You are killin' me here. I'm thinking that's not a such a bad thing." Coop took a step toward Noah.

His friend shook his head. Noah hooked his finger in the loop of Cooper's pants and pulled. "Always so damned impulsive." He chuckled before pressing his lips to Cooper's. Coop let him in, eager, excited, fucking hungry to taste him again.

"And you're a tease." Cooper winked at him.

*This should be freaking me out more than it is. Why aren't I losing it?* Those thoughts were cut off when Noah's tongue stroked his own. When his teeth closed around Coop's bottom lip and he bit, before sweeping his mouth again.

Cooper's cock jerked behind the fly of his jeans. He needed to get off so bad he could have lost it right there. But as quickly as it started, Noah was pulling away. "Relax. You don't have to be in such a hurry. I'm not going anywhere."

The muscles in Cooper's body deflated...but not his dick. That was still hard and so fucking ready. "You're a tease."

Noah winked at him. "You like it. You don't think I know the best thing to do is to keep Cooper Bradshaw on his toes?"

Coop smiled at that, liking that Noah knew him so well, but then he let the grin slide away. Was that really how Noah saw him? He thought Cooper was always looking for the next most exciting thing?

*Is that how I am?*

"Come on. We're not missing this game. Don't pretend you don't remember one of the last games we watched. I'm winning this one."

Cooper had forgotten, but now the memory flooded his thoughts.

*"I'm gonna win, Noah. There's no way the Broncos are missing this field goal, and then I get to pick what we do tonight." He didn't get why Noah wouldn't want to sneak out to the girls' slumber party, anyway. It would be way more fun than staying in the tent all night, just the two of them.*

*"Are you kidding me? It's too far. The Cowboys came back to take the lead, there's no way we're losing on a field goal."*

*As far as Coop knew, Noah had never even been to Texas. He only loved the Cowboys because it was his dad's favorite team. He guessed he understood that, though.*

*"Remember our deal, though. If you win, you get to pick if we go or not, and if I do, it's my choice." Noah smiled. "I mean...just because I don't wanna get in trouble."*

*"We won't get in trouble. We haven't gotten caught yet."*

*Both their eyes were on the TV screen after that. Cooper and Noah had watched as the Broncos kicked the field goal. Watched as it flew through the air. It was like slow motion or something, and he wished he could hit fast forward.*

*And then, it sailed between the poles. "Yeah!" Cooper jumped in the air. "I told you I'd win. And don't worry, you'll have fun tonight. It'll be perfect. I heard Gabby thinks you're cute."*

*Noah shook his head, looking down at the ground. Cooper was about to ask him what was wrong when he looked up and shrugged. "Yeah, I guess you're right."*

*They hung out with Cooper's aunt and uncle and ate dinner after the game. The whole time Noah was acting like he was mad at Cooper or something. He knew once Noah snuck out with him they'd have a good time. They always did. That's why he'd rather hang out with Noah than anyone else.*

*They screwed around in the tent, playing games and talking, until it was late enough for Vernon to be asleep. Coop could tell Noah was still bummed out. He hated it when Noah was bummed.*

*"We should probably go." Noah reached over and grabbed his shoes.*

*Hadn't Cooper just thought he would rather hang out with Noah than anyone else? It wasn't like they wouldn't have fun camping out. They always did.*

*"Where we goin'?" Cooper asked.*

*"To see the girls. You won."*

*"And since I won, I get to pick what we do, and we're staying right here."*

*Pride swelled in Cooper's chest when Noah looked at him and smiled.*

# CHAPTER THIRTEEN

At random times throughout the game, the memory from all those years ago popped into Cooper's head. Even back then, had Noah wondered if he was gay? Was that the reason he didn't want to meet the girls? Hell, even at thirteen, Cooper had been too horny for his own good. It could have been that Noah just hadn't thought with his dick the way Coop did. Or maybe he really was scared of getting in trouble.

*Or maybe he wanted to hang out with me…*

"What the hell are you thinking about over there? You're not watching the game." Noah hit Cooper's knee with his own.

Coop just shook his head and turned to the TV again.

It went like that through most of the game. There were periods of time where Coop would be as into it as he should be, laughing and talking shit with Noah. But then, there were those times when he'd look over at his friend and remember the things they did when they were kids, or studied Noah's body, or imagined what it would be like to take Noah in his mouth the way he had Cooper.

Thinking about it made his heart rate jack up in excitement, and also in fear. He hated being afraid of anything, but he also didn't want that to be the driving force behind this thing between them.

And then Noah stretched. Cooper watched the way he moved. Saw the outline of his cock pressing against the cloth of his sweats, and his mouth fucking watered.

No, fear wasn't what was driving him at all. That was all Noah.

Maybe that something had always been there, even if they didn't know it. Even back when they were kids.

"Hell yeah!" Noah jumped to his feet, startling Cooper. Jesus, what was wrong with him? He almost forgot about the damn game again.

Cooper turned his attention back to the TV, watching the replay of the Cowboys score. Watching Noah celebrate and not caring about his loss the way that he should.

Noah turned to look at him as Cooper still sat on the couch. "What do you have to say about your loss?"

Coop didn't give a shit. He shrugged. "I guess I have to say you got lucky."

Noah's brown eyes went even darker as he stared down at Cooper. Was it that obvious that Cooper wanted him?

"Maybe I'll get lucky again."

Noah closed the short distance between them. "Tell me...am I going to get lucky, Coop?"

Before Cooper could reply, Noah straddled his lap. Roughly, his mouth came down on Cooper's. The kiss didn't last long before his mouth trailed down Cooper's neck.

Cooper tensed when Noah's teeth bit into his neck. "Jesus." He dropped his head back. "That feels so fucking good."

Noah did it again. Deeper, not enough to break the skin, but enough that Cooper felt a sting of pain pulse through him. "I love that...love the roughness."

Noah pulled back, grabbed the hem of Cooper's shirt and pulled it over his head. Noah's mouth immediately went back to Cooper's neck, licking, sucking and biting.

He realized he was wasting the opportunity to touch. Slowly he reached up and ran his hand up Noah's chest. Fingered the piercings as Noah rolled his hips, putting his weight on Coop's dick.

"Fuck...wanna...touch you. You make me so fucking hard." Cooper pushed his hand under Noah's sweats and wrapped it around his cock. He loved the feel of it. The hard rod, covered in soft flesh. Running his palm up the length, hearing Noah hiss when he paid attention to the head.

Cooper groaned when Noah pulled away, but then his hands went to the button on Coop's jeans and he thought he might be the luckiest guy in the whole fucking world.

"God, I wanna suck you off so bad. Wanna taste you again. I love having my mouth fucked."

Cooper's pants were completely open by then and he had to press down on his own prick, trying to hold himself off. "No."

Noah looked up at him, his whole body frozen, as though he thought Coop changed his mind.

But he hadn't... No, Coop wanted Noah in his mouth this time. Wanted to know what it felt like to have his lips stretched around Noah's cock. "It's my turn. I...I wanna blow you."

Noah's eyes went wide at that.

"Just look at it as celebrating the win."

"But I won," Noah countered.

"Are you saying you don't want a blowjob to celebrate?"

Coop grabbed Noah and pulled him down to the couch beside him. In almost the same movement, he slid to the floor and lowered to his knees in front of Noah. Immediately, he went for Noah's sweats. Noah lifted his hips so Coop could pull them down. As soon as they got to Noah's knees, he realized his mistake.

"Shit, I don't know what the hell I'm doing here." Coop moved to one side of Noah so he could get his clothes off before settling between his legs again. Without a thought in his mind, other than the need surging through him, Cooper ran a finger up Noah's shaft.

"You're doin' just fine if you ask me," brushed past Noah's lips.

Coop ignored him and spent his time studying Noah's prick instead. He definitely wasn't small, not quite as long as Cooper himself, but bigger around. Pre-come already pearled at the tip of his purple-ish, throbbing head.

"You don't have to," Noah told him.

"Shut up." Lust rolled through Cooper, overpowering the nerves. He leaned forward, tentatively running his tongue over the tip of Noah's erection. He tasted precome, and though a quiet voice in his head told him he shouldn't like it, he wanted more.

So he took it. He pulled Noah's cock into his mouth. He tasted salty, strong. Coop lowered his mouth, trying to take as much of him in as possible, but gagged when Noah's dick got too far.

"Fuck. I'm screwin' this up." Cooper shook his head. He wanted to get this right. Needed to.

Noah threaded his fingers through Cooper's hair. "No you're not. Go slow. Get used to it. I promise you, I'll like whatever you do to me."

Cooper wrapped one hand around Noah's shaft, and then took him into his mouth again. This time he didn't go as deep, but used his hand to work Noah at the same time. He went slowly, sucking and licking, until he found his rhythm.

Noah's hand tightened in his hair. "That's it. That is *so* fucking it," Noah said.

The pleasure in his voice fueled Cooper on, made him go faster, try to take him a little deeper while stroking at the same time.

"Lick the head," Noah told him, so Cooper did, pulling back enough so he could swirl his tongue around the tip of Noah's dick.

When he felt Noah's hand push gently on the back of his head, he started to suck again. In the back of his mind, he knew he should feel some kind of conflicted emotions about this, but all he could focus on were the sounds of pleasure slipping past Noah's lips. The slight sting to his head, where Noah's fist tightened in his hair. The salty liquid, slowly leaking from his hole.

"Christ, that's good. So fucking good, Coop." Noah flexed his hips slightly, making Cooper take him a little deeper than he planned. He almost gagged again. "Shit, I'm sorry."

That made Cooper jerk back. His eyes met Noah's. "Don't you fucking do that. Don't go easy on me. If I can't take something, I'll tell you." He hated that shit.

Coop wrapped his lips around Noah's prick again, determined to show his friend that he could take it. That he could make Noah feel as incredible as Noah had made him feel. Cooper palmed Noah's balls, tested their weight, treated them how he liked his own touched, as he tried to take Noah deep again.

"It helps if you swallow—aw fuck yeah—just like that."

Coop tried not to smile around Noah's cock, loving the ecstasy that coated his friend's words. He was going to do this. Cooper couldn't wait to drive Noah wild.

***

Noah was trying his damndest not to come. Everything inside him was screaming for him to let go, to blow his load in Coop's mouth, but when he did this would be over, and he wanted nothing more than for it to last forever.

He moved his hips a little, fucking Coop's mouth but trying not to give him too much. He was a natural, though, sucking and taking Noah's dick deep into this mouth. He alternated between jacking him off and playing with his balls.

As much as Noah loved sucking dick, the feel of Coop's warm, wet mouth blew that feeling out of the water.

Looking down, Noah watched Cooper's head in his lap. Watched as his childhood best friend, hell the best friend he ever had, pleasured him. Watched his lips stretch around Noah's cock. His hair in Noah's hand.

It was fucking beautiful.

Coop lowered again, taking him deep, then he looked up, his blue eyes grabbing onto Noah's. It was the sexiest sight he'd ever seen.

"I'm gonna fucking blow, Coop. If you don't want it, you better move. Now."

Cooper sucked him again. Noah's balls drew up tight as come erupted into Cooper's mouth. He expected Coop to pull back, but instead he lowered his mouth again, making another jet of semen shoot down his throat. Cooper swallowed it all down, then ran his tongue over his tip before pulling away and looking up at Noah.

His eyes were a little wide for a minute, a tense look on his face as though he'd just realized what he did. But then Coop grinned. "I think I'm pretty damn good at that."

"Pretty damn good doesn't even begin to cover it. Now it's my turn." Noah's body was dead, but there was no way he would let Cooper walk away without tasting him again, too. He pulled Cooper to his feet, then pushed him backward for more space. When Noah could get down between Coop and the couch, he fell to his knees, pulling Coop's pants with him as he went.

"I've wanted your cock in my mouth again all day." Realizing he left Cooper's boxer briefs on, he pulled those down. He didn't know or care if Cooper stepped out of them. All that mattered was the long, hard cock in front of him.

Noah immediately took him deep. Felt Coop at the back of his throat as the rough hair around the base tickled his face. He inhaled, taking in that musky, masculine scent that he loved so fucking much.

He welcomed it when Cooper pumped his hips, when he felt the end of his dick hit the back of his throat, over and over.

Noah used one of his hands and let it wrap around Cooper's body. He ran his finger down the crack of Coop's ass. When he felt him stiffen, he let his hand slide down the back of his leg instead.

*Too much, too fast. Don't fuck this up, man.*

So he touched his balls instead. Rubbed his thumb on Coop's taint before giving his sac a gentle tug.

Coop's cock jerked in his mouth—hot, thick, sticky heat filled his mouth.

"Fuck, ah fuck," Cooper groaned above him. Noah kept sucking, kept milking him dry, until he'd swallowed every last drop.

And he wanted more.

"Holy shit, I don't know if I can walk. I can't believe I came that fast." Cooper grabbed the arm of the couch. Noah couldn't help but smirk.

"I think I'm pretty damn good at that, too."

He was surprised when Cooper ran his hand through Noah's hair. "Pretty damn good doesn't even begin to cover it."

The look in Cooper's eyes was soft, expressive, in a way Noah wasn't sure he'd ever seen Coop look at him. "I've had practice." He tried to make a joke, but Cooper groaned.

"Don't remind me. I had my first case of jealousy not too long ago, when you brought that guy home. I think I'd like to pretend this is new for both of us."

Noah stood, trying not to overthink the comment. Hell, they'd only been messin' around with each other for a day now. The last thing he wanted to do was to start making this into something it wasn't. Getting emotionally involved probably wouldn't end well, which wasn't usually something he had to worry about. The only person he'd ever been semi-serious about was David, and that relationship had lasted over a year.

But then, this was Cooper. They'd always been emotionally vested, in one way or another. How could he shut that off?

Bending over, Cooper pulled up his clothes. Noah grabbed his sweats but didn't put them on.

"It's early, but I'm tired. You comin' up?" Cooper asked.

Noah let bed distract him from his previous thoughts. "Yeah." He walked over and hit the button on the TV.

"We can get this mess in the morning." Coop nodded toward the food and then headed for the stairs, turning off lights as they went. When they hit the landing, Noah turned to go into his room. Coop surprised Noah by asking, "We're sleeping in there?"

Noah just assumed they were sleeping in their own rooms. He would put money on the fact that the woman who'd been here the other night wouldn't have slept in his bed till morning. "It was only this morning you told me we'd be normal and if things happened, they happened," Noah clarified. He was pretty sure sleeping in the same bed every night put things on a different level.

"Yeah, and a few minutes ago, I had your dick in my mouth. Considering the fact that we live together, I'm thinking that means we're okay to sleep together. I mean, won't that make it easier if I want to do it again?" Cooper grinned, a dimple under his mouth showing. That was always the smile he used to get his way.

But if they were doing this, Noah needed him to understand a few things. He took a step toward Cooper, then another. His friend didn't back down.

"If this is happening, we need to get a few things straight. I don't share, Coop. Especially not you. If I'm going to be in your bed at night, that means no one else is ever there until one of us tells the other this isn't what we want. I'm not pushing you to get into a relationship with me, because I know this is new for you, but I also don't want anyone else's hands on you until after you say we're done. I don't care if it's a woman or not. Is that something you can handle?"

Noah could tell Coop almost gave him a sarcastic reply, but then his blue eyes softened. He knew exactly why Noah was making sure he understood this. Maybe he didn't know about David, but he knew about Noah's mom.

"You know I'd never play games with you, man."

Maybe not intentionally, but from Coop's own mouth he knew every sexual relationship Cooper had came with an expiration date. Only, typically they came with the understanding up front that either person wasn't tied to the other. And even if they didn't, it wasn't like Cooper would ever get serious with another man.

"But it goes both ways. I won't share you, either."

Noah chuckled at that. "I have a feeling you're going to be hard enough to handle."

Coop returned his smile and pushed Noah toward Coop's bedroom.

# CHAPTER FOURTEEN

"I don't think this back room is big enough for me to work." Noah looked around the small space. There was a possibility he could make it work, but it wasn't what he wanted.

"I was wondering about that." Cooper stepped up beside him. "I mean, there's a lot of surface with the counter all the way around the room, but I don't know how much of that you need. The room is small, and it doesn't leave you much ground in the middle."

Noah sighed. This was the third and last place they had to look at. Blackcreek was a small town, so there weren't a lot of options. Sure he could go closer to Denver, but he also didn't want his business too far away from home. "I guess I didn't really think about shit like this when I packed up and came home." He shook his head. "If I look closer to Denver, I should probably look for a house there as well."

"What? Why would you want to do that?"

"So I wouldn't have to drive in every day. If this place is going to be mine, I don't want to be an hour away from it." Noah took care of what was his, and he didn't feel like he could do that as well from a distance.

"Yeah, but you have time. It's not like you have to make that decision now. Something else might come up here."

Noah pushed Cooper's shoulder. "Always the fucking optimist."

"I'll help you look. We'll figure something out. Don't go makin' any rash decisions."

They turned to head out. "It's hard sitting around for such a long time. I'm used to being busy. Especially the days you're at work."

Before Coop responded, they stepped outside. "What do you think?" the realtor asked.

Noah shook his head. "The front is great. I love the display window, but the back is just too small."

The woman smiled at Noah. "Don't give up yet. I'm definitely not going to."

Cooper nudged him. "Yeah, that's what I said."

Noah chuckled and asked her to call him if she found any other possibilities, and then they were climbing into Noah's Mustang. They'd spent the past two weeks since the football game together. Coop went to work, but when he wasn't there, they were watching TV, working on the house, whatever they could find to do.

Cooper gave head like he'd been doing it his whole life now, and Noah was thankful every day he got to be the one Coop gave it to. The only time he didn't sleep in Cooper's bed were the nights Cooper worked. It felt wrong for some reason. When Coop was home, it was so they had access to each other. What reason did he have when his friend wasn't there? Noah already worried they teetered along a very steep edge; he wanted to keep the lines wherever he could, without missing out on Coop.

As they drove down the road, Cooper said, "You never did tell me why you wanted to move so fast."

"And I don't really want to now."

What man wanted to admit getting cheated on? Especially someone like Noah, who should have seen it coming?

"Come on, man. This is me you're talking to. Tell me. You said back there you didn't really think about your work when you packed up and came home. Makes it sound like it was a spur of the moment thing."

Noah sighed, knowing Cooper wouldn't give up on this. It wasn't the way he was built. "I was dating this guy—David. He's still in the military and was closeted."

"Serious?" Coop asked.

Noah paused for a minute, considering the question. "I thought so. It'd been over a year."

"You were in love with him?" Cooper shifted in his seat, his voice holding a surprised edge to it.

"No." That answer came easily. "But I was committed to him. I thought he was committed to me."

Beside him, Cooper mumbled, "Shit."

"Yeah. My reply was a little harsher than that. I could have killed them both when I walked in on them together. I never saw that as me, ya know? Being the kind of man someone thought they could take advantage of and get away with it."

"All his cheating says is that David's a bastard, not that there's anything wrong with you. And you didn't let him do anything. You walked away. You're not your dad."

He wasn't surprised that Cooper knew exactly what he thought—how he felt. He never wanted to be that man. The one who let someone walk all over them. "You'd think I'd know the signs, though. I saw it enough, Coop. Since David hid his relationships—well, I guess, hid ours—that made it easier for him to do what he did. No one knew we were together, and, therefore, I didn't know he was with someone else, either." Noah's hands squeezed the steering wheel, his knuckles turning white.

He'd sworn when he walked away from David he would never hide who he was again. Not hide who he was with. And what had he gone and done? Found himself in an even worse situation. Noah not only had to keep his relationship a secret, hell, he didn't even know if it was one. He wasn't with a man who was in the closet, but a man who considered himself straight. Who'd always been straight, until they started fucking around.

Noah flinched when Coop's hand squeezed his thigh. The grin on his face said he didn't see where Noah's thoughts went. Didn't see the similarities. "You're better than him. It wasn't anything you did."

Noah appreciated the sentiment, but he was also very done with this conversation. His body hadn't loosened up since Coop started talking, and now Noah was drawing lines between Cooper and David that didn't need to be drawn. They were only fucking around. Cooper didn't even consider himself gay. He needed to remember those things. "I'm hungry. You wanna go grab a burger or something?"

Cooper's smile grew. He could always be distracted by food. "I could eat." He still had his hand on Noah's leg, and Noah had the urge to stop the car and distract him with something other than food.

*Not in public, though. No touching, because no one can know what's going on.*

"Why am I not surprised about that?"

Noah drove to one of the small diners in town. A really local place that everyone who lived here came to. They used to get ice cream here when they were kids. The building looked like it had been painted, the sign still saying, "Blackcreek's."

When they walked into the place, Noah stumbled a little, surprised at the differences. The Formica was gone, replaced with new tables and counters. The floors were redone, and the walls had been painted from the old aqua color they used to be.

It was all warm browns, a very masculine feel to it.

"New owners," Coop told him. "They moved here a few years ago and updated the place. The food's a whole hell of a lot better, too."

Before Noah could reply, the hostess asked, "Two?"

"Yeah," Noah answered and followed her and Cooper as she led them toward a both in the back. Cooper sat down first and then Noah across from him.

About halfway through their meal, the warmth of Cooper's leg pressed against Noah's under the table. At first he figured the other man was stretching, shifting, something like that, but it didn't move—the rough hair and Coop's leg rubbing against his own.

Across the table, Noah made eye contact with him, and Cooper gave him a small shrug before looking down to take another bite of his food. It was such a small thing, and crazy fucking thing, to like, but he did. It wasn't something David would have done, yet already Coop did. Maybe their friendship made the difference.

Maybe somehow this would turn out okay.

***

Cooper hated the guilt that churned in his gut. He shouldn't put off visiting Uncle Vernon and Aunt Autumn like he did. Watching Vernon now, as he carried a plate of lunch in to Autumn, who sat in her favorite living room chair, he forgot why he did.

The graying man across from him put his hand on Autumn's shoulder. "Is everything okay, dear? Do I need to get you any more of that no-salt seasoning?"

Autumn's legs didn't work as well as they used to. They swelled a lot and filled with fluid. Neither of them were incredibly old, but they hadn't been blessed with the best health, either.

"I'm fine, Vernon. Thanks," she replied.

"What about your tea?"

She leaned over and kissed his hand. "I'm *fine*."

Cooper respected Vernon for the way he loved Autumn. He'd never loved anyone like that. It wasn't the only reason he had to respect the man. No, he wasn't perfect. He had a bit of a temper and was strong-willed, and not very forgiving, but the man treated his woman better than anyone Cooper knew. He'd been a good cop, and he'd taken Cooper in and raised him as his own. It had always been important to Cooper that he did the man proud.

Vernon sat on the opposite couch to Cooper. "It's been too long, Cooper. We live in Fenton, not on the moon." There was laugher in Autumn's voice. He loved the woman. She had the kindest heart of anyone he knew.

"I know. I'm sorry, Aunt Autumn. Between work and then fixing up my house, things have been a little crazy." No they haven't been. *Not with Noah's help. He's worked just as hard as me. You remember Noah? My best friend from childhood who I haven't told you moved back? The one you let practically live with us and then never wanted to talk about when he left?*

Which made another healthy dose of guilt settle in his gut. It was wrong of Cooper to hide Noah. Hell, they'd spent almost all their time together for three years. But then, Noah hadn't been gay then. Coop *hadn't been sucking his cock.*

And Vernon and Autumn had both been strange about Noah and his family after they had left. Who could blame them, though? His aunt had always complained about Noah's parents dragging him around to a different state every few years.

"How's it coming along?" Vernon asked.

"Good. We got a deck built, planted some trees out back. I'm thinking of putting a Jacuzzi in. I want to get the outdoor stuff going, before the weather gets cold. We can work inside the rest of the year."

"Who is this 'we' you're speaking of?" Vernon shoveled a forkful of potatoes into his mouth.

Fuck. He hadn't even realized he'd said that. "People who help. Friends and guys from the firehouse." Luckily, since they'd moved outside of Blackcreek, the chance of his aunt and uncle finding out he had a roommate were pretty small. Vernon kept up with the police force but he doubted they talked about Cooper very often.

He hated lying. Hated that he felt the need to. Mentioning Noah at all made him raw. Like he opened a window inside himself and that his family would be able to see everything. That they'd somehow know.

"We're so proud of your, Cooper. Even if you don't come and see us enough." His aunt smiled.

"Wasn't always sure," Vernon added. "You were an emotional thing when you were a kid."

"Vernon," Autumn warned.

"I'm not saying anything the boy doesn't know, dear. He always was a little sensitive to things, and damn did you like trouble." He smiled at Cooper. "A wild thing, you were."

Coop didn't know whether to smile or be pissed. Was it wrong to be emotional about losing your parents? That he hadn't been able to get over it quickly? *That I'm still not over it.* But then...he liked the comments about being wild. He'd always been that way. Just wanted to have fun and live life to the fullest. He and Noah did some crazy shit that they'd been much too young to do.

*We're doing crazy shit now...*

Stuff that he loved.

"But your aunt is right. We're proud of you. You grew into a good man. A damn good fire fighter as well."

Pride pumped the length of Cooper's body. "Thank you. That means a lot to me." It meant everything to him.

They finished eating lunch, talking and visiting. Autumn showed Cooper a new quilt she was making, and Vernon talked about fishing and how bored he was now that he retired. He'd always kept busy. He used to take Cooper, and sometimes Noah, on all sorts of camping trips when they were younger. Vernon always said a man belonged outside, and he lived his life that way as well. Cooper knew it had to be tough for him, not to be able to do as much and to need to be here with Autumn.

Cooper had been there for a couple hours when Autumn asked, "What time is it? Beverly is supposed to be here this evening."

"I didn't know you were having company. I could have come another day," Cooper told her. Beverly was one of the women his aunt sewed with. They'd met since Vernon and Autumn moved to Fenton and were really close.

"It was slightly a spur of the moment thing. She just called yesterday, and I didn't want to cancel. She's going through some things with her son and needed to talk."

"Ungrateful bastard her son is, if you ask me. It's wrong what he's doing to his mama," Vernon added, with an angry lash of his tongue.

"Oh, Vernon, stop. It's none of our business. It's their concern. It's easy for us to point fingers from the outside."

"Point fingers? What the hell else is there to understand, Autumn?" Vernon looked at Cooper and shook his head. "The guy comes to dinner at his mama's house with another man. Says it's his boyfriend and she needs to accept it or have nothing to do with him. He damn near gave her a heart attack. Poor woman has been in tears for days. How's she supposed to act when he springs being a faggot on her?"

Ice filled Cooper's veins. His jaw tightened as he fought the urge to grind his teeth together. He hated that fucking word. He wanted to tell his uncle to watch his mouth. His instincts exploded inside him to defend this guy he didn't even know.

*Because now I'm like him?*

No, because it was the right thing to do.

"You know I don't like that word, Vernon. And like I said, it's their business. I'm just going to be there for Beverly. She loves her son. She doesn't understand what happened to him...where she went wrong."

Autumn's words were an echo in Cooper's head. Is that what they would think if they found out he was with Noah? That they'd done something wrong in raising him?

Not that he was really *with* Noah.

*No, I just have him in my bed every night, and love nothing more than when he has his hands or his mouth on me.*

"It's not her fault her son is letting his own family down," Vernon told her. "What kind of man comes to his mama and drops something like that in her lap? He's a grown man. If he was a fag, he would have been before now."

The urge to vomit crawled up Coop's throat, questions he asked himself before this thing with Noah started, but he had since pushed from his mind, finding their way to the forefront again. He'd always been with women. Loved women. How could he be interested in a man now? It wasn't who he was. This whole thing wasn't Cooper.

*But the way he makes me feel...*invincible. Incredible. Fucking buoyant.

But could he do it? It was like he'd tried to live in a bubble with Noah the past couple weeks. Could it go any further than that? Hell, Cooper didn't even know how to be gay. Not that that made any sense, but everyone knew he was always with women. If things kept going, how could he ever step out with Noah? People wouldn't get it. *He* didn't get it, and the thought of letting Vernon down after all he'd done for him made that ice inside him start to take over again.

"Well, let's just stop worrying about it because it's not our problem." Autumn interrupted his thoughts. "Why are you stressing about it if you don't have to?"

But they would have to stress, worry and deal with it if Cooper kept up with whatever he was doing with Noah.

# CHAPTER FIFTEEN

Noah was surprised to hear the kitchen faucet running when he came downstairs. He hadn't known Cooper was home from his uncle's. It wasn't like Coop not to make his presence known, and it definitely wasn't like him to come home and start washing dishes. From the clanking going on in the other room, the man obviously wasn't in a very good mood.

That goddamned uncle of his. Noah's body got tense just thinking about him. He didn't doubt the man loved his nephew, but he always found a way to make Cooper feel like shit, too. Noah always felt at odds when it came to Vernon. In some ways, the man gave Noah things his own family didn't, but just as often, he was a jerk.

Heading straight for Cooper, Noah stepped up behind him, the front of his body lined with Cooper's. Automatically, he reached his hand around, palming the bulge under Coop's zipper, and put his lips next to his ear. "Need help relieving that tension?"

Cooper went rigid against him. Hell, Noah didn't even think he was breathing. He should have known this would happen. Actually, he had known it would eventually, but he didn't want to believe it.

Noah pulled his hand away from Cooper's dick and stepped back.

"Sorry. Not in the mood," Cooper mumbled before turning off the water and drying his hands. He twisted to face Noah, his square jaw dusted with stubble. Damn, he was sexy. This would be a whole hell of a lot easier if he wasn't.

"Not in the mood, huh?"

Cooper tossed the hand towel to the counter. "Yeah. That okay with you? We said we'd see how things went. This is different for me, Noah. You can't just come up and put your hand on my cock any time you want to."

Noah crossed his arms. "I don't know the rules if you don't tell me. I've had my hands and mouth all over you. You've had yours on me, too, if you don't remember. I've slept in your bed every fucking night for weeks, and now you're suddenly pissed when I touch you? You seemed to like it all the other times."

Anger shook his insides, threatening to take over. He shouldn't be this fucking mad, but he was. Not because he couldn't pleasure Cooper right now, because that's not all this was about.

He knew what this meant. Knew it was already over, even though he didn't think it was what Coop wanted. He sure as hell knew it wasn't what he wanted.

"Fuck you, Noah." The words shot from Cooper's mouth, fast, deadly like a bullet. But then, Cooper dropped his head forward and sighed. "I don't want to fight with you. This is...this is new for me."

Noah fought the urge to go over to him, with wanting to give Cooper the space he needed. "It was new to you before as well. If you don't want to be touched, you have that right. You know I fucking believe that, and if you want to stop, we stop. I've said that from the beginning. But I find it a really big coincidence that you came in my mouth just this morning and after one visit to your uncle's, you don't want me to touch you."

It was Coop who then walked over to Noah, who stood next to the kitchen table. It was Cooper who put his hands flat on that very same table, so his arms were around Noah. It was Cooper who dropped his forehead to Noah's shoulder, and Cooper who inhaled a deep breath as though wanting to take in the scent of Noah.

And that made Noah hard as a rock. He loved the scent of a man. Loved Cooper's, especially. He ached to believe that Cooper wanted to take in Noah's scent as well.

Finally, Coop spoke. "They're the only family I have, Noah. They took care of me when my parents died."

There it was, the truth Noah always knew anyway. Still he had to ask, "So you believe what we're doing is wrong, because they don't approve?"

Cooper paused before replying. "I'm not gay, Noah. That's all that fucking matters. I...I don't know what was going on with me. Maybe it was curiosity or having you back in my life, and being close to you again. Who the hell knows? But I'm not gay. I've never wanted a man before."

"You want one now." Noah grabbed Cooper's hips and held him. Didn't pull him closer, but needed to touch him. Maybe he shouldn't have said anything. Maybe he should have just walked away, but he needed to hear the words. Yes, Coop did want him. And Christ, he wanted to feel him, even if it was for the last time.

Cooper sighed, his breath warm on Noah's neck, before standing up straight again. "Wanted."

That one word pierced a hole through Noah's chest. It was all he needed to hear. "Then there's our answer." Noah dropped his hands, backed away. "It was fun while it lasted. Would have been nice to get a fuck out of it." He winked, giving Coop a half smile he didn't really feel.

"You're never happy with what you get." Cooper didn't even try to smile, but shook his head. "We can go back? Be friends like we always were?"

The vulnerability in Cooper's voice tied Noah in knots. Cooper was usually the sure one. He always knew what he wanted, and always figured things would just work out. Noah needed him to be that way about this, too. "Come on, man. You know us better than that. Plus, even if I didn't want to be your friend anymore, you'd bulldoze your way in like always. You're too damn used to getting your way."

Finally, Cooper smiled. "Asshole," he muttered.

"Takes one to know one." The air between them was awkward, stiff, no matter how hard they tried not to make it so. This wasn't something they could get over by teasing each other.

"Okay, I'm going to finish up these dishes." Cooper stepped back toward the sink.

"I was about to run some errands. You need anything?"

"Nope, I'm good." He didn't look at Noah when he spoke. It wasn't until he got to the door that Cooper's voice stopped him. "Noah?"

Pausing, he turned to look at his friend. "Yeah?"

"I'm sorry...I fucked it all up."

Noah felt the weight of those words in his chest. Felt them, because he knew Cooper took responsibility for so many things in his life that he didn't need to. Noah didn't want to be one of them. And hell, he didn't want to feel Cooper so deeply at all. But he did. Probably always had.

"You didn't fuck anything up. Never have."

Without another word, Noah walked out the door.

***

Cooper hated being weak, though he guessed that's exactly what he was. Calling it off with Noah like that. Caving in to the, what? Urge, desire, head fuck, in the first place. Whatever it was, it was over now, the way it should be.

They continued to watch football together and work on the house. Noah left often and Cooper didn't ask where he was going. Didn't know if he was looking for a building for his store, or maybe even a new place to live. He had every right, even though it drove Cooper crazy not to know. Maybe that was best, anyway. Things would get twisted real quick if Noah brought a guy home again, and Cooper didn't even *have* the urge to bring someone home.

In the weeks since his visit with his family, Cooper had been working in the old building on the far side of his property. He wasn't sure what it had been used for, and it needed a lot of work, but it gave him an escape, a reason to not be in the house with Noah too much, which made him a real bastard.

Coop sat on the couch at the firehouse when Braden came in and joined him. "Why do you look like someone ran over your kitten, man?" Braden laughed.

Cooper shook his head. "Fuck you."

"Slow night."

"Slow nights are good." Had it been a slow night when his house caught fire? Had the men sat around like this being bored but grateful for that feeling until that bell rang?

"No shit. I was just saying."

It was a little over a week until the anniversary of his parents' death. He fucking hated that day. The nightmares would probably start up again soon. Talk about making him feel weak. Nothing did that like waking up in the middle of the night screaming.

Coop shifted on the couch. He was working an extra, partial shift today and would be getting off soon. He wasn't sure if he looked forward to that or not. *Fuck, I'm being a pussy.* He needed to get over it and get over it now.

"What are you doing tonight?"

"Don't have any plans. What's up?" Braden asked.

"Feel like getting out? Have some beers or something? It's a Friday night."

A slow grin spread across Braden's face.

*Jackpot.*

Braden was always up for a good time. If the guy was off, he was almost always looking for something to do. "Do you ever have to ask me if I want to go out? The answer is always yes."

Cooper nodded. This was exactly what he needed. It wouldn't bring back that connection he missed with Noah, or the friendship that was slightly strained, but maybe if he went out, had a good time with a woman, it would get wanting to have Noah Jameson out of his head for good.

# CHAPTER SIXTEEN

Noah really needed to get out of here. It wasn't that he and Cooper weren't getting along since the day Coop came home from his uncle's. No, it was that Noah still wanted to fuck him. Maybe wanted him more than he did before, though it didn't make much sense as to why that would be. All he knew was he noticed Cooper all the time. Maybe it was because he now knew what he tasted like. He knew the feel of Cooper's cock in his hand...in his mouth, and also how the other man turned him on when he did those same things to Noah.

It was different before...just the wondering, the curiosity of being with the first person who he'd ever really trusted. And now he knew, if only from the brief teasing pleasure, just to have it snatched away.

*That's* why he'd been scouring Blackcreek and nearby cities for a place for his store, and *that's* why he let Cooper put space between them when he locked himself in the building outside for hours. Added to that, there was the question if he should even stay in Blackcreek after all of this. Would it be too awkward between him and Cooper?

It was fucking killing him.

He just plain missed Cooper. That was the worst part of it all. He missed a man who he lived with and saw every day. That was the real reason he needed to get the hell out of this house. No good could come of the emotions trying to push their way to the surface from deep inside him.

Noah kicked his feet up on the deck railing, pulled the little piece of paper out his wallet, before leaning back in the chair.

Wes answered on the third ring. "Yeah." There was a tiredness to his voice that Noah could practically feel.

"Hey, Wes. This is Noah. From the bar."

Humorlessly, Wes chuckled. "I know who you are."

"How's everything going?" Noah didn't have to ask to know. He could hear it in the way the man breathed. In the sadness that somehow seeped through each exhale of breath.

"I'm more interested in how you're doing, man."

So, he didn't want to talk about it. Noah could respect that. He also didn't really have shit to say. Calling was a spur of the moment decision. The way things were left between them still made Noah feel like crap. He stalled, trying to figure out what to say next, when Wes took the decision out of his hands.

"Ah, so you don't want to talk about life, either? The roommate?" For the first time, there was real laugher in Wes's voice. Dealing with a sick sister, he figured the man could use a little more of it.

Noah ignored his questions. "Wanna hang out or something tonight? I'm not lookin' to fuck," he clarified. "Just have a beer or something. Maybe play some pool." Just like figuring out what he was going to do outside of living with Coop, he figured this was equally important. Coop was the only person he spent any time with in Blackcreek. He needed to get out, meet some more people, and stop lusting after his straight, bi-curious best friend.

"Yeah…yeah, I think I could use that," Wes said, softly.

They made plans to meet and Noah told him about the bar here in town, only to find out Wes actually lived right outside of Blackcreek. Closer to here than where they'd met the first night.

"Lied when we first met. You never know, and I didn't want shit to come down on my sister. Once we made it to your house and I knew ya a little better, didn't think where I lived really mattered for what we were planning on doing," Wes said.

Noah figured he was right about that.

He showered and got dressed in a pair of jeans and a white T-shirt. He finger-combed his wet hair, letting it fall wherever the hell it fell. He couldn't help but notice Cooper wasn't home yet. Since his friend was only working a partial shift, he expected him by now.

*Not my business. I need to remember that.*

Fighting to push Coop out of his mind, he shoved his wallet into his back pocket and grabbed his keys and cell before heading out the door.

When Noah walked into the bar not long later, he noticed Wes right off the bat. He sat in the back corner at a small table, with a pitcher of beer.

Noah's shoes crunched on peanut shells and whatever else littered the ground as he walked over, pulled out a chair, and sat across from him. Wes raised his whiskey-colored eyes to look at him, making Noah wish like hell things had worked out with him. It would have been easier than dealing with this shit with Cooper. Not that Wes had the time in his life right now, but maybe it would have helped, would have been a way for him to forget.

Wes nodded his head toward the pitcher. "Have at it."

Noah poured beer into the empty cup in front of him.

"She wants me to keep her daughter," he mumbled.

The mug almost tumbled from Noah's hand, not expecting the other man to say something so serious, especially so quickly.

Before replying, Noah took a much needed drink before setting the mug down. "Christ, that's huge, man. What do you think about it?"

"I think I don't want her to die." The anguish in his voice squeezed Noah's heart. His problems were small, like nothing compared to what Wes was dealing with.

"I know you don't. You feel helpless, I'm sure. Maybe it will help to focus on the things you can change. If you can't alter the outcome with your sister, you move to the thing you can, which is her daughter."

Wes drained his beer before pouring another. "Why would she want me to keep Jessie? It doesn't make sense. I'm a single, gay man. We have another sister. Did I tell you? She lives local, too. She has two little ones herself. Jessie would be much better off with Lydia."

"But she wants you to have her. There must be a reason. She's her mama. She's going to want what's best for Jessie, and she chose *you*." Noah was running on pure instinct here. He had no idea if he was doing or saying the right things or not. He sure hoped so.

Wes rubbed a hand over his forehead. "What if I fuck it up? What if I fuck Jessie up? Chelle, that's my sister, she raised Lydia and me. She gave up so much to take care of us, and now she's dying. I don't know how to not have my sister there, and I'm scared to fucking death I will screw up with Jessie. I couldn't stand to do that, not only to that little girl, but to my sister." Wes dropped his face into his hands. Sat. Didn't talk. Just breathed.

"Fuck, man. I wish I knew what to say. All I can tell you is she wouldn't want Jessie to be with you if she didn't think that was the best decision."

It took Wes a few minutes to reply. Finally he lowered his hands from his face, lowering a mask into place, looking more like the man Noah'd seen eying him from across the bar the first night they met. "Sure you don't wanna fuck?"

Noah laughed. "I wish like hell we could." But he wasn't sure Wes needed that. Didn't want to risk doing the wrong thing, because something about the other man told him they'd end up friends. If Wes needed him with all this shit he was dealing with, he didn't want sex to hang between them. And Noah definitely knew it wasn't what he needed. Not with Cooper still so fresh, so...prominent in his mind.

"Then I guess I'm going to get shit-faced drunk to try and forget my problems. Tell me about your problems. I need to feel sorry for someone other than myself."

Noah blew out a heavy breath, figuring he owed the man. "I want my straight, best friend. Want him so fucking bad, I can hardly stand it."

"And?" Wes drank some more beer.

"And he can't do it. He tried, but he can't. Things are...different with us. They always have been. I didn't trust many people as a child. I probably only trusted him, and now...? Now, I fell right back into that, only I want to fuck him on top of it."

Wes laughed.

"But I still don't trust very well, and when it comes to a lover, I expect things that even if Cooper was gay he might not be able to give." Noah swallowed, unable to believe he'd said all of that to Wes. He didn't do shit like this. "It's not like I'm on the hunt to settle down or anything, but I expect loyalty, commitment, and he likes quantity. So yeah, we were fucked from the start."

"Doesn't stop your dick from getting hard for him though, does it?" Wes asked.

Noah picked up his mug of beer. "No shit. I'll drink to that." They clanked their beers together and both took long, deep swallows.

Wes's eyes peered over his glass and toward the door. When he lowered the drink, he grinned. "We've got company."

Noah didn't have to turn around to know who it was.

*Fuck.*

*** 

White, hot anger fried Cooper's insides. What the hell was Noah doing here with the guy he tried to fuck in his living room?

Forget that he'd come here hoping to find pussy, to screw Noah out of his own head. Noah was here with the man he'd had his mouth on. The one who'd had his mouth on Noah. Cooper's hands shook.

"You plannin' on standing in the doorway all night, man?" Braden asked.

"Oh, look. Noah's over there. I thought you said he was busy tonight?" Jules peeked over his shoulder.

Cooper opened and closed his mouth before he replied, hoping his voice didn't come out tight. "He is. I just didn't realize it was here."

"Should we join him?" Jules sounded hopeful.

*No. He likes cock, sweetheart. You don't stand a chance, and I turned him down. I should keep far a-fucking-way.* "Yep."

Cooper, Braden, Heather, Jules, and Danny all headed toward Noah and whoever-the-fuck he was.

Cooper stopped right next to Noah. "Didn't know you were going out tonight." *Shut up. Shut the fuck up.* It was like someone injected cement into his body, Cooper was so tense.

"You, either." Noah looked to Heather first, who had her hand on Coop's arm. "Heather." His eyes lingered there before he turned to the rest of the group. "Hi, Jules. Danny."

Braden reached a hand out. "Hey, man. I'm Braden. I work with Cooper. Nice to meet you."

Noah shook his hand before turned to his friend. "This is Wes. Wes, meet Jules, Heather, Danny, Braden and Cooper."

Was it just him, or did Wes stare hard? Curious?

Wes smiled. "Nice to meet ya. Any friend of Noah's and all." And then the bastard winked at him.

*Motherfucker.* Coop's hands balled into fists. He wanted nothing more than to knock the man out.

"Wes," Noah said, warning in his voice.

Wes winked at Noah this time before drinking some of his beer. "Pull up a table. Have a seat."

It just happened there was an empty table beside them. Cooper grabbed one side and Braden the other. Once they had it in place, Cooper sat in a chair right beside Noah, who was next to the wall. Heather sat beside him, Jules next to her, with Braden and Danny on the other side with Wes.

The waitress came by and they ordered a couple more pitchers of beer. Cooper, suddenly having lost his thirst, didn't pour a glass.

"So, how have you been, Noah?" Jules struggled to look around Heather and Cooper to speak to him.

"Doing well. How about you?"

"Doing very well, it seems," Cooper interrupted. Jesus, what was wrong with him? He was acting like an idiot, and he knew it but couldn't seem to stop himself.

"Yep, I can't complain." Noah didn't look at Coop when he spoke, but Cooper could have sworn he felt a blast of heat from the other man. He was pissed. Yeah? Well, so was Cooper.

*But I don't have a reason to be. I told him I couldn't do it. I don't want to do it. I want to be with women.*

"You live around here?" Braden asked Wes.

"Not too far." His reply was cryptic. He then took another drink. "You?"

"I work at the fire station with Coop."

"Oh, I hadn't heard Cooper was a fireman. Haven't been told much about him."

Cooper's pulse jack-hammered. He wanted to fucking kill Wes...but something about the way he spoke told Coop he might want that. He was itching for a fight. That much was for sure.

Noah pushed to his feet. "Play a game of pool with me, Wes."

Without a word, the two of them walked away.

"Holy crap, Noah Jameson grew up to be gorgeous," Jules said to Heather. Cooper ignored them as they discussed Noah. He practically had to bite his tongue not to tell them Noah was gay...but then, if they knew that, would they wonder about him and Coop? He almost didn't care. Wanted to tell them he'd touched Noah, and tasted him, and seeing him in those low-slung jeans and tight tee did nothing to showcase the body beneath.

*I need to fucking stop this shit. Why can't I stop?*

Danny started talking to the women as Coop fought to keep his eyes away from the table where Noah and Wes were playing pool. Instead, he caught Braden raising a brow at him. "You okay, man? You're acting a little strange." He spoke softly enough that only Coop could hear him, but that didn't stop the panic from shocking his system. How obvious was he being? Did anyone except Braden see it? Did Braden get what was going on here?

"I'm just tired. I'm not feeling too hot all of a sudden."

It wasn't long until Noah and Wes came back. Noah didn't say a word to Cooper this time, and Coop tried not to notice the almost outdoorsy scent of Noah, or concentrate on the sound of his laugh, or the feel of his leg when it brushed against his. Despite everyone laughing, talking and drinking around him, Coop felt like he was losing it. The longer he sat here, the further away from his life he was drifting.

The thought of Noah with Wes made him want to hurt someone. Each inadvertent touch made his cock harden. Fuck, even when Jules spoke to Noah, he struggled not to tell the woman, *Noah was his.* He hadn't even spoken a word to Heather in…he couldn't say how long.

This wasn't ending, and he didn't know if it would ever end, and Coop didn't know if he wanted to celebrate, cry, or destroy the whole fucking world.

He didn't know how, or why, but he knew he couldn't get over Noah. It was such a foreign emotion. He hated it. Wanted it gone. Wanted his normal life back. How dare Noah come back into his life and fuck things up so badly?

Wes said something to Noah and he laughed. The grip on his chest tightened. Dizziness made him spin.

Through blurred vision he saw Wes fumble with his glass. Heard Noah ask him, "How many beers you had, man?"

"Don't know."

"I'm driving you home," Noah told him, making the grip turn into a vice, squeezing everything out of Cooper. Noah would go home with Wes. Noah was *his.*

*No he's not, no he's not, no he's not.*

"Fine by me," Wes answered, his voice smooth. Cooper knew that voice. How many times had he used it on women?

"I gotta go." Coop started to stand but Noah's grasp on his arm stopped him.

"Coop."

He ignored the warning in his voice. Fuck that warning. "I have something to do. Let me go, man."

He realized Julie, Heather and Danny had all left the table. They were dancing, and Coop hadn't even realized they had left. Braden's eyes burned a hole through him. Noah's hand set him aflame. And fuck if he still didn't want to put his fist through Wes's face.

"Coop," Noah said again.

Cooper pulled his arm free. He didn't give a shit if Braden realized what was going on here.

"Why don't you and Braden play a couple games of pool or something? I'll take Wes home and then come back, and we can talk." Noah's voice was steady, even as always.

"I'm not drunk. I can drive myself. I don't need you to come back for me." But if he came back, it meant he wouldn't be fucking Wes.

"I know you're not drunk, but I don't think you need to be taking off, either. Not like this."

# CHAPTER SEVENTEEN

Noah ran through the woods, sweat dripping in his eyes as he went. He ignored it. Ignored everything except his need to find Cooper.

"Coop!" he yelled, his voice echoing out. The look on his face when Pete had accused him of being a sissy, of letting his parents die. Noah had never seen that level of hatred in someone's eyes before. Especially not Coop's.

He hadn't been able to stop his friend's fist from slamming into Pete's face. And now he couldn't find him, as he'd run off alone.

"Coop! It's just me. No one's with me. Where are you?" His feet slammed against the ground before he suddenly forced them to come to a stop. Cooper sat, his back against a tree, leaves all around him, a lighter in his hand.

Noah's heart dropped, sunk down into the ground. "Coop?"

"He knew I let them die. He knew I'm a pussy. I shouldn't have run."

Slowly, Noah walked over to him. Slowly, he lowered to the ground. "You're the bravest person I know, Coop." And he was. He had lived.

"I hate myself for what I did. I should have died with them." Over and over he lit the lighter. Fear skittered down Noah's spine. This wasn't like his best friend.

"If you would have died, I wouldn't have my best friend. I know it's not the same, but... you help me deal with stuff. You make people laugh. Everyone loves you, Coop. This town wouldn't be half as fun without you in it."

I wouldn't love it without my best friend in it.

Cooper lit the lighter again. "I've thought about it, ya know. That maybe I was supposed to die with them. That maybe I should go the same way. With my family... But then I think about all the fun we have, and I don't have the guts to do it. That just makes me feel guilty because I shouldn't put how much I like hanging out with my best friend over being with my family." The flame burst to life again.

"Give me the lighter, Coop." Noah could hardly speak over the blood rushing through his ears. Thirteen was too young to talk about dying.

When Cooper didn't move, he said it again. "Give me the lighter."

*Still nothing, so Noah decided to take it. He put his hands on Cooper's. Coop trembled. Noah almost let go but didn't. He...liked the feel of Cooper's hand in his.*

Just cuz he's my best friend.

*"Gimme the lighter, Cooper." Slowly, Noah started unwrapping Cooper's fingers from the black lighter. Each one went a little easier than the other. Then Cooper's hand was open, the lighter in Noah's, but he didn't move. Didn't let go. "Don't talk like that ever again. Your mama wanted you to live. Your dad would have, too. I...I need my best friend."*

*At that, Cooper's blue eyes locked on Noah's. This time it was Noah who shivered, and he could have sworn it vibrated through Coop, too.*

*Coop stared, then jerked his hands away and started to cry.*

"God damn you, Noah." Cooper's voice snapped Noah out of the memory as they still stood by the table. The same memory that he knew Cooper was probably remembering, too. Because this was the only time other than that day he'd seen that pain, that much devastating hurt in Cooper's eyes.

"Go. I'll take Wes home," Braden told them. He nodded at the man, then peered down at Wes, who did the same, telling him to go. They had to be wondering what was going on. Why Cooper was acting the way he was, and why they'd both stood there for so long.

"Thanks."

Cooper pushed his way through the bar. Noah didn't catch him until they were outside. "We're taking my car," he told Coop.

"I can fucking drive."

Noah grabbed his arm and pulled him toward Noah's Mustang. "I wasn't asking. Get in the fucking car, Cooper."

He was surprised when Cooper did as he said. Coop slammed the passenger door behind him as Noah climbed into the driver side. Noah revved the engine, his tires squealing as he peeled out of the parking lot.

The inside of the car was silent, thick with tension. Neither of them said a word as Noah sped home. The second he pulled into the driveway, Cooper was out of the car, the window rattling when the door hit.

Noah was going to kill him.

He was out of the car right behind Coop. Noah's hand shot out to catch the door to the house as Cooper tried to slam it behind himself. It stung his hand but he ignored it.

"You're acting like a fucking kid."

Pacing the room, Cooper didn't reply. The heavy fall of his steps and the flex of his muscles shouldn't be sexy, but goddammit it was.

"What the hell is your problem?" Noah crossed his arms. "I was in your bed every fucking night, Cooper. You're the one who kicked me out of it. You're the one who said you couldn't do this, and now you're going to throw a temper tantrum because I'm not sitting around waiting for you?" Not that he'd planned to have anything with Wes, because he hadn't. But if he had, it was none of Cooper's damn business.

"You think I don't fucking know that?" Coop shouted. "You think I wasn't telling myself to chill the fuck out the whole time? That I didn't know you had a right to be with him? That I don't realize it's my own fucking weakness that leaves me aching for you every fucking day? I *know* that, Noah."

Noah hated admitting it, but his heart went crazy. His dick got hard. Christ, he ached for Cooper, too.

"But my uncle...I owe him—"

"Fuck your uncle. *You* made the decision. I don't blame you for it because I know this comes with a whole set of problems you've never had to deal with, but you still fucking made the choice, Coop. And I won't wait around for you. I won't be my father, wanting someone who only wants them when it's convenient. I'm not here to play fucking games, man. I don't do the back and forth shit. We're in or we're out."

He'd witnessed that too many times. His mom loved his dad when she messed up, when he threatened to leave her, but she seemed to forget that love when it suited her.

Cooper took a step toward him. Then another. "I don't only want you when it's convenient. I want you all the damn time!" Another step. Then another. "Jesus, I jack off thinking about you, and I remember what it felt like to be in your mouth and how you tasted in mine. God damn you, Noah. Damn you for making me want you. For the fact that my eyes are always on you, and my mind always with you."

He stood so close to Noah now, he felt the other man's breath.

"Damn you for making me jealous when I've never been fucking jealous in my life. For knowing I would have gone bat-shit crazy if you didn't walk out of that bar with me tonight, just like I would have lost it if you didn't find me in the woods all those years ago." A muscle ticked in Cooper's jaw. Anger in his eyes. Anger at himself, or Noah, he didn't know. But Noah saw something else there, too: desire.

"Damn you for making me want you, too, Coop. For making me *want* to keep someone off that edge when I've never cared about being that person for anyone else before. Just. Fucking. You."

Noah went to push around him, but Cooper blocked him. Before he realized what was happening, Cooper shoved him against the wall, his mouth coming down hard on Noah's. They battled each other, fought each other for dominance. Noah pulling Cooper closer, Cooper doing the same to him. Their tongues each trying to probe, to gain control of the hard, wet kiss. Their bodies collided, grabbing and grinding as though they were starving for each other.

*What am I doing?*

Noah grabbed Coop's face, pulled him again. The other man's chest heaved heavy with breath. "You decide now, Coop. You're in this or you're out. No more games. No more changing your mind. You touch me again, and you won't have a choice. You'll be mine."

***

A blast of heat shot through Cooper. A shiver raced down his spine. He wanted that. Wanted to be Noah's, and Noah to be his, so fucking bad he thought he would go crazy without him. He wanted to fuck him. To own him, and for none of the other shit to matter. He'd make none of the rest of it matter.

"I tried. I tried so damn hard not to want you, but I couldn't do it. I don't understand it. My brain keeps telling me it'll go away, but then I look at you and I don't want it to." Cooper grabbed Noah's face as well, a hand on each cheek. "It scares the fuck out of me, Noah, but that fear doesn't have anything on seeing that bastard with you tonight. It doesn't have anything on my need to make you mine."

Cooper covered Noah's mouth with his own. He let his tongue slide between Noah's lips. Noah's hands immediately went to Coop's ass, pulling Cooper against him so their cocks rubbed together.

Coop pushed his hands under Noah's shirt. Pulled it up, separating their mouths just so he could get the damn thing off. Before the shirt hit the floor, he rasped his tongue over Noah's pierced nipple. "Jesus, this is so sexy. Damn you for being so fucking sexy." He shoved himself hard against Noah. The bitterness in his own voice made Cooper see red. He shouldn't be pissed at Noah because of how he felt. He shouldn't be pissed at all, but the anger was there, intertwined with the need, alternating which one gained control at any moment.

Noah's hand slid around and covered Cooper's erection. "Make up your mind. Are you mad at me, or do you want me? You feel like you want me, Coop. I know you do. Does it get you hot that you can take your anger out at me? That you can be rough with me? Maybe you're not really pissed that you want to fuck me, you just like that you don't have to go easy on me."

There was some truth to that. Noah's strength turned him on. The fact that they matched each other in so many ways turned him on. He never thought he would find something like that, so...erotic.

"Fuck you, Noah. Fuck you for turning my whole world upside down." As he spoke, he thrust his hips, let his dick rub against Noah's hand.

Coop's fingers went to the button on Noah's pants but the other man stopped him. "I didn't come to screw things up for you. I never wanted that for you... but I can't be sorry for it, either. Not when it brought us here. You can use me if you want. Take it all out on my body, Coop. I can take it. I want it all from you."

*Fuck.* Cooper almost came right there. He ached, his underwear and pants suddenly too tight. Suffocating him. The reaction shocked him but excited him at the same time.

He wanted to burst free of all his confines. He wanted all of Noah. To experience everything they'd done and more.

Coop tried to drop down to his knees but Noah stopped him. "No. Upstairs. I don't only want our mouths on each other tonight."

New panic burst, came alive inside Cooper. "I don't...I don't know if I can... If I can let you..."

"You can have me. Use me. I just want you."

*That* he could do. Cooper turned and went for the stairs, Noah right at his heels. There was lube in his room from the nights Noah spent there, and Cooper had condoms already. Cooper pulled off his shirt. Storms raged down inside him: lust, need, hunger, fear, anger, confusion. He didn't know what to focus on so he fought to shut it all off. To do what Noah said. To take him. To. Fucking. Have. Him.

Cooper's mouth came down on Noah's. Holy shit he'd never been much for kissing, but he wanted to taste Noah all the time. He grabbed Noah's bottom lip between his teeth and pulled before letting his tongue swim in his mouth again. As they kissed, they both unzipped each other's pants. With rough hands, Cooper shoved the damn things down, Noah doing the same to him.

He wanted skin-to-skin and he wanted it now. He kicked out of his jeans and noticed Noah somehow beat him in doing the same. Then he wrapped a hand around both their erections. Cooper groaned at the feel of Noah's hard, hot, prick against his own.

"God, that feels so good. Why does it feel so good, Noah?" His own vulnerability angered him further.

"Don't question it. Just feel. You're running this show, remember? Take what feels good, Coop. Take what you want."

This man tied him in knots. Wrapped him so tightly, Cooper wasn't sure he would ever break free. With a hand on Noah's chest, he shoved him backward. Noah grinned as he fell to the bed. Coop wanted to kiss that smile off his face.

Instead he opened the drawer in his bedside table, pulled out the condoms and the lube, before tossing them beside Noah.

*Holy shit. I'm about to fuck a man.*

He almost took a step backward but then Noah's cock, long and hard, flexed against his stomach. Cooper watched him, remembered how it felt to have him in his mouth. How much he enjoyed having Noah there. Cooper wanted that more than he should.

Straddling him, Coop let his mouth take over. He kissed Noah's neck, shoulders, chest. "Fuck, I missed this, Noah. Missed you."

Noah's body stilled beneath him. Coop peered up from where he'd been kissing Noah's stomach when Noah said, "You have no idea what it does to me to hear you say that."

*Me, too...* Knowing how it affected Noah affected Cooper deeply.

Noah rolled his hip, rubbing them against Noah. Pleasure lit him up like a damn fireworks display, a sensual buzzing under his skin.

"Tell me what to do. Shit, I don't even know what to do." Cooper never thought he would utter those words during sex.

---

"You've never had anal sex?" Wrinkles formed around Noah's eyes, the cocky bastard.

"Anal sex isn't something women usually do when they know they'll only be with you a night or two."

Noah's whole face lit up when he smiled. "You're in for a fucking treat. Use the lube. It's been a while for me, so you're going to have to get me ready, Coop. I could do it for you—"

"No! Fuck that." There was no fucking way Cooper would let Noah do that. If Coop did this, he wanted to experience it all.

He flicked open the lube and poured some on his fingers. After scooting down off Noah, the other man opened his legs wide, his knees up and his feet flat on the mattress.

Coop's eyes went straight to Noah's cock. To the purple-ish head, down to his heavy balls…and lower to his hole. It didn't matter that he'd never touched a guy there, his body ached, pulsed with the desire to penetrate Noah.

He leaned forward, pressing kisses to Noah's shaft as he circled his pucker with a finger.

"Fuck…! Push in. Just do it. Need to feel you, Coop." The words breathlessly tumbled out of Noah's mouth.

So he did. Pushed passed the ring of muscles until he had a digit inside his friend. "Shit. You are so damn tight. I swear I'm going to bust the second my cock is inside you."

"Use more lube. Deeper. I'm going crazy for you, man."

Not as crazy as Coop was going for Noah. He poured more lube onto his fingers, onto Noah's hole, before he pushed deeper, pulled out and again, and then pushed his finger in as deep as he could.

Noah's hips moved as he rode Cooper's finger. It was the sexiest fucking thing he'd ever seen.

"It's not enough. Two. Gimme another one. Wanna feel you."

Coop did as Noah said. Noah panted as Cooper worked him, as he fucked him with his fingers.

He watched as they disappeared inside. Focused on the feel of Noah's body squeezing, wrapped around him. With each pump of his fingers, he felt Noah's body loosening.

Coop's heart thudded, slammed against his ribcage like it wanted to burst free. "I can't fucking wait. I want you so bad, I can't handle it."

Steady and serious, Noah said, "Then do it."

Cooper fumbled with the condom wrapper, finally having to rip the damn thing open. He rolled it down, sheathing his cock. He then coated himself in lube before kneeling between Noah's spread legs. He pushed them open further; his hands, one hooked beneath each knee.

And he fucking trembled.

Noah wrapped a hand around his own dick and started to stroke. The muscles in his stomach flexed, tightened as a moan slipped past his lips.

"You're so hot. I just wanna fuck you."

"Then, fuck me."

Slowly, Cooper pushed forward. Noah's hold was so tight he almost stopped, but then his head pushed past the ring of muscles. "Holy shit. Fucking hell. You are so tight." Deeper, Cooper worked himself deeper. Each inch he pushed in he thought he was going to lose it, thought he would explode, before he even got all the way in.

Noah kept jacking himself off, his eyes on Coop as he said, "I thought you were going to fuck me? Change your mind?"

That was all it took for Cooper to slam his way in. He cried out as he buried himself balls deep inside Noah. It was like a fist, a fucking glove tight around him. Already his balls started to draw tight, so he pulled out before slamming forward again.

Noah called out. His eyes squeezed shut as he started to moan.

*In. Out. In. Out.* Cooper watched himself disappear in Noah's hole. "Noah...shit...I'm gonna lose it. I'm not going to last. You better fucking come, too."

Over and over he slammed into Noah, watching as the other man stroked his own cock. Coop wanted it, too. With one of his hands, he palmed Noah's balls. Tugged on them a little as Noah's hand started to move faster and faster.

"Ah, fuck. Harder, Coop."

He played with Noah's sac as he slammed in harder. That was all it took. That one more thrust before Noah shot white cream out of his prick, flying all the way past his rock-hard abs.

And then, Cooper was joining him. Filling the condom with semen as he kept pumping.

His vision fucking blurred, and he felt lightheaded. He emptied himself before collapsing on top of Noah, sweat and spunk making them stick together. He couldn't believe how it felt, naked and on top of Noah. Intense. Different. Erotic.

It was fucking incredible.

# CHAPTER EIGHTEEN

The heavy weight on Noah was welcomed. Cooper breathed deeply, his thumb making lazy circles on Noah's chest. He couldn't believe he was lying here with Coop. Couldn't believe he'd let the man fuck him.

But then, there wasn't much he wouldn't give to Cooper Bradshaw. Saying anything different would be a lie. It had probably always been like that when it came to Coop.

"I gotta get rid of the condom." A shift from Cooper, and the weight on him was gone. Noah watched as he pulled the rubber off and tossed it in the trashcan by his bed. "I'll get something to clean us up."

"I don't need to be cleaned up." Noah grabbed Coop's wrist and pulled him back to the bed. He came easily, but this time, as he went down beside him, he faced the other way. Noah tried to ignore the ache in his gut.

After a minute, Coop spoke. "Is it strange that I don't feel weird about this? Don't get me wrong, there's that voice that tells me I slept with another man, but...it was you, so somehow it just feels... Hell, there's a part of me who just thinks, *finally*. But then, I don't get it. I know we've gone over this, but I've never even thought about another man, Noah. I know we were only kids the last time we saw each other, but even then I didn't..." He shook his head. "Even then, I damn sure noticed girls. I feel like I should have known then."

Noah rolled onto his side, Cooper's words swimming around in his brain, before falling to his chest. He touched the back of Coop's neck, then let his fingers brush down his spine before traveling up again. "I don't have an answer for you, man." He leaned forward and kissed Cooper's shoulder before letting his fingers take the journey up and down his spine again. "I would give you one if I could. But I can tell you, I'm glad you're here. Not just because you fucked me crazy, either."

Like Noah knew he would, that made Cooper roll to his back and look up at him. He had that cocky grin on his face, the grin that turned Noah on so much. "Put all your other boyfriends to shame. David doesn't have shit on me."

Noah winked at him. "That's cuz David never fucked me."

This time, it was Noah who tried to pull away, but Cooper grabbed him, holding him in place. "What do you mean he never screwed you?"

Noah shrugged. "I don't usually bottom. I did a couple times in the beginning, but I've always preferred being a top. It didn't always go over well, but David knew I wouldn't let him have me."

Coop's blue-eyed stare pierced him, seemed to dig deep like he was trying to find out Noah's secrets. Wasn't like Noah wouldn't give them to the man, either. All he had to do was ask. Noah had always told him everything.

Again, Noah tried to look away but Coop grabbed his chin the way Noah'd done to Cooper earlier. "You didn't say anything. I just thought... Why didn't you tell me?"

Noah jerked free of his grasp. "Come on, Coop. You know the answer. If I had told you, if I'd said I wanted to fuck you, would we be here right now? Hell, when I said I wanted us to fuck you got nervous because you thought I wanted your ass. And I do, make no mistake about that." Noah curled a hand under Cooper. "But I get it. You're still trying to work your way through being with me at all. You weren't ready."

This conversation was getting to be too much. Cooper wanted to pass the hell out like he usually did after sex, or get started again. The talking he couldn't handle right now.

"And being with me was more important than anything else, huh?" There was laughter in Coop's voice but seriousness in his eyes. Noah could see him trying to work it out. Trying to play things lightly but also really wanting the answer...and probably fearing it, too. Would it make him run? Too much too fast, or put strings around Cooper Bradshaw, when everyone knew he didn't want them?

The thing was, Noah wasn't a runner. Cooper asked, so he was going to give him the truth. "Yes. I've already broken my own rules to be with you, Coop. That was just another one. Just like when we were kids, I can't deny you anything." He didn't want to.

"What are you doing to me?" Cooper asked, before pushing a hand through Noah's hair, leaning forward and kissing him. He pushed forward and Noah let him take control until he was on his back with Cooper on top of him. "Everything about you...I feel it on a level I've never had with anyone else. It's not the way we touch or how you taste or the way we look together. It's you, Noah."

"That's good," Noah smiled. "Because I told you earlier, if we did this, that made you mine."

"But what if I want you to be mine?" Cooper moved his hips, their cocks touching and hardening again.

"Are you sure that's what you really want?"

"Fuck yes..." Cooper closed his eyes, thrusting his hips harder. "Which means, that bastard needs to stay away from you."

Noah cupped his friend's ass, holding him in place. Coop opened his eyes again. "I wasn't there to fuck him. I wanted you. His sister is dying and he needs a friend."

Emotions washed over Cooper's face before he gave Noah a simple nod in understanding.

Noah smiled. "Now get me off again or let me go to sleep."

Coop chose the former.

*** 

A couple days had passed since Cooper came to terms with the fact that at thirty, he was not only in his first relationship, but it was with another man. He didn't know if it made him gay or what. All he knew was that he wanted Noah. He needed Noah.

They still had things to work through. Noah seemed to understand that Cooper was in this as much as Noah, but he wasn't ready to go public yet. It made his gut twist to ask that of Noah, but he didn't know what else to do. He had so much to figure out—how to deal with the guys at the station when they found out. And his uncle. Even though things were fucking incredible, they were still a mass of confusion in his head.

And he needed to talk to Vernon and Autumn first, something Cooper had to do the right way, at the right time.

He knew that, and though he hated it, Noah agreed with him. They were figuring this whole thing out between the two of them, before they went public.

*"But not long, Coop. I won't do it for very long..."*

Coop knew he shouldn't have to. And he wouldn't. Cooper would find a way to make this all work out so his family would understand—he didn't give a shit about anyone else. That didn't mean he wouldn't have to be careful about how he went forward, but ultimately, he didn't give a shit what they thought.

Cooper stood under the spray of the shower at the firehouse. They'd gotten back not long ago from a call. Sooty water trickled down the drain beneath him. His body was hot, overheated little flashes of the red flames dancing behind his eyes.

He shook his head, trying to dislodge the picture. He loved his job. Loved being the one who went in now, rather than the one who ran out, but that didn't mean each and every fire he'd been in wasn't engraved into his mind. That each one didn't remind him of the one he ran from.

Once he was clean, Coop turned off the water and grabbed a towel. He wrapped the towel around his waist before sitting on one of the benches by the lockers. He dropped his head back and closed his eyes. One week. It was a little over one week until the anniversary of their death.

"How ya doing, man?"

He looked over to see Braden fall down beside him. He'd already showered and wore a pair of jeans and nothing else. "Tired. It was a long night."

"Yeah...yeah, me too."

This was the first shift they'd worked together since the night at the bar. Jesus, he'd embarrassed himself that night. He could only hope Braden didn't realize what had been going down. But if he did, Cooper wanted to know, now. "Thanks for taking Wes home the other night. I was a little off my game. Got some shit going down."

Braden nodded. "You don't have to thank me. I didn't have to take him home. He came home with me." The other man winked at him and everything inside Cooper froze. Was Braden saying what he thought he was? He'd gone out with Braden a hundred times. The man did women. Always.

He must not have realized Coop was losing his shit, because he continued, "I don't know." Braden shook his head. "I mean, not that I'm complaining. He was a good fuck, and it's not like I'm into the whole next day thing, but I was shocked when I woke up and he was gone. The bastard would have had to walk back to the bar for his vehicle. I was thinking, maybe if you or your guy have his number or something?" It was then that Braden made eye contact with Cooper again. He must have noticed the look of—hell he didn't even know what on his face, because he added, "Ah fuck. Don't tell me I just screwed up here. I thought—"

"I've always seen you with women."

"I could say the same to you."

"How do you know that's not still the case?" Stupid question, but he had to ask.

"Because I have eyes in my head? Nah, that's not it. I don't think anyone else realized it because it's not something they'd expect. I guess because I've always swung both ways, it's easier for me to spot. Not that I ever would have thought that about you, until I saw you that night with Noah."

Cooper looked around them toward the door to make sure no one lingered, and then managed to find his tongue. "That's because it's never been that way for me, man. Never. Not until him."

Braden's eyebrows went up, looking skeptical. "Never? I mean, no attraction or anything? I always knew I was bi. Even before I really knew what that was, I noticed males and females. Freaked me out a little when I was a teenager, but bodies are beautiful. Both sexes, and I enjoy the hell out of both of them. You're saying you never felt it before? I call bullshit."

"Fuck you. Why would I lie?"

Braden shrugged. "Guess you're right. That probably has your head all fucked-up. No wonder I thought you were going to go postal in the bar the other night. You've been missing out, though." Again, Braden winked. "There's nothing like being with another man, which is why I want Wes's fucking number."

Coop almost told him to back off, that the other man was dealing with a dying sister, but he didn't know if it was his place. If Wes had wanted him to know, he would have told him. "I'll see what Noah thinks. Can we get back to the part that you're bisexual and I never knew it? Why is that?"

Honestly, a man being bi wasn't something he had ever thought about before. Maybe it made him sound like a prick, but before Noah, he wouldn't have said it was possible. If a man wanted women, he only wanted women. Now, he knew that wasn't true. But hell, did that mean he was bi? Like Braden said, he should have known it.

There were some sounds and laughing in the hallway. Both men clammed up until the voices faded to a whisper before disappearing altogether.

"It's not something I hide, but it's not my first line when I introduce myself, either. There aren't a lot of options in Blackcreek, so I guess it's always women who I've found to hook up with. Before Wes, that is."

He guessed that made sense. And Braden had only lived around here going on eight months, so it wasn't like they'd known each other for years or anything. Cooper leaned forward, elbows on his knees. It was different talking to Braden than Noah. Easier, probably, since Braden wasn't the one he'd been fucking for three days. "Was it hard for you? I know you said it was when you were a teenager, but... How the fuck do I tell people I'm with a man? Hell, I've never even had to introduce a real girlfriend to someone, and now I'm supposed throw a man into that place. But...I want him there. More than anything, I want him there."

Cooper was cracking the hell up, that's what he was doing. He'd never talked to anyone like this in his life. But he didn't want to screw this thing up with Noah, either.

"You just do it." Braden spoke slowly, firm, with a seriousness Cooper didn't often hear from him. "For the life of me, I will never understand why people give a shit who someone else loves."

Love? Cooper had never been in love in his life. But then...this was Noah. Noah had always been different. He'd always been *more*. The fact that they were together at all proved that. His pulse kicked up and his hands began to sweat. Could he be in love with Noah?

Braden stood. "Or, I guess I should also say, why people care who someone else fucks." He held out his hand. Cooper took it and they shook. "I'm out of here, man. Let me know what your guy says about the number, and if you ever need to talk, I'm here."

All Coop could do was nod.

# CHAPTER NINETEEN

Noah was on the back deck when Coop got home. He'd spent most of the day working outside and had just finished his shower before coming back out. "I heard about the fire. Everything okay?" he asked, as the man leaned against the deck.

"No one was hurt, if that's what you mean."

It was partially what he meant but not all of it. He had no doubt Coop knew that, too. A big fire close to the anniversary of his parents' death couldn't be easy for his friend.

"I don't feel like talking about it right now. I had the craziest conversation with Braden today. He fucked your friend the other night."

Noah's cell almost tumbled out of his hand. "He's gay?"

Coop shrugged. "Bisexual, I guess. I didn't know until today. He wants Wes's number. I said I'd see what you thought. The guy bailed on him while Braden was sleeping."

Noah didn't reply to that. He wasn't sure what to say. He could usually tell when someone swung his way, and he'd had no idea about Braden. And Wes had given Noah his number that first night, even after he'd pretty much kicked him out because of Coop. If he'd wanted Braden to have his number, he would have given it to him.

"I'm tired." Cooper rubbed a hand over his forehead before licking his lips. "I'm going to go shower. I'll be back in a few."

When he walked by Noah, he grabbed his wrist. "Come here."

Cooper's blue eyes held a stormy haze, sadness and thought. Still, he came easily, bending toward Noah so he could take his mouth. Noah kissed him slowly, teased Cooper's lips with his tongue before delving inside. Cooper moaned into his mouth before their tongues dueled.

When Noah pulled away, Cooper leaned his forehead against Noah's. "I needed that."

"There's more where that came from. Go take your shower. I'll be here when you get back." His already throbbing erection begged him to follow Cooper upstairs. To join him in the shower and show him exactly what he needed, but more than that, he knew his friend...his lover... He knew Coop needed some space right now. Otherwise he wouldn't be going upstairs to shower when he'd obviously had one at work.

When Noah let go of Cooper's hand, the other man walked away. Christ, he was in over his fucking head here. Noah wouldn't put a word to the emotion spreading through his chest but he knew it was there. It had always been there, because he'd always cared about Coop in ways he didn't anyone else. But now? Now it pulsed through his veins, giving life to his lungs.

He'd never really had to fight to hold his emotions in check before. Noah knew what he wanted out of life. He wanted companionship, loyalty, and incredible sex. Interspersed with that was his need to keep that cage around his heart. It had always come easily to him, but then, he'd never been with Coop before, either.

"Hey, you in there, man? I asked if you wanted a beer." Cooper's hand came down on his shoulder.

"Nah, I'm good."

"Yeah...me, neither." Cooper stood beside him, freshly showered in a pair of low-slung shorts with no shirt. Noah watched those sinewy muscles move as the other man stretched. Fuck, he was sexy as hell.

"The place looks good. I feel like shit that you're out here working on my house without me." Coop's eyes didn't veer Noah's way.

"Keeps me busy. I miss working with my hands. I miss making things. I need to figure this shit out before I go crazy."

At that, Cooper turned, peering over his shoulder at Noah with a sexy-as-sin smile on his face. *There* he was. The storm in his eyes had been washed away. "I got something to show you."

"What is it?" Noah crossed his arms.

"Get off your lazy ass and come see." Coop took the few stairs leading off the deck. Curious, Noah stood and followed as Cooper walked around the side of the house. He headed toward the edge of his property, to that old building he'd spent so much time in, alone.

"I had an electrician come and check everything out before I started." Coop's feet crunched in the leaves that had just begun to fall. "He had to make a few upgrades, but nothing major."

A surge of energy zipped through Noah. Had Cooper done what he thought he had?

Before he could ask, Cooper unlocked the door. He stepped inside, with Noah right on his heels. "I didn't know exactly how you'd want things set up. I guess I should have asked, but... fuck, I'm not even sure if I knew what I was doing this for when I started."

Noah cased the room with his eyes. The freshly sanded counters, the benches. A few cabinets that looked like they'd been newly painted hung on one of the walls, with another, unfinished set on the ground that needed to go up.

Cooper had even thought to put a sawhorse and racks for tools. Yeah...he was really fucking lost over his man.

"It's not perfect, and I know it still needs some work. It's not a store, but it's yours if you want it. It gives you a place to get back to, work at home... Or hell, make all your stuff here. Then you can check into that shop in town we saw. It might be a hassle hauling stuff back and forth, but we have my truck. You can use it whenever you need."

Each of Cooper's words did two things to Noah: made his cock hard, and made that feeling in his chest, the one he didn't want to name, expand and grow until it damn near took him over.

He turned. Cooper was rubbing the back of his head, his arm bent, those shorts riding so low, making Noah want to trace the spot where they met his skin with his tongue.

"You don't let anyone drive your truck." He wasn't sure why those were the words to come out.

"I said I didn't trust anyone enough to let them drive her. Maybe I do, now." Coop dropped his arm.

So many damn questions exploded inside Noah. What did this mean? Was Cooper saying he didn't want him to go? All he knew was this: what Coop had done took a lot of thought. It was putting himself out there, and he'd done it for Noah.

Noah didn't reply. Couldn't. He just stared at Cooper as Coop did the same to him. His whole body buzzed with need. Want. Desire. And that stupid fucking emotion he didn't want to name.

"This counter is pretty long. I figured you'd need a lot of space." Cooper walked over to the tabletop he spoke of. "Maybe put the other cabinet above? I'm sure you're going to need a whole hell of a lot more shit, but that's on you. I already worked my ass off enough." Cooper laughed. Noah wasn't laughing. He was heading straight for Cooper.

Holding Coop's face in his hands, Noah slammed his mouth down on his. His mouth opened as Noah's tongue took over. The kiss was fast. Hard. Noah's body was stiff with overwhelming need. "Christ, what you do to me, Coop. Do you have any fucking idea?"

"I have to ask you the same question."

Noah smiled at that, liking the idea that they were in this together. "Turn around," he told Cooper, while at the same time pushing the other man to do as he said. Coop went easily. Noah wrapped his arms around him, hugging his bare chest, pushing his chest to Cooper's back.

"I want you all the time." He bit the muscle where Coop's neck met his shoulder. "I let you inside me. Fuck, I like you there." He kissed the red mark from his teeth before moving to the other side. He ran his hands up and down Cooper's chest, feeling and pushing him tighter and tighter against himself.

"None of my rules matter with you. I want to burn anything to the ground that keeps me from having you." His teeth dug into Cooper's skin again.

"Ah, *fuck*. That feels so good. Everything you do to me feels so fucking good."

And Noah wanted more.

He dropped to his knees behind Cooper. Rubbed his cheek against the other man's ass. "Let me make you feel good, baby. I promise you'll like it." He palmed one of Cooper's cheeks. "Let me taste you here."

And then he prayed like hell Cooper told him yes.

*** 

Coop's nails dug into the wood beneath his hand. His body froze up, stiffened.

But it was in there, too... He felt it. That low buzz of energy and desire that was curious about what Noah asked. He felt it dig its way to the surface as Noah squeezed his ass again.

"We'll start with my tongue. And that's all if you want. I won't try to fuck you. Not yet."

Coop's knees actually buckled, his grip on the counter and Noah's hands what held him up. He wanted this. Holy shit did he fucking want this.

"Yes."

"Thank God." Noah chuckled but his hands were already moving. He pulled Cooper's shorts and boxer briefs off. He slapped his hand down on Coop's skin before kneading. "You have such a hot ass." One of Noah's hands slid in front of him and wrapped around his dick. "You're hard for me. You want this. Tell me you really fucking want it, Coop."

He ached. Looking down, Coop saw pre-come leaking from his slit. He thrust his hips, so Noah stroked him. "I want it. I so fucking want it, Noah."

He growled when Noah let go of his cock.

"Gimme a second, baby. I'm not leaving you hanging. You're going to like this just as much."

As if it had a mind of its own, Coop pushed his ass out and toward Noah.

"Bend over the counter a little, okay? And spread your legs for me."

Cooper did as Noah said. He felt both Noah's hands on his ass again before he spread the cheeks wide.

Coop seized up at this, his body flushed. Noah was looking at his asshole—a part of him he never thought anyone would see. He moved his feet, ready to pull away, but then Noah spoke. "Don't. Don't be embarrassed. You are so fucking sexy there."

He flinched when one of Noah's fingers brushed over his hole. He didn't have time for anything else before a wet tongue took the place of the finger.

Pleasure popped and cracked inside him. "Fuck...oh fuck. Do that again."

And Noah did. Over and over he ran his tongue over Coop's hole. Fast, slow. Hard, soft.

Cooper had never felt anything like it. One of his legs went weak but he locked it at the knee to continue to hold himself up.

"You're as good as I thought you'd be. I'll never get enough of you." Cooper shivered with Noah's words.

Noah spread his cheeks farther, buried his face between them as his tongue licked and pushed at Cooper's hole. He didn't know when he'd started, but he was moving against Noah's face now. Smiling at the feel of the day's growth of facial hair as he rubbed his skin.

"I'm gonna put a finger in, baby. Just one, okay? Wanna fuck you with my tongue. This will make it easier."

Fear or embarrassment couldn't find their way in around the pleasure. "Do it."

He heard Noah spit, then felt the probe of one of his fingers. "Bend a little more. That's it. Right there. I want my tongue inside you so fucking bad."

"Me too...yes...fuck, Noah, I want that."

Noah's tongue joined his finger, saliva making him wet. That's when he felt Noah push. Coop tensed up.

"Relax for me." As soon as the last word left Noah's mouth, his tongue was back to work at Cooper's hole as he probed with his finger again.

"Fuck...fuck, fuck, fuck."

Coop felt it when Noah's finger was inside him. It was...he didn't even know what to call it...a little uncomfortable.

Noah spit again, making it easier as he slowly pushed and pulled with his finger. "I am such a prick for doing this without lube. We're keeping some in here from now on. In every room of the house, and spread all over the property."

He was trying to distract Cooper. He knew that. And, damned if it wasn't working. His asshole loosened, Noah's finger fitting more easily inside.

And then it was gone and Noah's tongue took its place.

"Fuck! Noah. That feels so good. More."

Noah spread his cheeks, his tongue fucking Cooper. It was like his whole body suddenly came alive. He was a live wire, surging with electricity. "More," he gasped, again. God, he couldn't believe how incredible this felt. How much more he wanted.

Noah's tongue pushed into him again before pulling almost all the way out. His tongue went slow and deep, fucking Cooper.

"I wanna come. Need to come so fucking bad."

Coop felt empty when Noah's tongue left him.

"What—Oh God." Noah's finger pushed into him again. He went deeper this time, touching his—"Fuck!" That quickly, come shot out of Cooper's dick. But Noah kept going. Kept rubbing inside him and Cooper just kept coming. It was intense. Like his whole body was being pleasured by a hundred people at once. "Noah...fuck... Holy shit." He could hardly breathe. Hardly speak. Could hardly think.

When Coop had been wrung dry, his legs went weak. Noah was there, holding him. He pushed to his feet and wrapped his arms around Cooper from behind again. "I've never...I haven't... I've never felt anything like that. What the hell was that?"

Noah kissed the side of his neck. "That, my friend," he moved to the other side, kissing it, too, "was your prostate. It's a man's best friend." And then he chuckled. "I told you you'd like it."

Cooper leaned back against him. Noah's hand played with his softening cock, rubbing his semen all over.

"'Like' isn't a strong enough word. I know I should get you off right now, but I swear to fucking God, I think I'm dying. I don't know if I can move."

Noah laughed again. "It'll be your turn to play with me later. That was for you, although hearing you come like you just did almost had me doing the same. This place...it means a lot to me, Coop."

Cooper shrugged, closing his eyes. "Don't want you to go. Figured I'd do what I can to make you stay."

Noah hugged him tighter. "Can you get a couple days off the weekend after this one? I wanna go somewhere. Somewhere no one will bother us, and we can lay around and fuck each other for days…"

Coop took a deep breath. "And that's all you want?" But he knew it wasn't.

Noah shook his head. "Wanna help you forget. Wanna make you feel so fucking good you won't have space for guilt. Or if you just wanna talk about them, we can do that. Whatever you want." Those last words were everything Cooper needed to hear. Completing him, sealing the deal on this thing between them. No one would care about him like Noah. No one would one hundred percent *get* him and what he needed the way Noah did. He supposed a part of him always knew that. From the second Noah came back into his life, on some level, he'd known.

Cooper turned and faced him, saying the only truth he had. "The only thing I want is you."

# CHAPTER TWENTY

Turned out Cooper loved having something in his ass. It had been three days, and Noah had had his fingers or tongue inside Coop numerous times now. He hadn't let Noah fuck him yet, but then Noah wasn't pushing, anyway. He loved and enjoyed any part of him that Noah could have.

The way Cooper rode his hands, breathless and demanding more, he didn't think it would be long until Noah was buried deep inside him.

"Noah...Ah, fuck." Cooper's hands fisted in the blanket as he moved against Noah. So close. Coop was so fucking close, and Noah couldn't wait any longer to get him there.

He hooked his finger down, looking for the spongy place inside him that he knew would push Cooper over that edge. When he found it, Noah rubbed the spot with his finger while his other hand jacked Cooper off.

"Fuck yes!" Cooper groaned as sticky, white fluid pumped out of his slit. Noah kept working him, wringing him dry before he flipped, pulling Coop with him. Without his needing to direct him, Cooper sucked Noah's cock deep into his mouth.

Christ, the man was good at that. Noah pumped his hips, the tip of his prick swallowed down the back of his lover's throat. He already teetered on the edge, his balls already tingling and ready to explode. He wouldn't watch Cooper get off without almost getting there himself.

He threaded his fingers through Coop's hair, losing himself in the wet, hot suction of his mouth.

"So good. You are so fucking good at that, baby," Noah growled, reaching for Cooper when the man's mouth pulled off of him. But then... "Ahhh. Yeah. That's it." A wildfire spread through him at the feel of Cooper's tongue lashing at his hole. Even though Coop had found he loved receiving, this was the first time his tongue had ventured there.

Noah spread his legs wider, giving Cooper better access. He didn't push in but this was enough for Noah.

He grabbed his own erection and began to stroke but then Cooper's hand batted him away. "It's mine. Let me do it."

Christ he loved the sound of that. "Then do it. Make me come, baby."

246

And Cooper did. He continued licking at Noah's pucker. Slow and hard. Quick and light. While his fist pumped up and down Noah's length. "Close... so fucking close," he gritted out, eyes closed. The heat spread throughout him, his whole body sensitive and alive to every touch.

He fought to hold it off, to do anything to keep the sensual assault going as long as he could, but the faster Cooper stroked, and the seductive, overwhelming feel of his wet tongue, was too much. Noah burst, his body tensed, cried out as he came all over his own chest. "You are going to be the death of me." He grabbed Cooper and pulled him up higher.

Cooper went down beside him, one of his arms flung over Noah's chest. "It's good, isn't it?" he asked cockily.

Noah rolled his eyes. "Yes. Incredible."

Cooper grinned up at him. "I'm good at this gay sex thing."

"You're a big head is what you are." He laughed, but Cooper didn't.

"I'm being serious. It's...right. I don't know if that's because it's with you or, hell, have I always been gay and just didn't realize it? Or bisexual, I guess, but even that...the sex, no not even just the sex, the connection was never like this with a woman."

*It's me...I want it to be because it's me.* Which was extremely selfish of Noah but he couldn't help it. Coop was his, and he wanted so much for Coop to want to keep him, too. For him not to care about what anyone else thought, so everyone could know they belonged to each other.

"Maybe it's because I'm just that good?" Noah tried to lighten the moment. It worked as Cooper's body vibrated in laugher against him.

"And you say I have a big head."

They were quiet for a few minutes before Cooper spoke again. "I need to talk to my aunt and uncle... Let them know I won't be around this weekend. Autumn will no doubt invite me over. She always does."

When they were kids, Noah had loved Cooper's aunt. She was always baking for them. She treated Noah the same as she did Cooper. And though Vernon had always been a hard man, they'd had fun with him. He was always taking Noah along when they were kids. Fishing, camping—he'd felt like he belonged with them. "I'd love to see them sometime."

Coop tensed against him.

"I'm not saying you have to tell them yet, Coop. We're still new. I can wait a little while. I just...I missed them, too, when I left. I'm actually surprised Autumn hasn't spoken to me yet. She was always like that. She used to invite me to dinner almost every night, even without you having to ask." Noah smiled at the memory.

"Yeah...yeah, I know they want to see you, too. We'll plan something, soon."

Noah hit the light on the bedside table, his eyes suddenly fighting to stay open. He didn't care that he was a mess from their lovemaking. Noah squeezed Coop, let himself start to drift off with the one man with whom he ever truly felt like he belonged.

***

*The second the car came to a stop in their driveway, Cooper opened the door.*

*"Where are you off to in such a hurry?" Aunt Autumn asked. The smile on her face said she already knew.*

*"I'm gonna go over and talk to Noah. I want to tell him about the game." Cooper had spent three days with his aunt and her family. Uncle Vernon didn't go this time and he didn't know why. But Autumn's brother had brought him to his first NFL game. It had been the coolest thing Cooper had ever done and he couldn't wait to tell Noah about it. He knew his best friend would think it was just as cool as Cooper did.*

"Don't be too long. I'm sure your uncle wants to hear all about the game, too." She ruffled Coop's hair.

"Thanks, Autumn." Cooper bound out of the car, slamming the door behind him. He ran to Noah's house. It was technically next door, but his aunt and uncle had a little bit of property, so he had to jog about a block down the road.

The little, white house was dark when he pulled to a stop out front, out of breath. Noah's parents' car was gone, but Noah had told him he'd be here when Cooper got home. He knew his best friend would have done everything to stay home, and his parents weren't really the type to make him go somewhere with them if he didn't want—which he usually didn't.

"Noah!" he called as his fist came down on the front door. When he did, it pushed open slightly, not having been closed all the way. "Noah, it's me. Get your butt out here!" He yelled again, not wanting to just go into the house.

When no one came to the door, Coop decided to peek inside. This was Noah's house. It's not like they would care.

With a hand on the door, he pushed. "Noah—" His words died off when he saw the living room almost empty. The couches were still there but the TV was gone, and the pictures off the walls. Cooper's heart started going wild, even louder than all the fans had been at the game.

"Noah?" He ran inside. Went to the kitchen first. The cabinets were all open, with nothing in them. Cooper ran for the hall, his feet tangling and making him run into a wall.

"Where you at?" He went straight for Noah's room.

And there was nothing inside.

Nothing.

Noah was gone.

He was a baby. Such a freaking baby, because his eyes got blurry with tears. They ran down his face, more following quickly behind them. All he could think was, Noah was gone. His best friend had left him just like his parents had. Noah was the only person who really got him. The only one who he talked to about his Mom and Dad. The guy who knew he had nightmares but never told, and never made him feel like a wuss because of it.

And then, that ache in his chest spread because he knew he'd let him down. Just like his parents, Cooper had let him down. He'd left for the weekend and Noah's parents had made him leave, when he knew Noah would never want to go. He'd promised if it ever came down to that, he would beg Autumn and Vernon to let him live with them or they'd run away. He hadn't been here, and because of it, Noah had to go away. He hated that he'd gone to that game and hated that he'd let Noah down.

And now, Noah was gone. What was he supposed to do without his best friend?

Cooper didn't even bother to wipe his tears away. Didn't bother to try and stop more from flowing as he turned and walked out of Noah's room. Down the hallway again and back to the front door. When he stepped onto the front porch, Vernon was standing there, smoking a cigarette.

"Your aunt told me you came over. I'd hoped you'd come home first so I could tell you."

"What happened, Uncle Vernon? Where did they go?"

The man shrugged. "His mama and dad decided they wanted to leave, so they did."

Cooper crossed his arms, still crying. "It's not fair," he whispered. He'd already lost Mom and Dad. Why did he have to lose Noah, too?

"That's life, kid. Better get used to that idea now. Life's not fair and there's nothing we can do about it. Crying over it won't help."

Cooper wiped his eyes, even though he didn't feel like it.

His uncle sighed. "I'm not trying to be mean here, son. I just think you need to be prepared for life. It dealt you a bad hand. I get that. And I don't know what I'm doing here, either. Kids weren't ever on the list for me, but your parents died and now we have to do the best we can. The sooner you get used to the fact that you never know what cards you'll be dealt, the better."

"Yes, sir," Cooper whispered. He was shocked when Vernon put his arm around Cooper's shoulders.

*"You're better off, if ya ask me. Not the most respectable family."*

*"What?"* Coop looked up at his uncle. *He'd never spoken like that about Noah before.*

*He dropped his arm from Cooper's shoulders. "They're just not the kind of people we need around, is all. All that fighting. We're...we're better off. Trust me on this, kid. And that boy was always a little soft, if you ask me. Always worried about him rubbing off on ya. Things will be much better now."*

*No, they wouldn't. Things would never be good again.*

Cooper tried to shake the memory from his head. Tried to forget how Vernon had taken him out camping that night even though it had been a school night. They went fishing and he'd tried hard to help Coop forget his friend. It was then he realized his uncle really did love him. He might not show it with kind words and he expected a lot out of Cooper, but it was because he wanted Cooper to do well.

They rarely agreed, but he had no doubt Vernon's heart was always in the right place.

Even though he'd wanted to cry that whole night, wanted to tell his uncle that Noah wasn't soft, and that he was Cooper's best friend. That he didn't care if his parents fought or his mom was wild. Noah deserved better. He *was* better.

So he'd waited. Noah had his address. He would write, and then once they found out where he was, he'd tell his uncle he would do anything if Noah could come live with them.

But Noah never wrote. Or called.

Vernon got upset every time Cooper mentioned them, until he finally stopped. And now, Noah was back. Noah was in his bed. He'd been dragged away, been unhappy, but he was here, again.

And Cooper was an even bigger pussy than he'd been as a kid. Because he hadn't even told his aunt and uncle Noah was back. Maybe it was because his uncle had had such a problem with Noah and his family, or maybe it was because he didn't want Vernon to think Noah was soft like he had said. Because that's what he would think. Noah was gay so he was weak, when he was anything but.

Or again, maybe Cooper was just a fucking asshole because he let Noah believe his family knew he was here. He didn't want Noah hurt, he told himself. Noah cared about Cooper's aunt and uncle, even though, like Cooper, he didn't often agree with Vernon. Yet Vernon thought they were all better off when Noah and his family left. That's all this was about, protecting Noah from being hurt by how Vernon really felt.

# CHAPTER TWENTY-ONE

Noah grabbed a hold of a rock and pulled himself up. He and Cooper had gotten to the cabin just a couple hours before. After dropping off their stuff, the first thing they'd done was go for a hike. They both loved being outdoors. Always had. The weather would be changing soon, winter keeping them from doing a lot of the things they loved to do.

"I still can't believe you don't like skiing," Cooper told him as they worked their way along the path. "I'm making you go with me this winter. You'll end up loving it."

Noah shook his head. He loved that Cooper thought he could do anything, but this one wasn't happening. "Didn't you tell me that when we were kids? It didn't happen then and it won't happen now."

"Eh, I guess I thought you were a little smarter now then you were then. What kind of Coloradoan doesn't like to ski?"

"The kind you're fucking," Noah tossed back at him.

Cooper shoved Noah's arm as he stepped over another rock. Noah grabbed a hold of him. "You put your hands on me and I'm not letting you go."

He wondered if Coop would pull away but he didn't. But then, it wasn't like there were a whole lot of people out here. It was just the two of them.

"How we going to climb if we're holding hands? I didn't know you were such a romantic, Noah."

Noah stopped walking, tugging Coop toward him. "I like my hands on you whenever I can have them there."

Cooper leaned forward and pressed his lips to Noah's. "You're good at this. Usually I'm the one using lines like that."

He tried to start walking again but Noah held him in place. "It's not a line, Coop. Tell me you know that."

The look in Cooper's eyes changed. Softened, but flared with heat, too. "I know."

Before Noah tried to take him right here in the trail, he let go, and they started hiking again.

"You haven't talked about your parents once since you've been back. I'd be lying if I said I wasn't a little curious," Coop said.

Noah was surprised Cooper had gone this long without asking. Wasn't like it was a huge secret, but he also didn't like talking about his family. He also was never very good at keeping things from Cooper.

"Dad died about a year ago. Heart attack. Went to bed one night, never got up the next morning." He was grateful when Cooper didn't try to stop hiking as they spoke.

"Shit, man. I'm sorry about that."

"Yeah," Noah said. "Me, too. I miss him. We always kept in touch over the years, even when I didn't speak to her. He loved her till the end. Didn't matter how many times she hurt him."

"Or you?" Cooper asked.

Noah looked over his shoulder and nodded. Those simple words cemented all the reasons Noah was in love with him. Because he knew he was. Trying to deny it wouldn't change it. In some way or another, he'd always loved Cooper Bradshaw. Now, he was *in* love with him.

"Or me."

It was another few minutes before Cooper spoke again. "And her?"

"She's alive and kicking. I went back home when Dad passed. He'd left me half of everything, so there were papers to sign and all of that. I planned the funeral. I wanted to do it for him. Not that she wouldn't have, but…I don't know why, but it was important to me, and she gave me that. I left the day after and haven't seen her since."

There were days he missed her, days he even thought about calling her, but then he'd remember his father and the pain he had endured all those years. He'd remember leaving different homes, leaving Cooper, and Noah just couldn't do it. He was so different than his father. The other man had forgiven her so many times; Noah couldn't bring himself to ever do it. He saw forgiveness as a weakness, a way to get hurt.

Cooper let the conversation go after that. They climbed for another hour and a half before they made it to the top. Noah took in their surroundings. The thick trees, mixed with rocks and the world below them that looked a million miles away.

"It's beautiful." Noah glanced at Cooper beside him to see him looking off at the distance.

"The air feels different up here. Like it's not the same air others are breathing."

There was this sort of awe in his voice that hit Noah right in the chest. He wanted to show Cooper everything. For him to see the world differently when they were together. It's what Coop had always done for him.

"My parents used to hike. Did I ever tell you that?" Coop asked.

Noah put his hand on the back of Cooper's neck, letting his fingers run through the hair at his nape. "No. I'm even more glad we came, then."

Without looking at him, Cooper replied, "I already was."

They enjoyed the view for a little while longer before having lunch. The hike down went much faster than the one up. When they made it back to the cabin, they showered before heading to a restaurant for dinner.

They were in a small town, about two hours from home. It reminded Noah of a movie from the past—an old-town feel that he'd always loved.

"I'm stuffed. Haven't had a steak that good in a long time," Cooper said as they walked down the street.

"I'm glad you liked it." Noah wanted to touch him. There was a little voice in his head that told him he shouldn't. He wasn't sure how Cooper would deal with it. The man was still adjusting to being with another guy. Touching in public might send him over the edge, but damned if he didn't want to stake claim to him in that way.

"Hey." Cooper nudged him with is arm. "We just went on our first date. I hope you don't expect me to put out."

Just like that, Cooper lightened the mood—despite the fact that Noah didn't fully grasp why it had been heavy in the first place. Reaching over, he grabbed Coop's hand. "You better put out," Noah whispered in Cooper's ear.

"I knew it. You're using me for sex," Coop tossed back at him. There was nothing except playfulness in either of their voices. And Cooper didn't pull away, either. He looked down, studying their latched hands as they walked.

"This doesn't feel weird, either." Coop squeezed. "Though it should, and not because you're a guy, but because I don't think I've walked down the sidewalk holding someone's hand since I was in high school."

"Is this your way of telling me I'm being clingy? Childish?" But he didn't let go. He didn't think that was what Cooper was saying, anyway. He only wanted to give him a hard time.

"No. I'm saying when I was a kid I did it because it was expected, and as an adult I didn't do it because I didn't want to give the person I dated the idea that what we had was more than what it was."

Noah nodded, Cooper's words landing right in his chest where they belonged. Trying to find out how in the fuck they got here, yet glad they were, he said, "Who would have thought, all those years ago, that the boy who made me steal magazines with naked women in them and wanted to sneak out and meet girls all the time would be here with me?"

Coop laughed. "Not me. Hey...I wanted to ask you that for a while, now. That night of the football game when we were kids. When we were camping and supposed to meet those girls but you didn't want to go.... did you know? I mean, I know you didn't really know you were gay then, but was there something?"

"Are you asking me if I knew I wanted you when I was thirteen?"

"You're always accusing me of being cocky. What do you think of me, man?"

Noah smiled. "I think I know you and you *do* want to know that. But I also think I don't care. It's who you are, Coop. But...." Noah tried to think of how to reply. "Yes and no, I guess. I didn't know I was gay, but I knew I didn't feel the same way about those girls as you did. I never had. I knew then that I'd much rather be alone with you than with them. That I would have rather been with you than anyone."

They reached Cooper's truck as soon as Noah finished talking. It was in the back of a parking lot they'd walked to, no one else around them.

Noah sucked in a deep breath when Cooper backed him against the truck, his hands on the hood, on either side of Noah.

"I might not have known then what it meant, but I would have rather been with you than anyone else, too, Noah. Always. You've always been what's most important to me. It's as if I've just been biding my time until we were together again. In some way or another."

He stepped closer. Lined his body against Noah's, all male and musk and so Cooper; he got dizzy from his presence.

Coop leaned forward until his mouth was right next to Noah's ear. "I wanna be with you. Want to feel you...inside me. I'm telling you right now, I plan to put out."

Coop's honesty, the way he just put himself out there, stole Noah's breath. Noah grabbed Cooper's hips, pulling Coop to him. "I'll make it good for you, baby. I'll love you so good."

He'd love him. Always.

***

Cooper's fingers shook slightly as he went for the button on his jeans. The second they got back to the cabin, they'd gone straight to the bedroom. Excitement and hunger enflamed him, but those nerves were there, too. This wasn't a finger or a tongue. This would be Noah's dick, inside him.

But he wanted it. Wanted it so fucking much, he could hardly stand it.

"No." Noah touched his hands and Coop looked up at him, afraid he would stop them. But then Noah added, "Let me. I wanna take care of you tonight."

Cooper nodded as Noah pulled the hem of Coop's shirt up and over his head. Then removed his own, showing Coop those piercings that drove him fucking wild.

With slow fingers, he unbuttoned and unzipped Cooper's pants before dropping to his knees in front of him. He slid his hand in the back of Cooper's jeans and cupped his ass before pushing his jeans and underwear down.

Coop thread his hands through Noah's hair, letting his head drop back, when Noah leaned forward, burying his face in Cooper's pubic hair. "You smell so fucking good." He sucked one of Cooper's balls into his mouth, then the other. He felt that one touch everywhere, making him weak. Cooper tightened his fist in Noah's hair, pulling slightly.

"You're gonna make me come before you even get inside me."

"Don't," Noah ordered. "Hold off. I wanna play a little. I'm gonna savor every part of you, baby."

Cooper moaned. Oh yeah. "I like the sound of that—Oh, fuck." He hissed when Noah took his prick all the way to the back of his throat.

Noah licked his head before saying, "I'm getting to the fucking."

"Get there quicker," Cooper gasped.

"No. Go lay on the bed." Noah walked over to his bag, pulling out the rubbers and lube. Coop went straight to the bed like he said, but wrapped a hand around his cock, stroking.

"That's my job." Noah tossed the stuff to the bed.

"Then get me off. I don't want to wait." His whole body felt primed, eager, frenzied. He'd decided he wanted this and he wanted it now.

Noah's hand covered his, making Cooper open his eyes to look at him. "Do you want me to hurry because you want me, or because you don't want to change your mind?"

That was Noah, always over-thinking, always wanting to make sure he was being the nice guy.

"Shut up and fuck me. If I changed my mind, you know I'd tell you."

A slow smile spread cross Noah's face. It took Coop's breath away.

"You asked for it. Roll over."

He almost said he wanted to do it face to face, but he trusted Noah. Cooper flipped onto his stomach, spreading his legs wide.

"Holy Christ you have no idea how fucking hot you look like that. So damn sexy, Coop."

Cooper's skin burned. His insides tingled. He was afraid one touch would send him over the edge. "Want you."

He watched over his shoulder as Noah took off the rest of his clothes, watched his prick—thick and hard, the head purple and — swollen—as he walked toward him. He lay on the bed, moved on top of Cooper, and said, "You have me."

Noah slid down Cooper's body, spreading his cheeks wide. Cooper moaned when his tongue traveled down his crack, settling on his hole. He licked and probed as Cooper started moving against him, needing more. His own cock rubbed against the comforter, creating a delicious friction he couldn't get enough of.

Behind him, Cooper heard the lube open, felt it cold on his asshole before Noah pushed a finger inside.

There was that moment of discomfort and then his body went loose. "That's damn good. *Fuck...*you inside me..."

Noah's fingers pumped in and out. "I gotta give you more to get you ready. Tell me if it's too—"

"Shut the fuck up, Noah. Don't treat me like I can't fucking handle this."

Cooper gasped as Noah's teeth bit into his ass cheek. "You're right."

Then his teeth were gone. More cold and… . "Fuck…yeah." Cooper didn't know how many fingers were inside him, how many were fucking him and loosening him up for Noah's cock. It was tight, stretching him in a way his body had never been stretched before. He couldn't breathe, couldn't move.

"You got this. Just enjoy it. I can't make you come yet or your body will be tight and it'll be harder for you."

*In. Out. In. Out.* Each time Noah's fingers fucked him, it hurt less. The fingers went in easier. And soon he was moving his ass so he met Noah's movements. He started to move faster, his body now wanting more. Wherever Noah was concerned, he always wanted more.

"I need you. Please…"

Behind him, Noah groaned and pulled away. "Turn over. I wanna look at you when I make love to you."

Those words made Cooper shiver with anticipation. He flipped just as Noah was rolling a condom down his cock. He poured lube on himself, then rubbed some on Cooper's hole. When he leaned over Cooper, his body lined up between his legs, Coop froze up for a second.

"Don't…I told you I'd make it good for you. Trust me, baby."

And he did. He trusted Noah with his life. He spread his legs wider, an open invitation. And then Noah was there, his prick pushing into him.

There was pressure, so much fucking pressure.

"Relax and bear down a little."

Cooper did what Noah said. They both gasped when the head of Noah's erection pushed inside him.

"So tight. So fucking tight I could come right now." Noah held himself over Cooper, looking down.

"You better not." He smiled and Noah started pushing in again, slower, farther, until he was buried completely inside Cooper.

He could hardly talk around his quick, short breaths. He felt so full. Ached...but there was pleasure in there, too. "Noah...fuck. Oh God." His eyes closed, probably rolling to the back of his head.

"Open them. Look at me. Look at us."

So Cooper did. He peered down, watching as Noah's hips pulled out before he thrust forward, disappearing inside Cooper's body again.

And it was incredible.

"More...give me more..."

Noah did. Pulling out and slamming forward, over and over. Cooper wrapped a hand around his own erection and started to stroke as Noah fucked him into the mattress. Each time Noah surged forward, Cooper gasped, felt Noah's sac slap against him.

His orgasm, already pricking at his balls.

Noah was gorgeous above him. All flexing, thick muscles. Coop sped up his movements, jacking himself as Noah fucked him.

Noah pulled out, almost all the way, then leaned more, making him hit inside Cooper at a different angle. When he slammed in again, Cooper crumbled apart, his insides bursting into flames as semen shot out of the end of his cock. Each time Noah pushed in, another jet flew onto his chest. It was like his orgasm would never end, pulling him under, wave after wave.

"So fucking beautiful," Noah moaned, and then he yelled out his own orgasm before collapsing on top of Cooper.

Coop just lay there and smiled. Fought to breathe. Neither of them spoke for the longest time, until Cooper ran his hand through Noah's hair and said, "I've never...I don't.... That was...Hell, I don't even know. I just can't wait to do it again."

# CHAPTER TWENTY-TWO

Noah needed a minute alone. "I'll be right back," he told Cooper as he stood up and walked into the bathroom. After getting rid of the condom, he washed his hands before running them, wet, over his face. Just like Cooper hadn't been able to, Noah couldn't find the words to describe what just happened. Christ, he hated getting emotional over this. It wasn't like he'd never had sex before...but he hadn't made love. And that's exactly what they'd done.

All he could think about was what if Coop decided he couldn't come out? What if he wanted to keep them hidden forever, or decided being with another man wasn't what he wanted? If he decided he didn't want to risk Vernon's wrath or deal with shit at work. It would kill him to lose Cooper again, to lose him in a way he hadn't before.

*Chill the fuck out, Jameson. You're losing it.*

After grabbing a towel from the rack, he wiped his face before going back out to Cooper again. He laid on his back, naked, his cock amazingly half-hard.

Noah's heart thumped, blood rushing through him. "I brought you a towel," he said, not sure what else to say.

Cooper turned his head and smiled at him. "You never cleaned us up before."

"That's because I like the evidence of what I do to you between us." He shrugged. "But I want—no, *need*—to take care of you, Coop." Noah walked to the side of the bed and wiped Cooper's stomach with the partially wet towel before tossing it to the floor.

"We take care of each other, yeah? Just like we used to." Cooper grabbed Noah's wrist and pulled him down.

He was lost. Fucking sunk. All because of the man in bed with him right now. "Come here," he told Coop, and he obeyed. Coop rolled over and wrapped an arm around Noah. The weight felt right there, heavy and perfect. Reaching over, Noah turned off the light. "Go to sleep. We have a busy day ahead of us tomorrow."

Noah felt like he'd just closed his eyes when his stomach growled, waking him up. Their room was already bright with light, telling him it was fairly late in the morning. He hadn't meant to sleep so late. They were going back home tomorrow morning and he wanted to spend as much time with Coop as possible.

*And here I go being a sap again. It's not like we don't live together.*

But today was also the anniversary of his parents' death. He wanted the day to be fun for Cooper.

Noah pressed his lips to the top of Cooper's head. "Wake up, baby. I need food." He knew Cooper would, too. The other man was always hungry when he first woke up.

Cooper rolled over, and then winced. "Fuck."

"I'm sorry you're sore." Noah kissed him again.

Coop's sleepy eyes caught his. "I'm not."

Noah leaned in. As their lips were about to touch, Coop's stomach growled this time, making both men laugh. "Food first. I'll kiss and make it better later." Noah winked, trying not to smile at the cheesiness of his own line.

Both men climbed out of the bed and went to shower together. It about killed Noah not to touch him, but he knew if he did he'd want to fuck Cooper again. He wanted him to get a break, because he definitely had to be even sorer than he was letting on.

He watched as Coop dried off then pulled on a pair of boxer briefs and shorts. His T-shirt stretched over the muscles that Noah loved so much, and damned if he didn't start to get hard.

"If you keep looking at me like that, we're never getting out of here." Coop's eyebrows went up.

"I can't help it. You're sexy."

"And you're not? Still, if we don't eat I might waste away, and then I won't have any energy left for tonight."

Noah laughed, pulling his shirt over his head. "We wouldn't want that."

They went to an out-of-the-way diner and had breakfast. Questions ate a hole through Noah. Was Cooper okay? Was he thinking about his parents and hiding it? Was this thing between them really going to work?

He kept them all locked inside, thinking there was a better time to discuss it than now.

After lunch they headed to the lake. They had fishing supplies, chairs, and whatever else they needed in the back of Coop's truck. They parked on the side of the tree-lined, quiet road before making the short hike down a hill to the water.

They had their fishing poles in the water for about an hour when Noah looked over at Coop in the chair beside him. He hated asking but couldn't stop himself. "How ya doing, man?"

"About which thing? Because of what today is or because of what we did last night?"

Noah shrugged. "I don't know. Both, I guess." His heart paused its beat, waiting for Cooper's answer.

"I know I should feel strange, because of last night, but I don't. I'm shocked I did it, and more shocked that I liked it so much. There's a part of my mind that still tells me this isn't what I should be doing. I shouldn't want you inside me, Noah, but I *do*. That part is stronger by a million times. I guess... ," he stopped as if to think over his words. "I guess it doesn't matter what I think I should want. What matters is what I need, and that's this, whatever this thing is between us. I feel more like myself when I'm with you than I ever have."

Noah's heartbeat began again. He reached over and laid a hand on Cooper's strong arm. "Such a fucking sweet talker," he teased.

"I know. I'm good, right?"

Even though it had been Noah who lightened their moment, he didn't let it last. "It might be different for me because I've been with men, but everything else is the same. I've only ever felt completely at ease when I was with you."

Cooper grinned. "See? I am good."

Noah shook his head. "You're an ass. Now what about the rest of it? Your parents?"

"I still miss 'em like hell, Noah. There's a part of me that knows it's been so long, I shouldn't feel it this deeply, but I do. I'm okay, though. I think they'd be happy to know I'm happy."

He had no doubt Cooper's words were true, but the tone of his voice and the look in his eyes said his lover was feeling things more than he wanted to share. That had always been Coop. He felt guilt for things that weren't his fault. And Noah knew Cooper would always blame himself for leaving his parents behind in that house, even though there was no way he could have saved them.

Before Noah could push the conversation farther, Coop's fishing pole jerked in his hand. "Well lookie here, Noah. Looks like I'm catching dinner."

***

Catching the fish couldn't have come at a better time. He'd known Noah would push things, and Cooper wasn't in the mood to deal with it. Not that he minded talking to Noah about it. The man was about the only person he really could, but not now. Not this weekend. He wanted this to be about them.

The fish had turned out too small to do much of anything with so they'd thrown it back. Cooper stood next to Noah's chair, ready to do something other than fish. "Go swimming with me." He nodded toward the water.

Noah didn't need to be asked twice. He reeled in his pole before taking off his shirt and dropping it on his chair. Cooper caught sight of that dragon tattoo on Noah's upper back that he loved so much. It continued to surprise him how sexy he found Noah.

After both stripping down to their underwear, they headed for the water. Coop watched as Noah dunked his head under before breaking the surface again, shaking out his dark, wet hair. Would he ever get tired of watching Noah? Even doing the simplest things like that?

They swam for a while before Noah snuck up behind him and wrapped his arms around Cooper's waist. They floated together, water running down each of their faces. When he looked at Noah, there was no doubt in his mind that this was it for him. That he really was in love with him.

It was scary but not nearly as much as he would have thought.

"Do you know how hard it is for me to keep my hands off you?" Noah kissed the back of his neck before pressing his teeth in.

Cooper shivered. Damn he loved the feel of Noah marking his skin. "About as hard as it is for me to keep mine off you?"

"Harder." Noah kissed him again. Then Noah was pulling him toward the bank. When they got there, he went straight to his knees, pulling Cooper's cock free and wrapping his lips around him.

"You are so good at that." He gripped Noah's hair as the other man sucked him off. It didn't take long for him to shoot his release to the back of Noah's throat.

When he tried to do the same for Noah, he wouldn't let him.

"You can owe me. Don't worry. I won't let the debt go unpaid." He smiled. "That was just for you."

"Sucking your cock would be for me, too."

Noah's face flushed with what Cooper recognized as desire. Still, he said, "Later."

They cleaned up their supplies and headed back to the truck. Cooper couldn't remember a time he'd laughed and had so much fun as they did that night. They went to dinner again before watching some sports on TV. They drank a few beers and talked about when they were kids and all the hell they used to raise together.

When they went to bed, Noah wrapped himself around Cooper, holding him. They kissed and touched, Cooper just enjoying the feel of all the planes of Noah's body. Noah kissed his forehead. "No sex tonight." Then his lips. "And no complaining." His lips pressed down on Cooper's chest next. "Because I'll give in, and I don't want to hurt you."

Cooper laughed, pulling Noah down so he rested all of his weight on Coop before closing his eyes and going to sleep.

*"Daddy! Where's Dad?" Cooper yelled. His whole body burned. His throat and chest hurt. And it was so hot. So hot he felt like he was cooking.*

*"Go, Coop. I need you to go." His mom flinched as the heavy beam shifted on top of her.*

*Tears flooded down Cooper's face as his mom started crying, too.*

*"I love you, kiddo. Just go. Now."*

*"I don't want to go. I don't want to leave you!"*

"Cooper, baby. Wake up. You're dreaming."

Noah's voice pulled him out of the past. His whole body shuddered as Noah pulled him closer. Flipped them so Noah laid on his back, partially sitting up, with Coop lying between his legs. His head rested on Noah's stomach as he fought to catch his breath. Goddamned dream. He didn't want to taint their time here. Didn't want to ruin it with the past that Cooper couldn't seem to let go.

"Shh. It's okay. I'm here. It was just a dream." Cooper relaxed into Noah as the man stroked his hair.

"It's been twenty years. Why can't I get over it, Noah?" His voice cracked on his lover's name. It made Cooper feel weak. He hated that.

"Because they were your parents. Because you still haven't forgiven yourself for living."

"I left her. I could have saved her, at least."

"No." He continued running his fingers through Cooper's hair. "You couldn't have. You were a child. You did what your mom told you to do. What she wanted you to do. You would have died, too. You couldn't have saved them, baby." Noah tilted his head up, so Cooper looked at him, the moon giving them enough light to see. "You didn't run. You didn't leave them. You lived, and that takes a whole lot of strength. It was the right thing to do."

Fuck, he wanted that to be true. Wanted Noah's words to be carved into stone, into his past, so maybe he could believe it. "Was it the right thing? Vernon always pushed me to be strong. To be a man. If I would have been stronger then—"

"Fuck that, Coop. Did he tell you that?" Noah's whole body was stone beneath him.

"No." *He didn't have to. I know he thought it. Vernon always did the right thing. He was always strong.*

"It's not your fault, baby." Noah's thumb brushed his cheek. "You are the strongest person I know. Even being here with me, that's so fucking strong, Coop. God, when we were kids, I looked up to you, so much. You were this light in the darkness, this bright spot that always made everything better. When you spoke, people listened. Everyone loved you. They still do. Why can't you see all that you are? When I left, that was what kept me going. You'd been through so much more than me, but you kept going. I wanted so fucking badly to be just like you."

Noah's words pumped through him. They echoed through his head, pulsed blood through his heart. "I ran straight to your house when I got home that weekend. I wanted to tell you about the game. It felt like I lost everything when I found that house empty. You say I was all those things to you, but you were them, as well, to me. I wonder," Cooper paused, but then decided he didn't give a shit how this sounded—it was real and honest and he wanted Noah to know it— "Hell, maybe in some way I was even in love with you back then."

Noah sucked in a deep breath. "What?"

"I said I'm in love with you, Noah. Don't pretend you don't know to hear me say it again."

Noah didn't laugh as he'd hoped. This would have been a lot easier if he did.

"I love you, too, Coop. I've always loved you."

Cooper let out a breath he didn't realize he held.

After that, the room went silent. Noah didn't move from under him, so Cooper rested his head on Noah's stomach again, still lying with Noah's legs around him.

They went to sleep holding each other, the way he hoped they always would.

# CHAPTER TWENTY-THREE

The two weeks after they got home, everything went at warp speed. Cooper worked a couple of extra shifts on top of his regular schedule. He was exhausted, but he also wanted to be there to help Noah as he put in hours into his new workshop. Cooper had wanted to do this *for* Noah, so it hadn't felt right that the other man spent time out there alone. So any time that he could he spent sanding, building and painting with Noah.

They'd gone in for Noah to fill out the paperwork on the lease for the store, so everything was lined up for him to get to work. He had to make a trip back to California to empty his storage unit, which held all his tools and also some pieces that he had already made.

"I feel bad you have to make the drive back by yourself," Cooper told him. Noah was flying to California, but then he'd rent a truck to haul everything back. "It sure would make the drive easier if you had someone else to take shifts with you." They were standing in the kitchen. Cooper had gotten off work not long before. He'd taken a shower, and then come downstairs to see Noah making dinner.

"Don't worry about it. You can't get the time off. The drive isn't going to kill me. I just made it a few months ago. Plus, I don't mind driving. It's sort of relaxing." Noah nodded toward the table. "Sit down. We'll figure out the bills and everything while the food finishes cooking."

Cooper rolled his eyes. Noah was insistent that if he was going to be staying here, well, they hoped forever, that they had the bills split more equally. "You're being ridiculous."

"No, I want this to be equal, Coop. I'm living in your house and working off your property. I don't mind. It's not that, but I also won't feel like I'm living off you. We're in this together, all the way."

"Don't want to be my, what? Kept boyfriend?" Cooper laughed. Boyfriend. Whoa. He never thought he'd have one of those. "You know how much money us firefighters make. You probably have more in the bank than I do."

Cooper sat down, putting his feet up on the chair across from him. Noah stepped up behind him, his hands on Cooper's shoulders. "That's not the point. Now shut up and humor me." He bent and kissed the side of Cooper's neck. "But I like hearing you call me yours."

Aaaand just like always, Cooper's dick perked to attention at the sound of Noah's voice. "If we're going to do this, we need to do it. I'd much rather fuck."

He never got enough of Noah. He'd taken Noah a couple times these two weeks, but usually it was Noah inside him. He loved knowing his lover had him in a way no one ever had, or would.

"Horny bastard," Noah said next to him. They wrote out all the bills and evened everything out. They'd halved the expenses, each of them paying specific utilities. In his way, he wondered if that was Noah trying to make things more permanent between them. Not that they weren't, but like he wanted it in stone. Cooper humored him, even though where he was concerned, they were already in stone, cemented, written in the fucking stars, or whatever you wanted to say.

There was only one dark cloud hanging over them—and Noah didn't even know the extent of it. Not only did his aunt and uncle not know he was in love with another man, but they still didn't know Noah was here. *That* made him feel like shit more than anything else. Noah had made another comment about how excited he was to see Cooper's family, Autumn especially, yet he didn't think Noah would get the reception he assumed. Well, from Autumn, maybe, but not Vernon.

Cooper crossed his arms, trying to focus on the smell of the stew in the crockpot instead of his guilt. "I'm talking to Vernon and Autumn while you're gone."

Noah leaned over and nuzzled his neck. "I don't feel right about your talking to them without me. It shouldn't all come down on you. I should be there. Maybe...maybe it'll help them understand better since it's me. They know how much we meant to each other. They practically helped raise me for three years. That has to count for something."

It wouldn't. Not with Vernon. What Cooper didn't understand was why.

Cooper shook his head. This was something he needed to do alone. He wouldn't risk Noah getting hurt by how things would very likely go down. "I need to do this. Plus, you leave tomorrow. I know you don't want to put off getting your stuff any longer than you already have."

"And what about everyone else? Are you ready for people to know? It's going to look strange, baby. I live with you. I have a shop on your property. It's going to look permanent."

"That's because it is. I don't give a shit what anyone else thinks. I'm not going to lie and say I don't want this to be okay with my family, because I do. It won't stop me, but...I don't want to lose them, either. Regardless, they raised me. And I'm not going to pretend it won't cause some shit at work, too. We both know it will, but this?" He put his hand on Noah's leg. "We're more important. Fuck everyone else. I love you."

He could feel the switch in Noah instantly. See the fire in his eyes and the need on his face. "I love you, too. Now get your ass upstairs. After tonight, it's going to be way too long before I get to fuck you again."

Cooper couldn't think of anything he wanted more at that moment.

*** 

Noah's hunger for Cooper never diminished. All the other man had to do was speak or breathe and Noah wanted him. "Upstairs." He nodded his head toward the stairs.

Cooper stood. "You know there's no one else I would allow to order me around the way you do, right?"

Grabbing his shirt, Noah pulled Cooper toward him. "Same goes for you, baby. Now go upstairs so I can fuck you." He gave Cooper a little shove. Not that Cooper needed it. Coop made it to the stairs in no time flat, taking them two at a time, with Noah right behind him.

As soon as they made it to the foot of the bed, Noah stopped him, his lips colliding with Cooper's. Their tongues battled, one surrendering, before fighting to take control again. He loved his power play with Coop.

When his guy shoved his hands under Noah's shirt, he pulled away far and long enough for his shirt to get pulled off before he was kissing him again. Cooper's thumb brushed over the piercing in Noah's nipple before he tugged on it, making Noah cry out.

"Wanna suck you." Cooper sat on the edge of his bed, making quick work of Noah's jeans. He felt twitchy, as though he would bust out of his skin if he didn't have something, *everything*, from Cooper right now.

When Noah's jeans and boxer briefs were gone, he was immediately enveloped in the hot cavern of Cooper's mouth. Coop took him deep before pulling back and paying special attention to the head. "Yeah. That's it. Christ, I love your mouth."

Noah ran his fingers through Cooper's short hair, rocking his hips so when Coop slid his mouth down again, Noah could fuck it.

His lover did everything Noah liked: sucked his balls, let his tongue probe the slit before pulling him to the back of his throat again. Pleasure built deep inside him, quickly finding its way to the surface, until he had to pull Cooper back. "Wanna love you," he said, before lowering his mouth to take possession of Coop's.

And then he pulled the other man to his feet. With slow hands he undressed him, showing him all that tanned, golden skin, stretched across hard muscle. "You are so fucking sexy."

Noah grabbed the lube and a condom from the bedside drawer. Their bed was high, making it perfect for the way he wanted to take Cooper.

After the rubber was in place, he looked back at Coop. Noah pushed him so he bent over. "Let me see that sexy ass."

Coop leaned over, his upper body held up by his elbows on the bed. When his fingers were lubed, he added a little to Coop's hole before pushing a finger inside. "Oh fuck. Yes..." A heavy breath fell from Cooper's lips. He'd never get tired of that sound. Never get enough of Coop taking his pleasure.

He used one, then two fingers to stretch Coop, twisting, turning, pulling, pushing. The man rode his hand, pushing back into it, alternating between making little gasping sounds and asking for more.

Noah flipped the lid on the lube with one hand, letting it leak over his cock, before pulling his fingers free and pushing inside. His body shuddered, savoring the feel of Cooper's tight hole, squeezing him.

"Harder. Give me more." Cooper moaned.

His. Fucking. Pleasure.

Noah leaned forward, wrapping his arms under Cooper's arms and pulling him tight against him. He hooked them together as he bent Cooper over the bed, no space between the two men.

"So tight...so fucking good," he whispered in Coop's ear before pulling out and slamming home again. Cooper's whole body shook, rocked, and Noah made love to him with swift, hard thrusts.

The bed rattled as he knocked against the bedside table, but he kept going, kept pumping into Coop. Each time he did, pleasure shot through him, higher and higher.

"Fuck...Noah..."

That just made him squeeze Cooper to him, tighter. Push deeper, fuck harder. Still with his arms hooked under Cooper's, his hands gripped the other man's shoulders, pushing him to meet Noah's thrusts.

"Oh, shit. I'm gonna come."

Noah let his hand drop, pressing tightly at the base of Cooper's prick so he didn't orgasm. "Not yet."

He couldn't stop the groan from passing his own lips when he pulled out. Noah flipped Cooper over easily, despite the fact that they were similar in size. As soon as he had his guy on his back, he thrust into him again, pushing Cooper's legs back so he could watch as his erection disappear inside his lover.

"Fuck!" Cooper yelled when Noah angled himself so he'd hit the other man's prostate. Then, pulse after pulse of creamy, white fluid jutted out of Cooper's dick and landed on his chest. That was all it took for Noah's orgasm to rock through him. He kept going, kept fucking as he filled the condom with his semen.

When his release took everything out of him, Noah, holding himself up with his hands flat on the bed, looked down into Coop's blue eyes. "Wanted." Breath. "To watch." Another one. "You come."

Then he lay down on top of Cooper, who wrapped his legs around his waist.

"How am I supposed to make it a few days without that?"

Noah smiled into Cooper's chest. Holy crap, did he love this man.

# CHAPTER TWENTY-FOUR

Cooper kept busy while Noah was gone. Between work and cleaning out space for some of Noah's things, the few days his guy was gone passed quickly. He still felt like shit that Noah had had to go to California by himself, but he'd make it up to him. In as many ways he could think of.

He wasn't embarrassed to admit he missed Noah. He'd never been surer of anything in his life than he was of Noah Jameson. It didn't matter that he was a man or that Cooper had never planned to settle down. Noah was his and he was Noah's, and fuck anyone who had a problem with it.

That didn't mean he wasn't nervous to talk to his aunt and uncle. There was still that voice in the back of his head that made Cooper feel responsible for others, that felt the need not to let down the people he loved. And there was no doubt in his mind: that was exactly how Vernon would feel.

He wouldn't understand it. He would see Cooper as weak and he would be let down. Because the way he'd see it, that wasn't how he'd raised Coop. Vernon would think himself a failure, and after the way his uncle had taken him in, raised him and cared for him as best he could, Coop hated the idea of that being marred by being seen as a failure.

Which was why he'd waited until the day Noah was supposed to be home to head to his uncle's house. Or, maybe it was because he knew he'd need the other man when he was done.

When his cell rang, Cooper reached over and grabbed it from the passenger seat. Braden's name lit up the screen. "What's up, man?"

"Waitin' on the phone number. You work your magic with your guy?"

Coop rolled his eyes. "I mentioned it to him once. What do I look like, your matchmaker? Why do you even want it so bad? You had a good time, and now it's over, just how you've always liked it."

Braden gave a humorless chuckle. "Did you see him? He's gorgeous. And that was with his clothes on. You didn't see—"

"—I'm thinking you should end it there," Coop cut him off. "The last thing I want to do is hear about what went down with you and Wes." Cooper knew it made him an ass, but he still wasn't real fond of the man. He felt bad for his situation, but he'd also wanted to fuck Noah. That was the part he had trouble getting over. "Holy shit. I still can't believe I'm talking to you about men. What happened to my life?" Cooper laughed.

"Nothin' wrong with exploring your sexuality. There's beauty in both men and women."

Even though Braden obviously couldn't see him, Cooper nodded. "I guess...though I can't see feeling that toward any other man but Noah." And he couldn't. He wasn't sure what that meant, but figured it didn't really matter. All he knew was he *did* go wild when he looked at Noah, and he loved the man. The rest of it was just labels.

"Look at you, you've turned into a romantic. So you get why I want Wes's number, or where he lives. I'm not adverse to showing up." Even though Braden laughed, Coop had no doubt the man was completely serious.

"So you spent one night with the guy and you're in love with him?"

"Fuck no. I'm in lust with him. Big fucking difference. And...I don't know. There's something about him. Like, he's completely alone."

The seriousness in Braden's voice tugged on Coop's guilt. All he wanted to do was talk to the man. What was the harm in that? And since Wes was losing his sister, maybe spending some time with Braden would do him some good. At least help him forget for a few hours.

"I don't have his number but I'll talk to Noah again when he gets home from California tonight. I'm pretty sure his last name is Jensen, though. Not sure if that'll help."

"Hell yeah. That's a start. What ya up to? Wanna go play some basketball or something?" Braden asked.

*I wish.* "Can't. I'm heading out to my uncle's. Shit, man, I'm going to tell him about Noah." Cooper's tires hit the gravel a little as he took a corner, but he corrected it quickly.

Braden was silent for a minute before asking, "And that won't go well?"

"No. It won't. Partly because he's going to have a huge problem with his nephew being with another man, but the fact that it's Noah won't help."

"Sorry about that. You need to go out for a beer or something after, let me know. I thought you grew up with Noah. Your family doesn't like him?"

"They did, that's what I don't understand. Noah was always at my house, but after they left, their family was off-limits for Vernon."

Cooper's heart dropped when the smell of smoke hit his nose. It wasn't something he could ever forget. His eyes ran over the mile marker sign before landing on a house off the side of the road, red flames engulfing it.

Coop slammed the breaks, jerking the wheel so he didn't miss the driveway. "House fire. Thirty-two mile marker off Old Stage Highway. Ah, fuck, this thing is huge, Braden. Call it in."

His foot slammed down on the brake as he skidded to a stop. Just like every time he saw a fire, his heart became a battering ram, slamming against his ribs.

Coop rushed out of the car as a little girl ran up to him. "Help! You have to help! My big brother!"

Cooper didn't hear anything else.

"Wait, Cooper. I just called it in on my other phone. Don't you fucking go in there!" Braden yelled.

But he had to. This is what he did. "And you wouldn't?" There was no doubt in his mind he would do the same thing.

Braden didn't reply and Cooper didn't have time to wait. He ended the call and put the phone in the little girl's hand, dirt and ash covering her. "You call your family if you can. I'm going to get him, okay? Is he the only one in there?"

"Yes!" she wailed.

"Where?"

"He was listening to his headphones upstairs. I was scared."

"What's his name?"

"B—Billy."

He touched the little girl's hair. "It's okay. You did real good. I'm gonna go get your brother. I promise you. Stay out here, okay? No matter what."

Without another word, Cooper ran for the house, determined not to fuck up this time. Determined not to run, not to leave someone else to die.

Heat scorched him the second he stumbled through the doorway. Holding his breath, Cooper went straight for the stairs. He knew he had to get in there, get the kid out, and go. He didn't have much time. Couldn't take many breaths.

Smoke billowed around him. The fire had obviously started up there, he just hoped like hell it wasn't in the same room as the kid.

Instinct took over as he hit the landing. The heat, the smoke, none of it mattered as much as finding that fucking kid. He took a breath. "Billy? Can you hear me?" he yelled as he went in the first room he came to. It was on the front side of the house, the fire all along the far wall, spreading, crawling through the walls.

Another breath. "Billy?" he called out. Sewing supplies burned all around the room. He doubted this was where the kid slept so he went to the next room. Loud popping and cracking mixed with the roar of the fire as Coop moved on.

*Save him, save him, save him.* He had to fucking save him.

Red and smoke was all he saw down the hallway. This fire was moving and it was moving fast.

The first thing he saw when he pushed his way into the second room was a small basketball hoop hanging off the wall, fire dancing all over it.

*Jackpot.*

"Billy? Are you here? I'm a fireman. I need you to come out, so I can get you out of here."

Cooper's burning eyes scanned the room before stopping on a figure huddled in the corner. As he went to walk toward the kid, flames lashed his arm, singeing him. *Fuck.* He had to move. Now.

Coop ran to the corner, lifting the limp kid in his arms. He couldn't tell if the kid was awake or not, but it didn't fucking matter. All that did was getting him out.

The floor cracked beneath him as he ran from the room. The hall, even more taken over than it was just seconds ago. Dizziness hit him but he pushed past it. Flames now blocked the stairs.

He felt Billy's hand tighten around his neck. Fuck, the kid couldn't be any older than twelve.

Looking behind him, Cooper saw fire, making an escape from the window impossible. Sirens called to him from a distance.

Ignoring his rapid-fire heart, he ran to the room at the end of the hall. *Thank God.* There was a window that faced the side of the house. The room was hot as hell, but he could get to that fucking window.

Cooper kicked it out, somehow keeping the kid in his arms. Another small favor. There was a section of roof below it. He only hoped like hell it could hold them.

A red engine pulled to a stop out front. He could see it when he stuck his head out. "Over here!" Cooper yelled, as more cracking and popping went off around him. The floor rattled. *Ah, fuck.*

"Help…" Billy's voice rasped in his ear. Help came running around their side of the house as if they heard him.

Above him came a loud banging sound. Cooper pushed the kid out the window just as something hit the back of his shoulders, pain piercing through him. Part of the floor next to him gave out as he went down, and Cooper's world went black.

***

It was dark when Noah pulled the rental truck into the driveway at home. He was tired as hell. All he wanted to do was crawl into bed with Cooper and pass the hell out. He'd made this trip much faster than he should have, just wanting to be home.

As soon as he pulled to a stop, he noticed the house was dark and Cooper's truck was gone. Before he could put much thought into it, Noah's cell rang. He almost didn't answer Wes's call, but then...what if something happened to his sister?

"Hello?"

"Where are you?" were the first words out of Wes's mouth.

"I'm at home. What's wrong?" Noah's gut cramped. Something had happened.

"I'm with Braden. We're going to come get you, okay? You stay right there. We're on our way."

The cramp became a fist, squeezing the life out of him. There was only one thing that would make Wes sound like that. "Where is he?" His voice cracked.

Wes cursed. "Wait for us and we'll drive you."

"Where the fuck is he, Wes?" Noah's hands shook.

"There was a fire," Wes told him. "He's okay. Fuck, it took Braden forever to find me. No one had your number or we would have called you earlier."

Noah's whole universe rocked. *Fire.* "Tell me where the fuck he is. Now."

Wes cursed again before rattling off the name of a local hospital. Noah ended the call the second he had the information. Noah ran from the rental to his car, knowing it would get him there a whole hell of a lot faster. It felt like two seconds and at the same time ten years later before he pulled up in front of the hospital.

Braden and Wes were already standing outside when he got there.

"I told him not to fucking go in. He was on his way to his uncle's. We were on the phone and he saw it," Braden said. All Noah cared about was getting to Cooper.

"What room?"

Braden paused before replying. "ICU."

Noah fought the bile threatening to crawl up his throat.

The two men flanked him as they ran for the intensive care unit. Double doors blocked the entrance. Noah went straight for the nurse's station. "Cooper Bradshaw." His voice cracked. "I need to see him."

"We only allow two visitors at a time, and there are already two people back there."

Noah's body tensed as he gripped the counter. "I need to see him. How is he? What happened?" He couldn't lose Cooper. Not again. Not permanently.

"Are you family?" she asked.

Wes and Braden both groaned beside him.

*He is the only family I have. I love him.* "He's my partner."

Her eyes widened before she smiled kindly at him. "Let me call back there and let them know you're here."

Noah's feet wouldn't keep still as he paced in front of the nurses station. "What do you know?"

It was Braden who spoke. "He saved a kid. He ran into that house and saved a little boy."

And as scared and angry as he was, there was pride there, too. That was his guy. He expected nothing less of Cooper.

"Just as he got the kid out. We don't know if something hit him and then the floor collapsed, or how it went down. He's got a puncture wound where a piece of metal went through his shoulder. He was knocked out, and there is obviously worries because of smoke inhalation."

When he heard the phone click behind him, Noah turned back to the nurse. The way her eyes cast down told him everything. They weren't going to let him see Cooper. "No one's stopping me from getting through those doors," he told her. As he did, they slid open and Vernon and Autumn stepped out.

*Thank God.* Noah rushed over to them. "Is he okay? They won't let me see him." Noah reached for Autumn, but she chewed her lip and looked away.

"What the hell are you doing here?" Vernon growled.

And that's when he knew. Things hadn't gone well when Cooper told them. "Listen, I know you might not agree with things between Coop and me, but now's not the time. We need to be here for him."

"His family needs to be here for him, and we are," Vernon replied.

No matter what they thought, Cooper was his family. Wes's hand came down on Noah's shoulder. He closed his eyes and took a deep breath to calm himself. "He'll want me there. I know this has to be confusing for you guys. I understand that, but I love him and he loves me. I can promise you he'll want me in that room with him."

Autumn gasped, leaning on her cane. Vernon's eyes turned to ice.

"There is nothing I wouldn't do for him. You might not like it but he feels the same way about me." Then he realized Cooper never made it there. They'd said he saw the fire on his way. Damn, this was a hard time for them to find something like this out, but there was nothing to do about it now. "He was going to tell you, today."

"Today, huh? You lying piece of shit. You show up, out of the blue, and tell me my nephew is in love with you? You haven't talked to Cooper in seventeen years! How the hell did you know what happened? What makes you want to push your way into that room the way your whole damn family shoved their way into our lives all those years ago?"

"Now, wait a minute." Braden stepped forward, but Noah grabbed him.

They didn't know. They didn't even know Noah had come back. Why wouldn't Cooper have told them that much? "You didn't know I was here? That I've been living with Cooper for months?"

Cooper had said his aunt wanted to see him. He looked at Autumn, hoping to see knowledge there, but she looked just as taken aback as Vernon.

Cooper had lied to him. He'd even kept their friendship hidden, just like David had.

"Whatever you thought was going on between my nephew and yourself, you're wrong about. I won't let you try to ruin his life like—"

"—Vernon!" Autumn cut him off. "It wasn't his fault. Noah was his best friend."

"I'm fucking in love with him!" Noah yelled. He didn't give a shit what any of them said. Even as angry as he was at Cooper, he wasn't leaving this hospital without seeing him.

Noah went straight for the doors. Vernon tried to stop him, a look of disgust on his face. A glance at Autumn showed him she was crying, a hand covering her mouth.

Noah just needed to see Cooper.

Before he could get a chance to do anything, security grabbed him. He hadn't even realized they were here. His muscles tightened—chest ached.

Both Wes and Braden started yelling, trying to defend him.

But none of it mattered. Noah wasn't family. Noah wasn't even officially Cooper's partner. Security escorted him from the building. He felt like he was cracking apart, his breath cut off. None of it mattered to them. There wasn't a damn thing Noah could do about it.

# CHAPTER TWENTY-FIVE

"Still no luck?" Noah asked Braden as the other man approached him. It had been two days since Cooper's accident. He came back every day but they wouldn't let him in. They didn't transfer calls through, and no one answered Cooper's cell. It was killing him.

No matter what happened between him and Cooper, he couldn't walk away without seeing him. Without witnessing with his own eyes that he was okay. He'd been forced away from Cooper one other time, and he wasn't letting that happen again.

He fought to push those thoughts away. Thoughts that no matter what Cooper wanted, he might not be able to go forward with this. Not if he hadn't even been able to tell his family Noah was here. Was he embarrassed of Noah being gay? Of what people would think of him? He didn't know, and it wasn't important now. Not as important as Cooper's well-being.

"His uncle told them not to let me in, either, which I knew he would do. They won't let him have any visitors. His uncle has been in touch with the captain but he won't share any information with us at work, either."

"Fuck!" Noah yelled. A couple looked at him and then scurried inside the building.

He could hardly keep still, adrenaline pumping through him as though it was on tap. What if he lost him?

"I'll be back. I have...just wait here and I'll be back." Braden walked away, but Noah paid no attention. He didn't care.

Wes came over and stood beside him. The man hadn't left his side since last night. "You should be home with your sister," Noah told him.

"She understands."

Noah wanted to tell him thank you. Who would have thought Wes would be someone he called a friend? He couldn't bring himself to do it right now, though.

"He lied to me, Wes. He didn't even tell them I was here. I've been here months and he didn't even tell them I was *here.* I don't think…"

"Now's not the time to think, anyway," Wes interrupted.

He wished he could turn it off like that. "Thinking is all I *can* do right now. He's not ready. I wanted to believe so bad he was, that it didn't matter that he'd never been with a man before. We loved each other and that's all that counted, but hell, he didn't even want his family to know we're friends again." Which confused the hell out of Noah. Vernon had been so fucking angry the other day. There'd been more to it than finding out about Noah and Cooper. A deep-seeded hatred that Noah didn't understand.

"I saw the way he reacted that night at the bar. He's in this just as much as you are. I don't give a shit if this is his first time with a man; he wants you. Don't think he doesn't."

Noah couldn't deny that. "I believe he wants me. I even believe he loves me. But that doesn't mean this will work. He kept everything about me hidden." Noah had seen people ignore the signs. Seen his dad ignore them, not wanting to believe his mother had cheated again. Hell, he'd ignored them with David, too. He couldn't ignore this. Actions spoke louder than words.

"I can forget the rest of it for now, though. I just need him to be okay." Noah ran a hand through his hair. "I can't fucking lose him like this."

It was then that Braden walked up with a redheaded woman. She looked around as though she was nervous stopping in front of him.

"Well, I'll be damned. So you're the reason Cooper Bradshaw told me he couldn't meet up with me anymore."

Noah dropped his head back. What the hell had Braden been thinking? Like he was in the mood to see a woman Cooper used to sleep with. Plus, this was Cooper's private business. He had no right to share it with this woman. But then he looked at her again, noticed the scrubs she wore. *Fuck yes.*

"Can you get me in to see him?"

She cocked her head. "If he wants to see you."

"He does." He did, right? Cooper would want to see him. Wait. "Is he awake?"

The woman, Adrianna, her nametag read, glanced away. He was awake, yet he hadn't asked someone for Noah? He hadn't called? *It's over.... He's decided he can't do this.*

"Look, unless Cooper tells me he wants to see you, I can get into huge trouble for this. Let me see what I can do. I'll try to talk to him today. Meet me at seven thirty, and I'll see what I can do, okay? That's usually when his family goes to dinner."

"Thank you," Noah told her. "And please, he hasn't...people don't know."

She looked sad again. "It's not my business to tell." Without another word, she turned and walked away.

Now if Noah could just forget the fact that not only had Cooper kept everything about him a secret, but he was awake and hadn't tried to get a hold of Noah, once.

***

Cooper's throat was killing him. He knew his shoulder should be, too, but somehow the pain medicine helped more with that. He hardly spoke because his voice only came out in a whisper and he knew he needed to rest his vocals, but still, he asked his uncle again, "No-ah...?"

How stupid could he be not to have Noah's phone number memorized? It was in his cell, and he remembered giving it to the little girl, but no one knew what happened to it.

The parents of the little boy and girl had been in to see Cooper. Billy had smoke inhalation, too, but like Cooper, the little boy was on the mend. He'd saved him, and as happy as that made him, he couldn't get his mind off Noah. Cooper needed him. How could he not be here?

"Now's not the time to worry about your friend. Focus on getting well. He knows you're here."

*Then why isn't he with me?*

Cooper fought to stay awake, to push his way through the fog of pain and medicine, but he couldn't do it. Just like every other time he woke up, he slipped right back into blackness in no time…

\*\*\*

Cooper had no idea how much time had passed when he woke up again. They'd moved him out of the ICU, he could see.

He let his eyes case the room, waiting for them to land on Noah, but again, the man wasn't here.

Cooper squeezed his eyes shut, trying to get a hold of himself. Had Noah decided Cooper wasn't worth the hassle? Did he change his mind? The pain in his shoulder traveled to his chest. God, he fucking needed Noah. He wanted him here.

When he heard the sound of the door, he turned his head, hoping to see the man he couldn't get enough of, but it was his aunt who slowly walked in.

"You're awake. How are you feeling?"

Cooper nodded, trying not to speak if he didn't have to. When Autumn sat in the chair beside him, he decided his throat didn't matter right now. He couldn't remember if he'd talked to Autumn or Vernon about any of this at any of the times he'd woken up, but he sure as hell couldn't stop himself now.

When he opened his mouth to speak, Autumn beat him to it. "Are you really in love with that boy, Cooper? Are you gay?"

They knew. But how? Had he told them? The only thing he did remember saying was that his friend was back, and he needed them to find him. "Love...him..."

Tears welled in Autumn's eyes. "Why didn't you tell me? Oh, God. Everything is such a mess."

Those words were like a bomb in Cooper's chest. Something had gone down he didn't know about. "Where?" When he tried again, his voice wouldn't come out. *Fuck!*

"We didn't know. You didn't even tell us he was back. It was such a shock to see him, and then he made all these claims. Vernon loves you. You have to understand. He doesn't want you to be hurt."

Hurt? Noah would never fucking hurt him...would he? He wasn't here. But maybe he'd tried.

"Where. No..." He was going to lose his fucking shit if he couldn't speak right. They said it would be a matter of time. That he just needed to let his throat heal. But Cooper couldn't wait.

"I should have said something. Seeing him just brought everything back."

Back? What could it have brought back?

"Autumn." Vernon stepped into the room.

Pieces of the puzzle started to form in Cooper's mind, yet still not forming the whole picture.

"He told me he loves that boy, Vernon. I don't care about anything else. I want Cooper happy. If he loves Noah—"

"Noah's just like his mother," Vernon shouted. "He weaseled his way into Cooper's life as a child and then clung onto him. And now he's back, pushing his way in just like his mother did. Cooper is not gay. He's never been, yet that man shows up, and suddenly he is? They're chameleons, all of them. Can't you see? I never would have hurt you like that if it wasn't for *her*."

The truth slammed into Cooper, finishing that picture as though it had always been there.

The cigarettes in Noah's backyard, when Vernon was the only one of them who smoked. Vernon not wanting to go away with Cooper and Autumn that weekend. Noah and his family disappearing out of the blue. Vernon and Autumn's sudden anger at Noah's family...and the tears. Autumn had been sad, hadn't she? He assumed it was because Cooper himself had been. Because their friends were gone. But it wasn't.

"Son...of...a...bitch." Vernon had had an affair with Noah's mom. She'd hurt her son and husband to be with Vernon, and Vernon had hurt Autumn with her. He'd lost Noah, his best friend, the man he loved, because Vernon hadn't been able to keep it in his pants. And he'd blamed Noah's family. Putting Noah and his parents down every opportunity he got.

"Don't you talk to me like that. Not after everything I've done for you. We raised you, and loved you. That boy clung to you just like his mother used to do with me. I should have known it, even back then. The way he would talk about missing you in those letters."

Cooper's heart seized at that. Noah said he'd written, but he'd never gotten the letters. For years after Noah had left, he'd felt like he'd let him down. Like he hadn't been there when Noah's parents tried to take him away, like he had promised, and he'd thought that Noah hated him for it. Why else wouldn't he have written?

But it was all because of Vernon. The man he respected and felt he owed his life to. The man who he looked up to for the way he'd loved his wife. And he cheated on her with Noah's mom.

"Out." He squeezed his fists together, angry that he couldn't form better words.

It was that easy. Vernon turned around and left the room, not that he expected anything more of the man.

He'd pretty much lied to Noah because of Vernon, when Vernon was the man who had actually hurt them all. His uncle had been the reason the man Cooper loved had to go, and Vernon had blamed it on Noah, instead of taking the blame himself.

Inside him, anger at Vernon blended with the pain of betrayal.

Still with tears in her eyes, Autumn looked at Cooper. "I know what he did was wrong. All of it, and he does, too. Especially what happened here the past couple days. But Vernon is a good man. He beat himself up over what he did. And he might not always be the best at showing it, but he loves me, just like he loves you." Autumn touched his hand. "Just like you love Noah. Love doesn't always make sense. Not whom we love or how we do it. But no one is perfect. I'll be back to check on you." And then Autumn hobbled out of the room, too, leaving Cooper alone. Still not sure where Noah was. Or if he was even coming back.

# CHAPTER TWENTY-SIX

Whether Adrianna could get him in or not, Noah was seeing Cooper. Tonight. The ache inside him had done nothing but grow with each hour, each second that went by.

"You know I could lose my job if this goes wrong. You have to promise me that if Cooper doesn't want to see you for whatever reason, you'll leave. It's one thing if his family is keeping you away from him. If this is Cooper's choice, he has the right to make it." Adrianna wrung her hands together as they stood at the entrance to the hospital.

She was right. But he knew that couldn't be true. Cooper would want him there. "If you just tell me what room he's in, I'll head up alone."

"I would, but I didn't get a chance to talk to him today. Like I said, I want to make sure this is what he wants."

It was on the tip of Noah's tongue to tell her it was, but he held it back.

"Just walk with me. I'm going to take the back elevator so we won't see as many people. Security has been watching out for you."

"Christ, what did I do that was so wrong? Because I want to go in and see the man I love?"

Adrianna frowned. "Everyone knows Cooper's uncle. He was a police officer here for years. If he said not to let you in, people will listen." She shook her head. "I never knew. How could Cooper be gay?"

Noah wasn't sure what to say to that, so he chose nothing. No matter what they planned, that didn't mean Cooper would feel the same after speaking with Vernon. No matter what the man was, he was Cooper's family. Noah wouldn't come between that.

He kept his head down as he followed behind Adrianna. The whole scene made him want to hit something. They treated him like he was a criminal.

"Hello, Adrianna," a woman said as she walked by.

Noah looked the other way as Adrianna told her hi.

They noticed a few more people on their way, most of them too busy to pay any attention to Noah and Adrianna.

They took the elevators to the second floor and headed west. As they rounded a corner, Adrianna froze. Standing in front of them was Cooper's aunt.

Noah let a heavy breath push from his lungs.

"Mrs. Bradshaw," Adrianna stuttered.

"It's not her fault," Noah told her before the woman could say anything. "I just...I need to see him." Noah didn't give a shit about the vulnerability in his voice. He needed to see the man he loved, and that was that.

"Then you should see him." Noah's eyes caught hers with her words. It was that easy? They were going to change their mind so quickly?

"He'll want to see you. In fact, he's been asking to see you, and I'm sorry we kept you away. It's just...we didn't know, and it was painful to see you. I'd thought I put it all behind me, but I guess I hadn't."

Put all what behind her? Noah had no idea what she was talking about. "What happened?"

Autumn shook her head. "I can't...just go see Cooper. I think...I think he needs you. Heaven knows he wants you, and he doesn't want to see his uncle or me right now. Not that I blame him."

Autumn tried to smile at him but she was crying too hard. When she tried to step away, she stumbled slightly and Adrianna reached out to grab her. She looked at Noah. "Room 2025. I'm going to help Mrs. Bradshaw downstairs. Just...I don't know you, and don't understand what's going on with you and Cooper. Even though I don't love him, I care about him. He's my friend, and I don't want to see him get hurt."

Cooper was Noah's first true friend. The first person he'd trusted. The happiest times of his childhood, or hell, his adulthood, the man had been a part of. "I would never hurt him."

Noah turned and headed for Cooper's room. Slowly, he pushed the door open. Coop's eyes were closed, the blanket pulled up. He had bandages and a sling on one of his arms. Noah's heart pinched seeing Cooper like this.

He was only a few feet away from the bed when Cooper's eyes fluttered open. The second he saw Noah, a smile spread across his face. Finally Noah felt like he could breathe.

With that fucking smile, they had to be okay. Had to.

"No..ah." Cooper's voice was pained, raspy.

Noah grabbed his lover's hand. "Does it hurt to talk?"

Cooper nodded.

"Do you want me here?" Again he held his breath, needing the answer to be yes.

"Ye-s. Fuck—yes."

*Thank God.* Bending over, Noah kissed his lips. "Then don't speak. Words can wait till later. I just want to hold you, baby, and make sure you're really okay."

He didn't pretend there weren't things they needed to discuss. Cooper might still want him, but that didn't mean he was ready. It didn't mean he could claim Noah the way he needed to be claimed by the man. But right now, all that mattered was feeling him and knowing he was really there.

Noah tried to sit in the chair but Cooper tugged on his arm and nodded his head toward the bed. Noah climbed in beside him, wrapping his arms around the man. There was nowhere else he wanted to be.

***

Cooper slept with Noah beside him. He internally cursed every time a nurse came in to check his vitals or give him medication. All he wanted to do was lie with Noah. It didn't matter that news would obviously spread after this. That people would find out before Cooper had the chance to talk to his work. He just wanted to lie with Noah. Needed to lie with him.

And so he did, as much as he could. For two days. Noah left to eat or change clothes, but he always came back. When Cooper tried to talk to him, Noah would tell him to wait, that they could talk later.

Braden came to see him with Wes, which surprised the crap out of Coop. Jules and Heather had shown up, too, both of the women surprised to see them together. Despite the fact that he'd never led Jules on, Noah had left to talk with her for a while. Cooper respected him for it.

He didn't know what went down to make it that suddenly everyone came in, when before he had no visitors, but he didn't care. Noah told everyone not to expect an answer from him, and growled at Cooper every time he tried to speak.

And Cooper growled right back at him. Cooper could take care of himself, but that didn't mean he also didn't like the fact that Noah was so worried about him.

Partially, he was glad he didn't have to talk much. When he did, he would have to tell Noah about his mom and Vernon. The thought made him ill.

On the third day, Noah sat on the chair beside the bed, running his fingers over Cooper's shortly cropped hair. "You scared the hell out of me, Coop. I know you go into burning buildings for your job, but this was different. You gotta stop holding yourself responsible for them. It'll make you screw up. You made a rash decision."

Cooper's throat was still tender and his voice off, but he managed to speak a little more easily. "Saved...that...kid."

"I know." Noah leaned closer. "And I'm so fucking proud of you, but that doesn't change the fact that you ran into that house to save your parents. You can't think that way. You're going to get yourself hurt."

"It's my job," he whispered softly.

"You know what I mean."

Cooper nodded, because he did.

"It wasn't your fault. I've said it before, but I don't think you'll ever truly be able to move forward until you accept that. Do you think that kid you saved could have gotten you out of the house? He's just a kid, man, and so were you. Their death wasn't your fault. Everything is not your responsibility. Just like dealing with my crap when we were kids wasn't, and making your uncle happy isn't. You can't control everyone's feelings and be what everyone else wants you to be, baby. And…," Noah squeezed his hand. "No matter what I said to you. When I told you if we moved forward you were mine, staying with me isn't something you have to do, either. If you're not ready, then—"

"No." Cooper winced, the force of the word making his throat burn. Noah was right about most of it. He understood that, but not when it came to how he felt about the other man. Those weren't the same. "I love you." He wished like hell he could speak louder.

"I know. I'm pretty irresistible." Noah winked at him, but when Cooper didn't smile, he continued. "That doesn't mean you're ready. I pushed you when I shouldn't have."

"Fuck...you..." If Noah thought Cooper didn't know his own mind, that he would let Noah talk him into moving forward if he wasn't ready, he was going to kick his ass. "You know me," he cleared his throat. "Better than that."

"You didn't even tell them I was back. Is it because I'm gay? If so, we're in a whole lot of trouble, baby, because for a while now, you've been with me."

*That's* where this was coming from. Cooper tried to sit up but struggled. Noah smiled before hitting the button so the head of the bed would go up.

"Stop getting all worked up. You're going to hurt yourself."

Cooper shook his head.

"I'm serious. I shouldn't have brought it up right now."

"Then I would have." Coop thought for a second, trying to figure out how to say this. "Vernon was angry when you left. At your whole family." It drove him crazy how slowly he had to speak.

"I didn't understand it. That was part of it. I know it's wrong, but I *did* feel like I would be letting him down, not just because I loved you, but because it *was* you. I didn't want to hurt you by telling you."

The set of Noah's jaw told him he'd done just that. "Why? I could tell he was angry at me when I tried to see you, but it doesn't make sense."

Cooper took a deep breath. Jesus, this would kill Noah. But he knew Noah better than to lie to him. He'd already done it on a smaller scale; anymore Noah wouldn't be able to forgive. Not after his mother's lies, and David's.

Cooper pulled on Noah's arm until he sat next to him, and didn't let go. "Your mom... and Vernon..."

Noah turned to stone.

"I just found out..."

"Christ. That's why we left?" Noah tried to pull away but Cooper wouldn't let him. Not that Noah couldn't pull out of his one-arm grasp, but he didn't. "That must have killed Autumn. How could she do that? She knew how much I loved you."

The pain in Noah's voice broke Cooper's heart. "So my mother slept with your uncle, and then I show up and seduce their straight nephew?"

"Thinking awfully high of yourself, aren't you? If I didn't want to be with you, I wouldn't be."

But they both knew that's how Vernon, and maybe even Autumn, saw it. Even when Autumn had come back into the room just before Noah the other day, she still struggled with it. She explained the whole story to Cooper. How Noah's father found out and they'd left. That his aunt hadn't known until they got home that weekend and Vernon confessed. She'd wanted time alone, so Vernon had taken Cooper camping.

That it had been hard, but she'd forgiven Vernon. That she knew her husband loved her. That what he'd done was wrong, but he'd tried every day to make it up to her.

It wasn't that easy for Cooper to forgive. Not when it hurt his aunt, had taken Noah from him, and shattered his vision of the man he respected.

"Your family treated me like I belonged. I practically lived with you. I was happy in Blackcreek. I begged my parents never to make us have to move, and she slept with your uncle knowing it would cause me to lose everything that was important to me?"

This time Noah did jerk away from him and paced the room. "Your aunt treated me like a son, and then my mother repaid her by hurting her that way? And then I waltz back into your life. Find my way into your bed and then shove my way into this hospital like I have some fucking right."

"You have *all* the right," Cooper told him.

Noah's eyes flashed to him at that, burning with that heat Cooper had become so used to from his guy.

"I will never forgive her for making me lose you, Coop. How will your aunt ever be able to look at me?"

"Come here," Cooper said. When Noah shook his head he continued, "Come here before I get out of this bed."

Noah sighed. Cooper knew he wouldn't risk Coop getting out of bed and getting hurt. When Noah got to Cooper's side, Coop grabbed the back of his head with his good hand and pulled Noah toward him until their foreheads touched.

"Because it wasn't your fault. Just like what happened to my parents wasn't mine, what your mom did wasn't yours. I'm not going to pretend it will be easy, and maybe it will always be a struggle, but it isn't your fault and you won't suffer for it." Noah suffered too much in his lifetime. Cooper had, too. They were due their happiness. Together.

"It's not the same thing. Don't pretend it is. I know it's not my fault. That doesn't mean it will be easier. I won't come between you and your family. I've already turned your life upside down as it is."

At that, Cooper smiled. He ignored the burn in his throat as he spoke. "If you did shake my life up, I wanted it. I needed it. I know we have shit to deal with. That it's going to be tough with my family, and officially coming out at the station, but I don't give a shit about that. None of it. I care about you."

"Coop—"

"No." Cooper shook his head. "There's nothing or no one I want in my life as much as you. Don't make this harder than it has to be, Noah. Twenty years ago you collided with me over that damn football, and my life was never the same."

"The same way you and your damn truck collided with me?" Laughter lightened the frayed edges of his voice. Noah was coming back to him.

"Guess that means we're meant to be. You were meant to be a part of my life, Noah."

"That's all I've ever wanted." Noah kissed Cooper's forehead. "One way or another, I've always wanted to be a part of you." His lips came down on Cooper's cheek and then the other one. "I have loved you since I was ten years old, and I'll be damned if I'm going to stop now."

Finally his lips landed on Cooper's. Their tongues did that familiar give and take, their battle and surrender. Neither of them was stupid. They both knew there were obstacles ahead of them, but they would deal with them together.

"I love you, too. Always."

# EPILOGUE

"Go talk to him." Cooper nodded his head toward Wes, who stood alone in a corner on the other side of the house.

"Thank you." Noah lead forward and pressed his lips to Cooper's, so fucking glad that he could do that whenever he wanted. It didn't matter that they were standing in a room full of people. Some of them were assholes about it, especially a few of the guys at Coop's firehouse, but they were dealing with it— together.

Noah ran a finger over the sling that held Cooper's arm, still sick to his stomach every time he saw it. He could have lost him. Lost his best friend. Lost his light. It had only been a couple weeks, but it was still all he thought about.

"I'll be back." Noah made his way through the crowded house. It was Wes's sister Lydia's house, which was bigger than the one Wes would now be living in alone with little Jessie.

"How ya doing, man?" Noah leaned against the wall behind him. Wes's eyes were sad, lost, but during the funeral or here at the service, Noah had yet to see the man shed a tear.

"Okay."

"No, you're not."

Wes shrugged. "She's gone, regardless."

Noah put an arm around his friend. "We're here if you want to talk. If you need help with Jessie, or anything. Not that I know the first thing about kids."

Humorlessly, Wes chuckled. "You and me both... I don't know if I'm going to do it for sure, Noah. I know that makes me a prick, but what the hell do I know about raising a little girl? I'm a single, gay man who likes my space. I don't want to screw her up...Lydia and I talked. We're going to take it slowly. We both want what's best for Jessie."

Noah's heart squeezed for the other man. "You'll do the right thing." And somehow, he didn't doubt that. There was something about Wes that Noah connected with on a friendship level, and he was glad to have met him.

"I hope so. I really fucking do."

Noah looked across the room at Cooper, who stood with Braden beside him. Noah smiled. "I doubt we'd be the only ones there if you needed anything."

A quick glance at Wes told him he was looking at Cooper and Braden, too. "I don't know why the hell he won't leave me alone. We fucked once. End of story. The bastard hasn't stopped calling me since he found me when Cooper was in the hospital."

No matter what he said, Noah doubted very much he wanted Braden to leave him alone. "Can't hurt to have another friend." If he was being honest, the whole thing surprised him just as much. From everything Cooper said, Braden like quantity. He was always going out and looking for a good time. Until he'd met Wes, at least. As far as Cooper knew, the man hadn't gone home with a woman or a man since Wes.

"I have too much going on to deal with anything else."

Noah shrugged. "Maybe it'll help. Maybe it's what you need."

Wes shook his head. "I'm not talking about this. How are things with you guys?"

Noah filled him in a little bit. They'd seen Autumn once since Cooper left the hospital. She was trying, even though she still struggled to understand what was going on with Noah and Cooper. Noah figured no one had to understand it. They were in love and that's all that mattered.

Vernon, stubborn as always, hadn't come around. In some ways, Noah was okay with that. He wasn't sure how it would be to look the man in the eyes knowing that he, along with Noah's own mother, had hurt all of them so much. But then...he didn't want Cooper hurt, either. Regardless, Vernon was his uncle and Noah would put his anger aside, for Coop.

Wes nodded in all the right places as Noah continued to talk to him, but he knew Wes wasn't into the conversation. He kept his head down, deep in thought, and every time his eyes rose, they landed on Braden.

When Coop left Braden's side, as Braden walked away, Wes's gaze followed him the whole time. It wasn't a second after Cooper made it to Noah, wrapping an arm around him, that Wes disappeared.

"He okay?" Cooper asked.

"I don't know. I hope so." He nuzzled his face into Cooper's neck. Sometimes people come quietly into your life. Not Coop. Twice, he'd collided into Noah's world. Years separated them—whole other lives—but they'd found their way back to each other. Found a way to leave everything except each other in the past. Noah pulled Cooper close and held him, thankful to have him in his arms, now and always.

The End

Return to Blackcreek in Wes and Braden's story.

Coming in 2014.

# Acknowledgement:

Noah and Cooper's story had been in my head long before I wrote it. The first person I need to thank is my bestie. Thanks for listening to me as I rambled on and on about Noah and Cooper. For dealing with me as I talked about how much I needed to write their story, before time allowed me to. I couldn't do this without you. Thanks to Ellis Carrington, Jessica, and Janette for reading, and for your enthusiasm. Also, a special thanks to Chris for your insight, and Marion for your skills with the red pen. And to Jamie for being awesome.

# About Riley Hart

Riley Hart is the girl who wears her heart on her sleeve. She's a hopeless romantic. A lover of sexy stories, passionate men, and writing about all the trouble they can get into together. If she's not writing, you'll probably find her reading.

Riley lives in California with her awesome family, who she is thankful for every day.

You can find her online at:

Twitter

@RileyHart5

Facebook

https://www.facebook.com/riley.hart.1238?fref=ts

Blog

www.rileyhartwrites.blogspot.com

Tumblr

http://rileyhartwrites.tumblr.com

44654935R00184

Made in the USA
Lexington, KY
07 September 2015